PRAISE FOR

SHOOTING DR. JACK

"In his first novel, Norman Green sketches such indelible por-
traits . . . the reader is drawn in."

—*New York Times Book Review*

"A self-assured debut. . . . [It] will invite comparisons to Elmore
Leonard." —*Publishers Weekly*

"A heart-catching novel of perception and intelligence. The language is fresh and poignant. With its moody underpinnings
and subtle redemptions, Green's book is a powerful and emotional story." —Perri O'Shaughnessy,
New York Times bestselling author of *Move to Strike*

"A powerful debut from a gifted new writer. It's got the narra
tive drive of a thriller, the unflinching reality of a literary
novel, and characters that come alive and stay with you after
the story is finished. You get the feeling that Norman Green
could go anywhere from here." —T. Jefferson Parker,
bestselling author of *Laguna Heat* and *Silent Joe*

"Norman Green has an original voice that takes us into the edgy
shadows of human nature. The blood of New York is so strong
in this book that you can feel it pulsing in your veins. *Shooting
Dr. Jack* should not be missed."

—Robert Crais, bestselling author of *Hostage*

"*Shooting Dr. Jack* is a stunner. Like Richard Price, Norman Green
brings an uncanny bare-knuckle vivacity to his portrayal of life
on the streets. Compelling."

—Jeffery Deaver, *New York Times* bestselling author of
The Blue Nowhere and *The Empty Chair*

John Wagner

About the Author

NORMAN GREEN reports this about himself: "I have always been careful, as Mark Twain advised, not to let schooling interfere with my education. Too careful, maybe. I have been, at various times, a truck driver, a construction worker, a project engineer, a factory rep, and a plant engineer, but never, until now, a writer." He lives in Emerson, New Jersey, with his wife, and is hard at work on his second novel.

SHOOTING DR. JACK

a novel

NORMAN GREEN

Perennial

An Imprint of HarperCollins*Publishers*

This novel is a work of fiction. Any references to real people, events, estab-
lishments, organizations, or locales are intended only to give the fiction a
sense of reality and authenticity, and are used fictitiously. All other names,
characters, and places, and all dialogue and incidents portrayed in this book
are the product of the author's imagination.

A hardcover edition of this book was published in 2001 by HarperCollins
Publishers.

HarperCollins books may be purchased for educational, business, or sales
promotional use. For information please write: Special Markets
Department, HarperCollins Publishers Inc., 10 East 53rd Street, New
York, NY 10022.

First Perennial edition published 2002.

Designed by Philip Mazzone

The Library of Congress has catalogued the hardcover edition as follows:
Green, Norman.
   Shooting Dr. Jack : a novel / by Norman Green.—1st ed.
      p. cm
   ISBN 0-06-018822-7
      I. Title
PS3607.R44 S55 2001
813'.6—dc21

                                               2001016841

ISBN 0-06-093413-1 (pbk.)

02 03 04 05 06 ❖/RRD 10 9 8 7 6 5 4 3 2 1

For Christine

The author wishes to thank Bill and the doctor, the Liberty Street Irregulars, Brian DeFiore, Marjorie Braman, R. Robert Toots, and last, but certainly not least, Kenneth Leroy Hand, 7/7/31–3/1/2000. Peace, baby.

SHOOTING DR. JACK

TROUTMAN IS A ONE-WAY STREET THAT RUNS FROM NOWHERE TO nowhere, from Metropolitan and Flushing Avenues at the north end, to Bushwick Avenue at the south, in between Brooklyn and Queens, in between neighborhoods, unwanted and unclaimed. It is not really Bushwick, not really Ridgewood, not industrial and not residential, not a desirable place to live and without the character of Harlem or Bed-Sty. It is a street of failures. Fall through the cracks of a better or kinder world, and you find yourself on Troutman Street. Dreams of a new world die in her sweatshops, cars and trucks die in her chop shops and junkyards, children die in her vacant lots, shooting one another for the right to sell crack on the two or three big intersections, junkies die wherever they happen to be when they shoot up—hallways, alleys, parking lots. Even the whores who work Troutman Street are failures, too homely, too scarred, too emaciated and wasted, too obviously addicted to be of much use as generators of profit. Even for endeavors such as prostitution and drug sales, there are better and more profitable places to do business. People who live on Troutman Street, businesses that locate there, and even the street people who make it their home stay because all of their other choices are exhausted. Troutman Street is a place of end games. From beginning to end, it is one of those places where whores, junkies, businesses, cars, and dreams go to die.

God, Stoney thought, must be like one of those kids who likes to catch flies and pull their wings off so that he can watch them crawl around and suffer until they die. It was the only possible explanation. The thought made Stoney's hangover even worse, if that were possible, each throb God's way of saying, Take that, you punk.

The brightly colored cars roasted in the sun, almost motionless on the New Jersey Turnpike, a long line inching to the north through the Jersey Meadowlands. He looked eastward across the ruined marsh, to where the bright towers of Manhattan rose over the low hills of the Palisades, a woman standing in a breeze to avoid breathing her own stink.

The bleat of a horn roused him, and he eased his car forward another six feet. He began to turn to give the driver behind him a one-finger salute, but he felt a sharp, stabbing pain shoot from his neck up through the top of his skull as he twisted in the seat. Grimacing, he turned front again, not even lifting his eyes to the rearview mirror, and for a second he thought he would pass out. Jesus, he thought, just kill me, don't torture me like this.

He reached under the seat for the bottle, and for one panicky moment he couldn't find it, but then there it was, stuck under the rear corner of the floor mat. He hefted the dark brown pint bottle, comforted by the familiar shape, slightly curved in his hand, full and heavy. Holding it below window level, he twisted the top off, listening to the crackle of the metal cap tearing loose from its retaining ring. He wanted to lift it to his nose, smell the smoky aroma, but he didn't. Everybody's a cop, he thought, everybody has a cell phone. He fished a paper cup out of the trash on the floor and poured three fingers into it. A snort, that's what his old man would have called it, not a drink, really, just a snort. He recapped the bottle and replaced it under the seat.

He took a swig, just a small hit from the cup, and his body rebelled. His stomach rolled, suddenly he felt dizzy, and he started to retch, but he fought it, muscling the bile back down into his stomach, gritting his teeth and gripping the steering wheel hard. He knew that if he kept the first one down he'd be okay, but if he lost it . . . He didn't even want to think about it. One more DWI and he'd do time for sure, and he was in no shape to handle it. His partner, Tommy, would run the business into the ground inside of six months or else he'd make them a fortune. No way to tell which, but he'd roll the dice, no question. Donna would divorce him, he'd lose the house, the kids would hate him even more than they did already. He took another sip and it went down a little easier, and he felt that spreading warmth, the throbbing in his head began to fade, and he leaned back into the corner of the seat. A year in the can, he thought. Maybe it wouldn't be so bad. Maybe it would be just what he needed. He loved his wife, but lately he could only make her cry. He tried to love his kids, but they were terrified of him. Even the cat hated him. If he walked into a room where the cat was sleeping, it would wake up, stare at him, and then get up and leave. He felt powerless to change any of it, other than to yield to the self-destructive impulse and just burn it all down. Donna and the kids would be happier, once they got over the initial shock. Donna would find another guy, easy, she still looked fine, and she could be so funny and sharp . . . His eyes began to burn, and he looked down into the cup to see how much was left, briefly considering a refill.

No, he thought. Don't get started. He drained off what was left and crunched the cup into a ball and pitched it into the backseat. He had been able to do it so easily once, find that cruising altitude and hang there, never quite drunk and never quite sober. Happy, or as close to it as he figured to get. He had lived in that zone for so many years, he couldn't understand why it now eluded him.

Last night it had happened again. He'd gone into Manhattan on a Sunday afternoon to go over some business with Tommy. They met in one of Tommy's hangouts down in the Village. Stoney couldn't understand why Tommy liked that neighborhood, maybe he had something going down there, Tommy always had something going. Stoney could remember the bar; kind of place, your shoes stuck to the floor if you stood too long in one spot, some kid playing a steel guitar. He hadn't meant for it to be anything more than that, just a few pops with Tommy and straight home again, but it had happened. He didn't remember leaving the bar, didn't remember drinking that much, one brief moment of awareness, hammering across the lower level of the George Washington Bridge, nothing else, then, waking up this morning on the cellar floor. Puking blood into the toilet bowl. Donna crying, slamming doors, hustling the kids off somewhere . . .

He'd never intended it to be this way. Who would choose this? Oh, yeah, I'm gonna go into the city, get blind fucking drunk, blow six hundred bucks that used to be in my wallet and ain't there now, drive home blasted, already on the revoked list. Pass out on the floor. Really impress the old lady.

Jesus.

Stoney just wanted to do what he'd always done. Have a few, just to take the edge off, go home, get up, go to work. That's all. He just couldn't seem to manage it. It was like someone else would flip a switch in his head, take over his body and his life, and he'd wake up the next day and have to face the wreckage. He had tried everything he could think of to get a handle on himself. Only drink wine, only drink beer, only two drinks a day, only drink on Fridays, smoke dope instead, only drink bourbon, don't drink at all. The last one had been a real trip, by the end of the first week he'd been so savage, Tommy, Donna, the kids, even the cat probably wanted to buy him a drink. So he'd started in again, carefully, oh so carefully, but then it had hit him, like he'd known it would, and that was the worst part, knowing, and being unable to hold it off.

He finally made it up to the tollbooths, and once through, traffic opened up a bit. When he got to where Route 80 splits off to the west, he had to fight the urge to turn off, head out to some new place. It wouldn't matter, he knew that, but God, the thought was seductive. Someday I'll do it, he told himself. Fuck everything and run. But this one morning he stayed in line for the George Washington Bridge, on his way to Troutman Street.

Tuco knew that they were both dead. How, specifically, he knew that, he couldn't have said, but he was sure of it the second he saw the two of them lying in the alley at the far end of the junkyard, past the parking lot, where, last summer, he and Jimmy the Hat had screwed galvanized metal sheets to the outside of the chain-link fence so that no one could see through. The girl was facedown, naked except for a T-shirt pulled up around her head. The boy was wearing jeans, too big and too long, expensive basketball shoes, Oakland Raiders jacket. His sunglasses lay broken a few feet away. Tuco looked around for the boy's hat, he had always worn a hat when Tuco had seen him in the past, but it was gone. Blown away, maybe.

Tuco sat on his heels feeling sad and sick. What is it, he wondered, what is it that goes away? He pictured the girl lying in a hospital bed, hooked up to all the machines to do the breathing, circulate the blood, to carry on all of the body's business, but it would not matter once that particular something was gone, taking her with it, leaving behind just this . . . Tuco, awkward and unskilled with women, was immensely sorry that they had stripped her of her clothes and her dignity, angry that he had to wonder if someone had done things to her, if they had forced the boy to watch before killing them both.

He had already seen enough of death in his short life. There was the guy, rolled up in a rug and dumped next to the Brooklyn-Queens Expressway last year, and the guy stabbed in the hallway outside his mother's apartment just months ago. His buddy had done it, guy lived on the same floor, the two of them were drunk and got into an argument, and the dude went and got a kitchen knife and settled it, stabbed his buddy thirty-seven times, went back in his apartment and passed out, blood all over him. Left the knife in the kitchen sink. When the cops had taken him away, he'd been crying for his dead friend. Hadn't remembered a thing.

Tuco stood up and backed away. If she were alive, he thought, she'd never let me see her like this. She would find me unattractive and uncool, she'd laugh and go find somebody better. It was okay with him, he'd gotten used to it. He was a Nuyorican, born in Puerto Rico but raised in Brooklyn, at home in neither place. He was just short of five-ten, broad, with a boxer's build, dark, wiry hair, heavy eyebrows, not much forehead. He turned away from the girl lying in the alley. It bothered him that she couldn't get up and get dressed, that he had to walk away and leave her there. He went around the corner and up the block, into the office.

The metal grating was still down over the office window, but the door was open. Inside a large and muscular black man with tips of gray in his hair was washing a coffee pot. He turned and looked at Tuco.

"Hey, ugly."

"Hey, dickhead." It was their habitual greeting. "Listen, Walter, there's two dead kids out around the corner, in the alley by the fence."

"You kidding?"

"No. Should I call the cops?"

"Tuco, listen to me. You ain't seen a t'ing, you don't call nobody, you don't know shit until Stoney get 'ere. You understand?"

"Yassuh, boss."

"Go on back and open up."

"Yassuh, boss."

Walter looked down at the kid. "What's the matter? They friends of yours?"

Tuco sighed. "Couple of kids from the neighborhood. Yo boys."

"Yeah, well. They in what you call a high-risk line of work. Maybe you don't enjoy getting your hands all dirty, but not too many people lookin' to shoot your ass 'cause you doing it."

Stoney was irritated before he even got his car into the parking lot. The gate to the lot was open. Chain-link fence, concertina wire, closed-circuit TV camera, everything but a guard tower, and they leave the gate open. He had seen, over the years, every conceivable human activity take place in this parking lot, from conception to death, with the single exception of a live birth, and he hadn't given up hope on that one. Sure enough, there was an old white guy in the corner behind the cars, preparing to shoot up.

"Hey, buddy, you gotta find another place to do that." The old man stood up, sticking his works in one pocket and some small bluish plastic bags into another. He had white hair, a short growth of white beard, and startlingly blue eyes. He half-grinned at Stoney.

"'S'okay," he said, "I'm gone." He walked out, not stooped over or beat-down looking, like most junkies, and he didn't watch

Stoney like Stoney expected him to, the way you watch a dog if you're not sure whether or not it bites. He just walked out through the open gate and headed off down the block, with that street-dude lilt in his step. I oughta know this guy, Stoney thought, I must have seen him around somewhere. He couldn't place him. He closed the gate and snapped the padlock shut.

He could see Walter watching him through the window, shaking his head. Walter would look at his hands when he got inside to see what kind of shape he was in. Mornings like this, Stoney thought, everyone's judging you, trying to decide if you've lost a step. The truth was that he had, and he knew it. He had started to get that Elvis-in-Vegas look, face all puffy and pasty white, muscle tone not what it was, belly starting to push against his shirtfront.

Walter, who was from Barbados, never seemed to change. The years had added a touch of gray to his hair, but that was about all. He was still hard as a rock, still had a grip like you got your hand caught in a car door. The thing about Walter was he had a round and open face, and he smiled easily. He seemed to have a gift for putting people at ease, off their guard. It was a gift that had proved useful, over the years. Same people look at me, Stoney thought, right away they wanna call the cops.

Stoney banged through the front door.

"Do I talk to myself?"

"Hey, boss—"

"Do I talk to myself? Does anybody listen to me?"

"Hey, boss—"

"Who left the goddam gate open again?"

"Boss, we got a situation."

"Why is it so fucking hard—" He stopped in mid-rave. "What situation?"

Walter explained about the dead kids in the alley. Stoney stuck his head through the back door of the office and bellowed, "Tuco, up front!" He turned back to Walter. "Anybody we know?"

"I ain't been to look. Tuco says they're neighborhood kids."

"Tommy's container still out back?" He wondered what difference it would make, either way, but when cops are coming, you have to cover your ass.

"Nope. Went out last Friday night, after you left."

"All right, call it in. You got the precinct number?"

"I dunno. Shouldn't I call 911?"

"It's no emergency, Walter, they're not going anywhere."

The cop didn't look like the ones that Tuco was used to seeing on TV. He was a big white guy, obviously worked out. He was almost as taut as Tuco. He wasn't wearing a suit and tie, either. He wore jeans, running shoes, and a Mets warm-up jacket. He had an automatic pistol strapped to his belt.

"So you were coming to work when you found them?"

"Yeah."

"You walk to work, Eddie?" He had read the name from Tuco's license.

"Yeah."

"And you live up on De Kalb?"

"Yeah, up by the hospital."

"And you came up Troutman from this direction?" The cop pointed with his chin.

"Yeah."

"Why were you coming this way? How come you didn't just walk down St. Nicholas?"

Sharp guy, Tuco thought. Be careful, tell the truth. "I don't go on St. Nicholas."

"Ah." The cop rubbed his chin with a big paw. He knew all about the street gang that worked out of one of the row houses on St. Nicholas.

"Dr. Jack," Tuco said with a touch of bitterness.

"Call them what they are, Eddie. Drug dealers, pimps, criminals. They got a beef with you?"

Tuco sighed. "One of them." My fucking cousin, he wanted to say. My friend, that I grew up with.

The cop regarded Tuco with renewed interest. He hated gangs, and he had a particular distaste for dealers and pimps. "What's the beef over?"

Tuco felt his face twisting up, wishing he could get that dead look that Stoney got when he was cranked, that look that told you nothing at all unless you'd seen it before and had learned to watch for it. He glanced at the cop, and wondered if he could ever know how it was, this big, rich, well-fed health-club white motherfucker from Long Island. How his best friend and cousin, Miguel, had joined and he had not, how they had hounded him and squeezed him and beat on him, even when they had known the whole time that he could never join, that he was different, set apart by his faith and by other limitations. He'd even wondered if they would take him at all, if he wanted them to. You can't be alone, his cousin would tell him, you can't live through it, and besides, you need us. We're not what you think, we're like a family. But Tuco had toughed it out, paying the price. A few scars, a nose not quite straight, a tendency to walk with his shoulders hunched and his fists balled, a bad case of nerves.

"Old news, man. Stuff from high school."

The cop didn't push it. "Are these two with the ones up on St. Nicholas?"

"No," Tuco said, thinking, This guy has to know the answer to this one. "He don't got their colors on."

"Oh, that's right. Green and gold." He took a card out of his pocket, ran his thumb along the edge. "So what do you think happened, Eddie?"

He knows this one, too, Tuco thought. "I dunno. Maybe they got caught where they don't belong."

"Maybe. See, my problem is, I gotta figure out what went down here, Eddie, and I got fourteen other cases already. I can use all the help I can get." He gave Tuco his card. "You hear any rumors, people saying this guy or that guy knows something, give me a call," he said. "Or even if you just wanna talk." Tuco took the card from him and looked at it. He couldn't read the words, but he could handle the phone number okay.

Tuco and Stoney watched as the EMS people zipped the bags shut and loaded them up. They both said a silent prayer to gods that they no longer believed in, Tuco more formally, the way his mother had taught him, Stoney more direct, no pleasantries. Jesus, God, he thought. Don't let me die on fucking Troutman Street.

2

THOMAS ROSSELLI, AKA TOMMY BAGADONUTS, AKA FAT TOMMY, pointed his Town Car uptown, two Styrofoam coffee cups beside him on the passenger seat, inside a cardboard box that kept them upright. He held a third cup in a massive left hand, drinking from it as he gunned the car up Hudson Street. Tommy hated foam cups, he much preferred paper, but if you wanted the best coffee in New York, you had to take the foam cups. It was just one of the little indignities that go together to make up the price you have to pay if you want the best. In a perfect world, his new favorite coffee shop would use paper cups, and Georgie's Bakery, the best dough-nut place in the known universe, would be a hundred blocks south, and Tommy would not have to drive all the way to buck-and-a-quarter street drinking coffee with no doughnuts. But Tommy was happy to pay the price.

He was a large man, of large appetites, a true gourmand, an epicure, a draft horse among fillies, the most improbably success-ful swordsman in New York City, and not necessarily just a big fat

bastard whose heart must surely be ready to give out, as his partner Stoney unkindly referred to him.

Tommy knew the best restaurants in New York, and how
much to tip the maitre d' in each one. He knew the bartender who
made the best martini, and the bars she worked in; he knew the
best wine shop. He was on a first-name basis with the cop who sold
the best dope this side of Big Sur. He knew where to buy the best
Polish sausage, the best (and biggest) pastrami sandwich, the best
homemade ice cream. He knew that the best chocolate croissants
in New York were actually made in a little bakery in Hoboken, and
could be had there at a substantial savings. He knew the best
whorehouse in New York, and the best massage parlor. The bar-
tenders at Lincoln Center knew Tommy's favorite drink, and they
knew it would be worth their trouble to have two of them at the
end of the bar at intermission. He knew who to call if he really,
really wanted you sleeping with the fishes in the bottom of
Newton Creek. In short, Tommy Bagadonuts Rosselli was the sort
of man who could show you the mistakes in both the Kama-sutra
and in Zagat's food sources guide.

Tommy had swum ashore from an Italian freighter coming
into Philadelphia, a young man with no advantages and no
prospects, speaking no English. He had gotten his green card by
the time-honored method of buying it from a lawyer in South
Philly. He learned some English, and not only survived, but pros-
pered by the use of his native intelligence, quickness, and sense of
humor. He never lost his accent.

Tommy owned a loft in Soho, part of a parking garage nearby,
a piece of a used-car dealership in Jersey, a couple of horses that
ate faster than they ran, a minority share in a massage parlor on
Third Avenue just north of Fourteenth Street. He also owned, with
Stoney, half of the junkyard on Troutman Street. It was the latest
in a long series of enterprises that the two of them used to work

the fringes of capitalism, those broad, gray areas where the rash and the unwary are prey to sharp teeth and sticky fingers. Tommy knew what auctions to go to and what auctions to go to a few days early. He knew who to see for theater tickets and for parking tickets. If you met Tommy, you'd remember him, but he'd remember you, your phone number, your wife's name, and what his chances with her were.

Tommy could always, always get it for you wholesale.

There was a new girl working the street. Tommy eyed her on his way past, and she him. He'd gotten sort of used to them standing around, watching the men go by, some with resignation, some with hope, some with vacant eyes that said nothing at all. They had become part of the landscape, they along with the steelworkers, the trucks, the factories, the Dumpsters, the empty crack vials, and the tiny blue plastic bags with the grinning skull imprint, ripped open at one end.

A few seemed to try to hold on to some vestige of normalcy, waving or saying hello to you if they were used to seeing you, as if to say, See, I'm not so different from you, good morning, how are you today. Some others always had their mind on the bottom line, Do you want a nice blow job, can you spare a dollar, how about a cigarette. They came in all forms, all colors, all shapes, having in common only that they were somewhat the worse for wear, like well-worn dollar bills. Some dressed up in traditional whore garb, short skirt, no underwear, high heels, scanty top of one kind or another, and a few would employ advertising of a sort, flashing the drivers who slowed down enough to seem interested. Others dressed in whatever, jeans or sweats, T-shirts and sneakers, and were generally less aggressive in pursuit of commerce, merchants content to open their doors and wait to see who comes in. On rare occasions Tommy would see one with a pimp attached, generally as run-down and as beaten as the woman.

Once he had noticed a girl who was all dressed up to look the part, but the clothes had looked wrong on her. She'd had the Irish look, painfully white skin, orange-blonde hair, pug nose. Tommy had guessed that she was a sister to one of the local dealers, there was enough of a resemblance. She'd had trouble with the role, only briefly making eye contact with the drivers going past, quickly looking down, turning away, the shame flaming brightly on her cheeks. She had walked the wrong axis of the corner, the accepted practice being to stick to the cross streets. He'd only seen her there that one time, and he had fantasized, since then, about her buying a pistol with the proceeds of her new venture, taking it home and blowing her brother's brains out for what he'd forced her to do. Of course, he'd assumed a lot, in that particular fantasy, but he had a good eye, and he'd lay money that he was fairly close to the truth. There had been no desperation in her face, so it was not her desperation that put her out there.

The desperation was plainest in the whores who were the most far gone, those clearly addicted, the ones who no longer took even the most basic interest in themselves, those too dirty and unkempt to attract many customers, even on that sorry street. Some would accost anyone who was out, they no longer cared about anything but the drug, and they would bargain over their rates as though it were the difference between ten dollars and five, or three, that made you turn away.

Tommy often wondered how their customers could manage a hard-on in the face of so much human misery, but then he would suppose that the customer would have his mind on his own appetites. Tommy felt more than a little guilty, and even though he could never identify with the situation of a prostitute, he would think of desperate things he had done, in desperate times in his own life, in pursuit of what he thought he needed, and he knew in his heart that, at least in part, it was blind, stupid luck that he drove and they walked.

By the time he got the car inside the lot, the new girl he'd spotted was just down the block, and when he got the gate closed and locked, she was right there. She was too pretty for Troutman Street. It is amazing, Tommy thought, what happens when someone gives the gene pool a good stir. Sometimes children of interracial parents turn out to be almost painfully beautiful, as this girl was. She was a shade darker than white girls get, a shade lighter than black girls get, her body a gift from God, Eve's face just after she met the snake, dark, dark eyes. She would not have looked out of place competing in a high school track meet, or as the mother of someone competing in a high school track meet. Tommy looked into her face and felt a bit of an urge. He silently lamented, not for the first time, the new age of AIDS, herpes, hepatitis, et al.

"Hey, sweetheart," he said as she walked by. "Whattayou do, down here? This isa no the street for you."

She smiled at him and he felt sad, knowing that if she stayed, soon enough there would be gaps in that smile, bags under those eyes, and that the bones behind that face would begin to show clearly beneath the skin. "You like to party, honey?"

"No, no. I'ma work here. This isa my corner," he said, with mock severity. "Nobody'sa work this block but me."

"Oh, look at you," she replied, cocking her head and smiling at his little joke, "you with your suit and tie."

"Maybe we alla prostitute, baby, but whattayou do, itsa no too smart. You gonna catch something bad, out here onna street."

"Not me," she said, turning her back on him, resuming her slow stroll. "I'll be fine."

•   •   •

On the other side of the fence, Tuco watched. At times he felt so bad and so hopeless that he thought the blackness inside him would well up and swallow him whole. This vision, this beautiful angel appears on the sidewalk, and Bagadonuts, the fat bastard, he walks up so cool, so casual, so calm, while Tuco could only watch from behind the fence, palms sweaty, his heart thundering in his chest at the mere thought of speaking to her. And what would he say? He was too rigid to admit to himself that he wanted her, and he could think of nothing to say to her, nothing at all, except maybe, Go home, please don't stay here, go home, because he, too, knew what a terrible price she would pay for staying. He knew in his heart that he would never be able tell her even that much.

Tuco thought back to a documentary he had seen on TV once, about a child whose parents locked her in a basement for the first ten or eleven years of her life. Social workers had finally discovered her, and they had taken her away. A team of doctors and scientists had slaved over her for several years, vainly trying to help her, to catch her up to where she should have been. But even though the girl seemed intelligent, they had only been able to make very minimal progress. By the end of the program, Tuco had guessed that it was hopeless, that when a child is at the correct age to learn to speak, to walk, to reach out to other people, there was only a limited window of opportunity, a brief span of life during which that child would have the necessary tools to learn those specific skills, and that once the chance was lost, it would never come again, and no matter how hard the doctors, the scientists, and even the little girl herself tried, it was no good. Too late. And so it was with himself, he felt. The isolation, the otherness forced upon him in childhood, the necessity of standing apart and being different had cost him some of those natural learning times, and he feared that it wasn't just the world of reading and book learning that was closed off to him, but that this terrible loneliness that he felt, this enormous distance, was permanent. Where Tommy was so open, so natural, he saw only silence for himself, and where Tommy connected so easily and so well with nearly everyone he met, Tuco could feel only longing, unspoken and stillborn.

Tommy B. saw Stoney through the front window, at the counter talking to Walter with his back to the glass. Stoney was smaller than Walter, but not by a lot, and while Walter seemed to be the kind of guy you'd invite over to have a few beers and watch the game, people were generally a bit nervous when they met Stoney. It was as though he constantly suffered from migraines. Hangovers, Tommy thought. Pale skin, circles under the eyes, a face that hadn't smiled in so long it had probably forgotten how. He wondered that Stoney had the constitution to stand up under what he put his body through and still show up every day, every day. He'd seen Stoney work like a dog when he had to be dying inside. Tommy, on those rare occasions when he did to himself what Stoney did routinely, would stay home and seek the comfort of bed and medicine, and hopefully someone nice to come make soup for him, but Stoney was merciless on himself, punishing, even, which Tommy B. did not understand at all.

Tommy was worried. He considered Stoney a friend, even if Stoney always seemed once removed, someone in the same room with you, but behind a pane of glass, so that you could converse with him, but never touch him, really, never really get a true smell of the man. Tommy had a difficult time not feeling bummed when he was around Stoney, because it seemed to him that Stoney never really enjoyed anything, never really jumped in with all of himself, and Tommy B. liked jumping in more than anything else in life. He

liked to laugh, to have fun, to treat himself well, and he wanted
Stoney to like those things too. He'd taken Stoney around a few
times, together they'd gone to some of the places that Tommy
would go to so much trouble to ferret out. Oh, yeah, this is great,
Stoney would say, but he'd never go back, he wouldn't even go
two blocks out of his way for something extraordinary. Sometimes
when Stoney got started drinking, something inside him would get
loose, something Stoney normally kept chained up in the basement, and then there was no telling what would happen. He
scared Tommy on those occasions, and Tommy would back off and
let him go, and then spend the night worrying that Stoney might
not survive the night. It had been getting gradually worse the past
year, and Tommy feared for his friend, but he also feared for himself, for his business. He didn't even want to consider the fix he'd
be in if Stoney died suddenly. It was not something they had ever
talked about. There should be contingency plans, Tommy thought.
If the business ever went into probate, if Donna ever got a lawyer
and started digging, God, the skeletons they would find! How
could he ever make them understand how things were?

And still, he couldn't bring himself to talk to Stoney about it.
Once again, he'd hope that guilt would do its work, that Stoney
would get hold of himself, that they would find a way to get by.

Stoney watched Fat Tommy come through the front door. He was
impeccably dressed, as always, smooth, confident, solicitous,
buffed, combed, polished, the very picture of overweight conti-
nental charm.

"Hey, Stoney, how you feel?"

Stoney shrugged. It was his biggest rationalization; if he
showed up for work every day, he was just like everyone else. "I'm
okay."

Tommy B. waved Stoney into his office. "We gotta few little problem. Maybe gonna turn into big problem." Stoney followed him, closing the office door as they went through.

"Okay, what's up?"

"Number one, Marty's dead." Marty had been their accountant, and he'd had that rare combination of technical expertise and street smarts.

"Holy shit! What happened?"

"I'ma no sure. The cops find him inna hotel room up inna Bronx, on White Plains Road. He wasa get shot, five, six times."

Stoney sat down on Tommy's couch. Tommy went on, telling him how one of Marty's partners had called to tell him Marty was dead, but offering no details. Tommy, of course, knew some cops in a neighboring precinct, and they had supplied him with more information. Meanwhile, the books for most of Marty's customers were in a state of confusion because his partners could not figure out his filing system or unlock his hard drive, and the end of the month, with its various tax-filing deadlines, was fast approaching.

Stoney did not care about taxes or paperwork. "Jesus. Do they know who did it?"

"All they tell me, he was there with another man, but they find him all alone. His wallet wasa still there, keys, car parked outside."

"Someone he knew, then."

"Maybe. But now, this bum he'sa work with, I never like that guy, he's tella me, "Oh, I don't know, we gotta figure out what's what, Marty wasa do things his own way. . . .""

"Oh, really."

"Yeah. He tell me they gotta spend some time, put everything together." Tommy rubbed his thumb and first two fingers together, palm upward.

"Yeah, all right." Stoney considered for a few seconds. "Okay, we'll wait, see what he comes up with. Anything else?"

"Oh, yeah," Tommy said. "Oh, yeah. We got a summons from the EPA."

"Who?"

"The EPA. You remember that business we did with Freon?"

Stoney thought back to a year ago. The previous year, due to environmental concerns, production of a chemical known as R-12, widely used in refrigeration and air-conditioning, had been outlawed except in a few developing third-world countries. Overnight, prices for the chemical had skyrocketed and a lucrative gray market had sprung up. It was illegal, of course, to import into the U.S. any R-12 manufactured in those third-world countries still producing it, and it was also mandated by law that everyone who used the stuff had to recapture it instead of simply dumping it into the atmosphere, and either reuse it or sell it to one of the companies that specialized in reprocessing the stuff and then reselling it. It had not taken operators like Tommy B. long to figure out that you could buy a thirty-pound drum of R-12 in India for, say, thirty bucks, ship it to the U.S. as "reclaimed" refrigerant, and it would be worth more like seven or eight hundred bucks. Vast quantities of the stuff came flying in under the radar. For about a year it had been second only to cocaine as an illegal import. The federal government tried to stem the tide, passing floor taxes, licensing requirements, record-keeping rules, and so on. A few very unlucky stiffs had gotten crucified as object lessons, but what had finally killed the trade was the insane price level, which had made it profitable for chemical producers to come up with cheaper substitutes. But for a while, it had been prohibition all over again, and Stoney and Tommy had made a lot of money. "Yeah, I remember, all right."

"You remember the freight company we wasa use?"

"Yeah."

"They wasa get caught with R-12 from someplace in Africa, was supposed to be recycle, but wasa still in original cans. So, the EPA, they squeeze 'em, they start giving up everybody they know, including," he said, "you and me."

"So now what?"

"So now they want to see record, where you buy, where you sell, license number from everybody who'sa buy, resale number, why you no pay the floor tax, and like that."

"Shit. So what happens now?"

"They gonna say, 'Okay, we know you buy so many pounds of thisa stuff, every pound, you gotta have document, license, where it went.' No papers, you geta fine, so much a pound."

"How many pounds?"

"Thousands."

"What's the fine?"

"Depend onna judge."

"So take a guess, for chrissake."

"Could be anything. Fifty thousand dollar, quarter million dollar, no way to know."

"Man, you're full of good news today. So how do we play this?"

"What I think, this business is incorporate, don't own much. They gonna try to get you anna me, we are officer of the corporation. I don't know, they can do or no. Depend onna what they can prove. They just have some truck driver says thatsa the guy, we say, uppa yours. They got more than that, maybe we sign for something, we gonna get stung."

"What kind of shape we in? We still flush?"

"I dunno. We could sell, you know, this and that. For now, we gotta wait, see what they got."

•   •   •

When they came out of the office, Walter was eyeing a blue rectangular piece of paper on the counter. "Stoney ain't gonna like this." He was talking to a guy who was known as Jimmy the Hat because he always wore a baseball cap to cover his bald spot. He was a bearish, barrel-chested man with thick arms and a double chin that he needed to shave twice a day. Black hair grew everywhere on him except where he wanted it to. He was sometimes called "Jimmy the Dope" by Stoney, who thought him dull and lazy. He had been hired by Tommy B. to buy used-truck chassis, a few to be repaired and resold, most to be broken into parts, containerized, and shipped to South America. Stoney thought that the only thing Jimmy had going for him was that he had connections inside a few big truck-leasing companies.

"Stoney ain't gonna like what?"

"Jimmy picked up a check," Walter said, "from that Italian ice cream guy on Staten Island." He moved away from the counter, leaving the check lying there.

"He picked up a check." Stoney walked over slowly and looked at the offending piece of paper. "Jimmy, what did Tommy tell you to do?"

"He said to stop and pick up the money on the way in."

"This is not money. This is toilet paper."

Bagadonuts insinuated himself between Stoney and Jimmy. "Stoney, he didn't know." He shot a look at Jimmy, hoping to keep him quiet. "We'll go straighten this out."

"I'll go, you stay." Stoney turned away, fighting to stay calm, but he turned back again. "You know what really bothers me about this? If we'da sent Tuco, who we pay squat, he'd have brought cash, or he'd have used his head and called in. But Einstein, over here, who gets big bucks, he takes a check." He took a step in Jimmy's direction. "What are you, a banker now?"

"Stoney, easy." Bagadonuts glared back at Jimmy, making sure he stayed quiet. Stoney turned away again.

"Yeah, all right." He folded the check and put it in his shirt pocket. "Get Tuco to come drive me to Staten Island." He walked out the front door into the bright sunlight. Bagadonuts turned on Jimmy.

"Whassamatta with you? I told you, hundreds. Ben Franklins. You don'a hear what I'ma say?"

Jimmy spread his hands and shrugged. "But, Tommy, that's a big place. They're no fly-by-night company. Besides, have you seen that guy's office? What was I supposed to say to him?"

Bagadonuts shook his head. "You think he's mafioso because he's gotta picture a Marlon Brando on his wall?" Sneering, he walked up face-to-face with Jimmy and grabbed the younger man by his crotch. "Maybe Stoney's right," he said. "Maybe you got nothing over here, you get scare off by a picture, fat movie star with cotton ball inna mouth." He released his grip and turned away.

Jimmy's face was beet red. "How was I supposed to know? That's a big company over there. You think they're gonna write a bad check? Jesus. I don't know anybody that does business like you guys."

"Big company my ass. They write more bad paper than the *News* and the *Post* combine. You better remember this," he said, enunciating carefully, emphasizing each word. "Business isa no friends. Business isa enemy. They get a chance to fuck you, they gonna do. Go get Tuco."

Tuco slid behind the wheel of Stoney's Lexus. He adjusted the power seat and the mirrors, started up the engine, and backed out of the lot. Stoney had the passenger seat reclined and was lying back with his eyes closed. Tuco got out and closed the gate. "New car," he said, sliding back into the gray leather seat.

"No," Stoney said. "I got it coming off lease, or my wife did, actually. I think she was embarrassed by the old one, thought I needed something better." Stoney was not into cars.

"Twenty thousand miles," Tuco said. "That's barely broken into."

Stoney opened one eye. "Really," he said. "You ever been out of Brooklyn?"

"I meant—"

"I know what you meant. Take the BQE to the Verrazano Bridge. Wake me up when we hit Staten Island."

Damn, Stoney's a slob, Tuco thought as he piloted the car down Flushing Avenue. He could hear beer cans rolling around on the floor in the backseat when he made the right turn onto Morgan. He loved the car, though, loved how silent it was, the way it soaked up the ruts and bumps. He always felt a little odd when Stoney asked him to drive. He often wondered if Stoney was trying to teach him something on these trips, but it was useless to ask, Stoney was not given to explaining his motives. Not that he wouldn't talk, sometimes they would have long conversations on their way to or from someplace. Tuco felt that Stoney moved through his world with a confidence that Tuco did not have. On his way to the BQE, Tuco would generally avoid Fifty-eighth Street, where the big cop garage was, because it was hard getting through, past all of the various cop vehicles, tow trucks, buses, vans, you name it, haphazardly double- and triple-parked on both sides of the street. Stoney invariably chose Fifty-eighth because it was shorter, and he would sit in the traffic honking his horn and cursing the policemen. "Why go this way," Tuco would ask, but Stoney seemed to enjoy the adrenaline. "Hey, it's a public street," he would say.

On the BQE, traffic reached that peculiar density that

demanded total awareness. Drivers dueled for position, seeking to cut into whichever lane was momentarily moving the fastest. Rarely did anyone leave more than a car's length of space between themselves and the car in front. Tuco focused totally on the road and the cars around him, even though he was not in any particular hurry, because he knew that at any lapse of attention he would be cut off, forced to hit his brakes and pray the car behind him noticed in time. It was like everything else: If you did not safeguard what was yours, even your space, it would be taken from you immediately. It made Tuco wonder if there were, somewhere, open and empty highways, someplace where there were fewer people than there were trees and animals, where he could turn on the cruise control and lean back into the seat, drive with one wrist draped negligently across the wheel, like Stoney did. Going over the upper level of the Verrazano Bridge, at the top of the arch, he looked to his left, out to sea, and he got just a glimpse of what it might be like, looking out over the expanse of empty ocean to where the blue sea dissolved into blue sky. It would be like that, he told himself, except for the colors. He resolved to take himself there someday, just to see it.

Stoney came to when they hit the tolls on the Staten Island side. He directed Tuco off the highway, down through the local streets until they got to the waterfront. Not all that different from Brooklyn, Tuco thought. Still a nasty place to be, but with shorter buildings. They pulled into a Burger King parking lot. About a hundred yards down the hill was a brown three-story cinder-block building in the shape of an L. In the open part of the L was a fenced-in parking lot, and to one side of the lot was a truck bay with its roll-up door open. Stoney watched the building in silence for a spell, then he directed Tuco down the hill, just around the corner and out of sight of the building.

"You wait here," he said. "Keep the motor running."

"You sure?"

"You come with me, there could be, ah, consequences."

"Tommy says it's a team sport."

"We go to jail for disturbing the peace, your mother is going to throw you out on your ass."

"She's getting ready to do that anyway."

Stoney sat back in the seat. "Really? Why?"

Tuco sighed. "It's a long story."

"Good. Come with me and you can tell me all about it on the way to central booking."

They walked through the gate, into the parking lot. "We gonna disturb the peace?"

"Damn straight. Just remember the first rule: Watch your ass." They ducked through the open truck-bay door, into a noisy, dimly lit machinery room. Tuco noticed a slight trace of ammonia in the air. There were no people in the room, no mechanics watching the machines. Compressors the size of small cars thundered away, circulating the ammonia that froze the ice cream and kept the holding rooms down to minus twenty degrees. The huge compressors, the motors that drove them, and the air handlers on the roof all combined to create a noise level that made Tuco think he was inside a working engine, listening to the roar. On the wall next to the open door was a belt-driven exhaust fan about four feet in diameter. The blades turned lazily, moved by the slight breeze blowing through the opening. Stoney took out a knife and sliced through the belt. Across from the door was a motor-control center, six feet high, topped by a gauge panel that showed the operating pressures and temperatures of the refrigeration system. Stoney pulled Tuco close to shout into his ear.

"You smell that? That's ammonia, that's what they use here. In a minute it's gonna smell ten thousand times worse. You're gonna have to breathe through your mouth, not your nose. Squint your eyes, they're gonna burn like hell. This is not gonna be easy, but don't panic, okay? We'll stay right on the inside of the door, and it shouldn't be too bad. As soon as it gets thick in here, the motor for that exhaust fan will kick in, and there might be an alarm. The intakes for the air-conditioning system are right over your head, and in five minutes everybody in this whole place will be out in the parking lot, and then you and I will go right down that corridor over there, into the office section. Ready?"

Tuco nodded, and Stoney picked up a pipe wrench from a workbench and smashed two of the big gauges on top of the control panel. The ruptured works behind the shattered glass began to hiss, and Stoney backed away hastily. "Okay, c'mon, over here by the door. Remember, breathe through your mouth, not your nose."

The stuff hit Tuco like a brick wall, and he was able to breathe only in very shallow gasps. He felt as if his throat was on fire, and it was all he could do to keep one eye barely open. Tears began to roll down his face. Stoney put a hand on his shoulder. "You okay?"

Tuco turned to look at Stoney, whose face was screwed into an exaggerated scowl. No tears, though.

"I'm okay," he croaked.

"All right. Won't be much longer." An alarm bell started ringing, added its voice to the din, and the motor that drove the exhaust fan hummed into life, but the drive belt lay on the floor, and the fan blades continued their slow turning. Tuco kept his face right next to the open door, trying to suck in the clean air coming through the opening. His discomfort began to level off, and he found he could see a bit better. Shortly after that he could hear voices shouting deep inside the building, and the sounds of running feet. "Just another minute," Stoney said. "Let them clear out."

Finally Stoney led him into the corridor, away from the

machinery room, and Tuco wiped off his face and began to breathe a bit easier, although his throat still felt raw. As they passed by a window, he caught a glimpse of the parking lot, filled with people milling around.

"How come they ran out so quick?"

"They hate the guy that owns this place. All it takes is one little whiff, they start complaining, hacking and coughing, they wanna go to the doctor, and like that. Get a nice big leak, the bell rings, they run like cockaroaches."

They went through the empty production area where the ice cream was made into dessert specialties. Conveyor belts clattered along, empty filler tables spun rhythmically, and extruders spit precise servings of product into empty space, splat, splat, splat. Stoney laughed when he saw it. The reception area and the main offices were similarly empty. They passed through the offices on the first floor and took the elevator up to the third floor. "Fat bastard," Stoney said. "You believe he put this in here just so he don't have to walk up two flights of stairs? I bet nobody uses it but him."

The innermost office on the third floor was dominated by an enormous mahogany desk. The walls of the office were wainscoted halfway up, topped with dark green paneling. There were bookcases along one wall, filled with matching leather-bound volumes that looked as if they had never been opened. On the opposite wall there was a wide-screen TV with a VCR. There were windows that looked down into the parking lot, and one that looked out over an alley on the far side of the building. Stoney opened the alley window wide, then went and sat down in the leather chair behind the desk. Tuco sat on a couch just inside the office door. The two of them sat listening to the noise coming in through the open window. After prolonged shouting, the alarm bell stopped ringing, and sometime later, people began to filter back into the building. Ultimately there were noises in the outside offices. Stoney held a

SHOOTING DR. JACK   31

finger up to his lips. Finally a short guy in a dark suit came wheez-
ing through the door. He fixed on Stoney and missed Tuco
entirely.

"What the hell are you doing here?"

Tuco thought he looked like a weight lifter gone to seed, a
hundred pounds too heavy.

Stoney had his feet on the desk. "Hey, Vittorio," he said, waving the check in the air. "You cash this for me?"

Vittorio stopped in the middle of the floor. "You get the hell
out of here before I call the fucking cops." He spat the words out,
his voice low and vicious.

Stoney laid the check carefully on the desk and dropped his
feet to the floor. "You gonna call the cops on me?" he asked, his
voice flat and calm. He put his hands on the desktop, palms down.
As Tuco watched him, Stoney's pale face turned dark red. Vittorio
twitched, just the beginning of a turn, and Stoney exploded out of
the chair and over the desk like a bull out of the chute. Vittorio got
his hands up but Stoney already had him by the shirt collar and
the belt.

"You gonna call the cops on me?" he bellowed, dragging
Vittorio across the room and running him into the wall next to the
open window. Vittorio let out a big whoof of air when he hit the
wall, but then as Stoney began to drag him toward the open window, he began to scream, short little screams because he didn't
have much breath, with a high, panicky note at the end of each
one, and as Stoney shoved the fat man's upper body through the
opening, the panicky note got longer, higher, and when Stoney
had him all of the way out, the panic was all there was, longer and
with an audible raspy intake at the end of each one.

Tuco sat transfixed, watching Stoney holding Vittorio, one
hand around one ankle, still bellowing, "You still wanna call the
cops?" The veins stood out on his forearm and on his neck, and

every visible part of his skin was flushed a deep, raw red. Jesus, Tuco thought. That guy has to be three hundred pounds. He remembered the first rule just in time, and when two younger, thinner copies of Vittorio rushed through the door, Tuco clipped the first one behind the ear with a cut-glass ashtray. The first one went down on his hands and knees, and the second one tripped over him, kneeing him in the head in the process, knocking him cold. A silver automatic went spinning across the floor, and Tuco went bouncing after it. He didn't know anything about guns, but he came up holding it the way Marshal Dillon used to, cocked in his hand, the barrel pointed up at the ceiling, more or less in the direction of Vittorio's son.

"Be cool, be cool," he said, holding his other hand palm out, fingers spread. "Nothing happened worth getting shot over, yet, okay? Just stay cool."

The kid looked at him, then at Stoney, back at Tuco again. Tuco saw him make his decision. "Sir," he said, his voice polite, but with urgency, "sir, bring him in, please? Sir, please? Bring him in, okay?" He looked back over at Tuco. "Tell him, okay? Tell him to bring him back in. Sir?"

Stoney seemed to wake up from a spell, and he looked at his hand, holding Vittorio's ankle, and he heard Vittorio, not screaming anymore, but just making that high-pitched keening sound. He grabbed the ankle with both hands and began to haul Vittorio back into the room, but it was much more difficult than getting him out had been. The kid, anguished, looked at Tuco and at the gun in his hand. "Go," Tuco said, gesturing with the pistol. "Go, help."

Once they got him back in, it became obvious that, during his inverted flight, Vittorio had lost control of his bladder, and gravity had done its magic. Tuco smiled, thinking it was the first time he'd ever seen anyone piss his pants and his shirt both. All three of the others stood by the window, red-faced and sucking wind. Stoney retrieved the check and handed it silently to Vittorio, who passed it to his son without looking at it.

"Go get the money for this," he said. The kid stood holding the check, looking at his father's shirt. Vittorio noticed him doing it and twisted his upper body suddenly, swinging his arm around and slapping the kid in the face, knocking him back several feet.

"You hear me? I said go get the money!" His face got redder than ever, but still he stood rooted in one spot. The kid recovered and went out. Tuco tried to read his face as he passed by but could not. Fathers, he thought, must be a mixed blessing. The three of them stood there silently, waiting, and in a few minutes the kid came back with a large manila envelope, stuffed fat.

"Count it," Vittorio spat. "I don't want to see you again."

"It better all be there, then," Stoney said, cradling the envelope in the crook of his arm, like a schoolboy holding his books. "You should have known better, Vittorio. You had to know I'd come."

"Just get out." Tuco looked at the kid again, on his way past, remembering how his face had looked when he'd pleaded for his father, but there was nothing of that there now, only a vast distance and the red outline of fingers on his cheek. They stepped around Vittorio's other son, stirring on the floor, and went out. Tuco wiped the gun off with his shirttail and left it in the secretary's trash can on his way by.

3

BY THE TIME THEY GOT BACK TO THE CAR, TUCO'S HANDS WERE shaking and his pulse was beating wildly, but Stoney pretended not to notice. He directed Tuco to drive them back to the Burger King parking lot. "Just wait," he said. The sirens began in the distance. "No cops," Stoney said, "just the fire department, so far. And the hazmat guys."

"I thought guys like Vittorio never called the cops."

Stoney laughed. "Guys like him? You think he's a wiseguy? I'll tell you what he is, he's a guy that sells ice cream, eats too much of his own product. Goes to too many movies, now he thinks he's living in one. He's an idiot."

"So he would call the cops."

"I'm not sure. He might, but he's got a couple of problems. One, he pissed himself, and two, the kids. How's he gonna look like a tough guy, smelling like that? The cops are gonna laugh at him, and he can't handle that. Right now, I bet he just wants to crawl in a hole. And the one kid, saw the whole thing, what's he gonna do about him? This guy loves money more than just about anybody I know, but if he goes to the cops, he's gonna look like a putz who tried to screw the wrong guys. If he lets the money go, he can go on pretending, 'Don't you worry, I'll get those fucks.'"

"And you ain't worried about him getting you."

"What's he gonna do, throw tartufos at me? The kid might try something, but I don't think so. I think he still buys the old man's act."

"After what he saw?"

"Not that one, you moron, the other one. The one you clipped with the ashtray, which was, I gotta say, very slick." Stoney grinned. "Very slick. No, the kid that saw the whole thing, he's in trouble now. You ever hear the story of the emperor's new clothes?"

"Yeah," Tuco said. "Guy's really naked, right? Thinks he's cool, but he's like, all hanging out."

"Not a pretty sight." Stoney shook out a cigarette, clicked it alive with a plastic lighter. "It's always harder to talk yourself into believing something after you've had your face rubbed in the truth. I read an article once about this guy, he was a college professor at some school out in Idaho, or Ohio, someplace like that. He gets a vision from God, okay, God tells him the world is gonna end, such and such a day, I forget what the day was. 'But I'll save you,' God says, 'you and whoever you can get to follow you, and we'll start over.' So the guy goes around preaching, the standard line, 'Repent, the end is near, the world is gonna end,' Fourth of July, or whatever the day was, I forget. Don't matter. Anyway, he keeps this up, he gets maybe a hundred people to believe him.

"So the big day comes, the day when the Big Kahuna is supposed to pull the cosmic flush handle. The people that are following him, they basically split into two groups. Half of them go home to make a last-ditch effort to save their families, and the other half stay with the professor to wait for the big one. They wait all night, nothing happens. The professor, he's despondent, he wants to kill himself, he goes up to his room to be alone, boom, he has another vision. 'Hey, I was just testing you,' God tells him, 'I had to find out if you were suitable, and the world is still gonna end, but I'll give you a little more time to convince people.' So the professor goes back downstairs to tell everyone, except now, being a wiser visionary, he doesn't tell anyone an actual date this time. Maybe next week, maybe next month, who knows.

"So here's what happens. The people who stayed with the professor all night, in his house, almost all of them buy the new story, you know, the end is still near, repent, whatever. The other ones, the ones that went home, almost all of them were like, 'Hey, you made a monkey outta me once, once is enough.' You see what I mean? Just because you talk yourself into believing some shit doesn't make it real."

Tuco shook his head. "Yeah, but why the difference? Was it just because half of them were all together, like?"

"No. The two groups had two different experiences. Like Vittorio's two kids. The one on the floor, he's still tight with the old man, even when he finds out what happened, he didn't see it, he didn't get his face rubbed in it, so he can still believe, if he wants to. The other kid, he's fucked. Every time the old man sees him, he's ashamed all over again, so the kid's on his own. Like in the story, he seen the emperor without his clothes, once he thought the guy was God, but he can't get this vision out of his head, you know, if he's a naked, fat, hairy bastard with a little, tiny schwantz, how can he be God? He can't. Even if he wants things to go back to how they were, it's no good, he can't do it. Like the professor's disciples, the ones that went home, they got their faces rubbed in it the next day when the sun came up. Too hard to go back to pretending, after that, this is real and that ain't."

"So what happens now?"

"Hard to say. Depends on the kid, I suppose. He ain't gonna face up right away, I don't think. He'll try to pretend, try to believe everything is like it was. He can't do it, but he don't know that. So for a while he'll keep it up, but he's screwed, no matter what he does. Either he quits or Vittorio fires him. No way he can hang in there. And here's the funniest part of the whole thing: say Tommy calls Vittorio next week, says, 'Hey, we can make some money, you in or out,' Vittorio might bitch and moan, but he's in. I guarantee you, he's in." Stoney turned to Tuco and grinned broadly. "That's why he didn't wanna pay to begin with. He might talk a lot of shit, but the only thing Vittorio really loves is money."

Tuco wanted to go home a different way, whether it was from paranoia or just to kill time, he didn't know. They went over the Bayonne Bridge and north through the local streets, heading for Jersey City and the Holland Tunnel. Tuco looked out his window in disgust. More tenements, more factories, giant apartment buildings, traffic lights, empty lots covered with old tires and broken glass. Stoney watched him in amusement.

"What?"

"Just like Brooklyn, man."

"What'd you expect?"

"I dunno. Trees, I guess. I thought Jersey would look different. How far does this shit go on?"

"Another half hour's drive west. Forty-five minutes, maybe."

"So, from halfway out on Long Island, all the way in through Queens, all through Brooklyn and Staten Island, all through these places here, and more, it's all the same."

"More or less. Some neighborhoods are better than others."

Tuco drove in silence. All right, he thought, so we're going north, not west, so there's no reason for any improvement, not if you figure this stuff has to spread out from a central point, like maybe it started in Brooklyn a long time ago, and maybe these places out here were nice then, but it spreads, like some kind of skin rash. It bothered him.

"Suppose you had to walk," he said to Stoney. "Suppose you started out from, like, our block. Imagine how far you would have to walk before you found a place didn't have somebody saying, 'This is mine, get out'?"

"You don't have to walk, you got a license. Plus, what about the parks?"

"You ever go into Prospect Park in the summer?"

"Yeah, okay. What's your point?"

"Didn't you ever feel like you should just take off? Like maybe you were missing out, staying here?"

"You wanna run away? That's all it is, running away. People from other places, they come here. Why do you think that is? My grandfather came here from Italy, so did Tommy, for that matter. From all over the world, China, Russia, you name it. They think they're gonna find something different when they get here. You ask them, you know what they'd say? 'The game is the same, anywhere you go. Ain't nothing free.'"

"You never feel like running away?"

"All the time." He flushed, remembering his urge to turn off the turnpike, just that morning. "You hungry? Pull over to this bodega, here. I'm gonna go in and get a beer."

Very carefully, Tuco did not look. "Okay."

"I'm just gonna get one, for chrissake."

"Wha'd I say?"

"Just pull over. Why don't you go into that place across the street and get yourself a sandwich or something." Stoney handed him a ten.

"You want something?"

"No, I'm not hungry." He caught Tuco looking at him side-ways. "I had a big breakfast," he said irritably. "Don't lock the door, I'll be back before you."

Stoney picked a quart bottle of beer from the back of the case, where they were cold. Up by the register they sold little bottles of vodka, like the ones airlines used. Stoney grabbed two of them and handed the guy behind the counter a twenty. He twisted the tops off and drained both vodka bottles at the same time as the guy behind the counter made change. "Hey, no drinking in the store, you're gonna get me in trouble."

"Yeah, sure," Stoney said. "Here, get rid of these for me, will you?"

They sat in the car in the parking lot at the Liberty Science Center, watching the Hudson River roll by, seemingly just inches from coming over the bank. Manhattan hovered improbably out over the water. Tuco ate his sandwich, Stoney nursed his beer. It went against his nature, he wanted to down it and go get another one, but then it would start up again, he could feel it hanging over him.

"You never told me," he said, "why Rosa's throwing you out. You think she's really gonna do it?"

Tuco was surprised by the sudden question. "Yeah," he said, swallowing a bite of sandwich. "Yeah, pretty soon. Only thing hold-ing her back, she don't think I could feed myself or get clean clothes or anything. She thinks I'd starve without her taking care of me."

"What'd you do?"

"Nothing. I didn't do nothing." He said it in a mildly wounded voice.

Stoney finished his beer and lit up a cigarette. "You musta done something," he said, half in jest. "You get a girlfriend?"

"No."

"Get drunk?"

"I don't drink."

"Smoke some shit?"

"No, never. You know I don't touch that stuff."

"Hmm. Maybe it's her. She get a boyfriend?"

"Nnnno."

"Aha. She got some guy coming around, she wants to go out, but you're in the way, and she can't go. Right?"

"She could go anytime she want. Besides, they'd only go to some church thing."

"Well, hey, what could happen at a church thing? Come on, man, give it up. What's up?"

"Well, this guy from the church did start coming around. At first he was coming after me, 'cause I quit going, but now I think he comes mostly for her."

"You quit going? Why?"

Tuco's face screwed itself into a scowl. "You remember when I was axing you about going to the country?"

Stoney blinked uncomprehendingly. "Huh?"

"Jesuchristo. Half an hour ago, I said, "How far do you have to go to get to the country?" You remember what you said? You said it was just running away."

"So I did."

"Well, that's all my mother is doing. She don' need to get a job, 'cause Jesus is coming. She don' need to go to school and learn nothing, she don' have to exercise, or even walk a little bit, find someone to go out with, go see the country, none of that. She just sits in that stinking apartment, getting fat and praying for heaven." Tuco was so mad he was ranting. "You believe in all that shit?"

Stoney could remember when Tuco had believed it, not so long ago. "Heaven and hell?"

"And God watching you, filling out your scorecard, counting how many times you fuck up?"

"I did at one time." Damn, Stoney thought, my son's only twelve, I thought I had a few years before I had to answer this. "Tuco," he said, "calm down. You spraying spit on the inside of my windshield." It was not what he had intended to say.

"Sorry." Tuco pulled his sleeve down over his hand to wipe it off.

"No, no," Stoney said, waving him off. "I was just busting. Listen to me. I'm gonna be as honest as I know how to be, okay? I'm not gonna tell you what I think, because what I think is wrong. What you think you know, that's wrong too. What Rosa thinks she knows is wrong."

"That don't make any sense."

"Look," Stoney said, reaching over, putting his hand on Tuco's arm, "this church of yours, the one you're not going to anymore, all the churches I ever been to, they ain't about what you think they are."

Italians, Tuco thought. They always gotta touch you when they talk, and they always gotta talk when they're beating the shit out of you. Tuco did not like being touched.

"What church is about is getting you to follow the rules. Look at you. You have a job, you dress normal, you speak good English. You keep going, by the time you're forty, you'll be driving a car like this one, voting Republican, playing golf on the weekends." Tuco did not look thrilled at the prospect. Stoney was having trouble coming up with the words he needed, and regretted the two quick hits in the liquor store. He tried again. "Listen. If you hadn't gone to church all those years, you probably couldn't ask the questions now, you know what I mean?"

Tuco shrugged, unsatisfied.

"You're just gonna have to find your own way. Meantime, I'll talk to Tommy B. when we get back, see if he can help you find a place, okay?"

"All right, just let me ax you one more question. This thing we did this morning. Making Vittorio pee himself. Making him hate his son. Are we gonna have to pay for that, you and me? Was that our fault?"

"Is it our fault Vittorio is a douche bag?" Stoney sat silent for a minute. "Everybody pays, in the end. Nobody gets away with anything."

In the sliver of afternoon that was left when Tuco and Stoney got back to Troutman Street, Stoney talked to Tommy Bagadonuts about Tuco's situation, and Tommy B braced Tuco just before leaving for the day.

"Stoney wasa tella me," Tommy said, "that you get a new girlfriend, she so ugly, she make you momma cry, and now she gonna t'row you out."

"Look at this face," Tuco said. "Does this look like the face of someone that girls would follow home?"

Somewhere back in Tuco's family tree, Tommy thought, there lurked a Mayan or two, and their genes had laid dormant all these years, and chosen this time to come out. In another culture, he might have been thought handsome. As it was . . . "Ha. You young guys, you so stupid, you don' know anything at all. You face isa no you problem."

"Aaaaah . . ."

"No. Is true. You see a nice girl, you know whattayou do?" Tommy let his mouth gape open and his tongue hang out, dropped his shoulders, bent his knees, and started making slurping noises.

Tuco had to laugh in spite of himself. "And then," Tommy continued, "you stare at the chest. I say, this isa no good. You look in the eye, say hello, make nice conversation. Nice day, oh what a pretty dress, you know, talk."

Tuco was red. He had always found it difficult to talk to Bagadonuts. To Tuco, who did his fifty push-ups and sit-ups every morning, there was something disquieting about the man. It bothered him that Bagadonuts expended energy the way a miser spends gold. He would drive around a parking lot four times looking for a closer spot rather than walk a hundred feet. Even when he cleared his throat, it was always with minimum effort, just a tiny ahem. Tuco noted that Stoney would generally hack vigorously and spit, and Tuco thought him more honest for it, more forthright. It was stupid, he knew, thinking that such a trivial thing had any significance, but the idea was planted already, and he was unable to change it.

Tuco liked to think that he understood Stoney, at least to some degree. Stoney did not generally bother to camouflage his intentions or opinions. With Bagadonuts, though, he always felt like an overmatched chess player, and no matter how careful or smart he tried to be, Bagadonuts always seemed to be five or six moves ahead of him, and he could never quite figure out what was happening in time to think about what his part should be. Tommy B. always got there first, figured the angles, and wrote Tuco's script for him. He couldn't say that Tommy had ever used him poorly, but he had used him, or at least taken the trouble to learn Tuco well enough to have a good idea of what he would do in a given situation. Maybe it was just that he did not like to be so transparent. But then, Tommy is a pro, Tuco told himself. This game is what he really makes his living at. People were always impressed with how quickly Tuco could open a locked car door or how well he could remember things. Why shouldn't Tommy be good at what he did? Fat Tommy was the front man, whose job it was to connect, to make friends and shake hands. That was why he always wore a suit, spotless white shirt, a tie with a matching hankie peeking out of the jacket pocket. I should be happy, he told himself, that Tommy is that slick, and that he's on my side. I hope he is on my side.

"Anyway," Tommy was saying, "I know a nice lady, she have an apartment building in Brooklyn Heights."

"You know a lot of nice ladies."

Tommy grinned. "You wanna know why? I talk. I look in the eye, she tell me her name, I remember what she'sa say. Later on, she wanna show me the chest, then, I look. Anyway, used to be a super in this building, live in the basement apartment. He'sa get run over with a truck, cross Flushing Avenue. The ambulance was'a take him to Woodhull hospital, he'sa catch infection, now he's dead. She gonna need a new super. It'sa nice job, no work, really. You gonna like."

"Why'd they take him to Woodhull? Nobody gets out of there alive. They shoulda took him to Wyckoff Heights."

"I think maybe he was drunk, the ambulance thinks he's a bum, you know, no job. So, that's where they take him. Anyway, basement apartments no good anymore, illegal. Nice place, but against the law. So, anybody'sa ask you, last guy was'a you uncle, that way, no problems. Give you nice place to live, save'a my lady friend some money. I talk'a to her. You go see, maybe you wanna do. Okay?"

"Okay. Thanks, Tommy."

"You wanna go, I'll stay and lock up."

Jimmy the Hat didn't exactly flinch, but he did stiffen up, and looking at Tuco sideways, he leaned away from him just a degree or so. It was almost like he was afraid, although he had no reason to be. It was puzzling to Tuco, because Jimmy hadn't always had that reaction to him. In the beginning Jimmy had always treated him like an underling, had not paid much attention to him except when trying to give orders. One day, though, Jimmy's body language had changed. "Yo, Jimmy," Tuco had said, and Jimmy had frozen up and waited stiffly for whatever he thought was coming. After Tuco had noticed it the first time, he'd done it a few times just for fun. He found it odd, though, because he could not think of even a faintly rational reason for Jimmy to be afraid of him. He'd gotten used to it, though, and did not wonder as much anymore.

Tuco was replaying the scene with Vittorio over and over again in his mind, especially the part where Vittorio had slapped his son's face. The kid had been the only conscious person in the room on Vittorio's side, but Vittorio needed to hit someone, and just because he could, he'd done it. Turned and smacked the kid as hard as he could manage. He watched Jimmy shut down his computer. "You get along with your old man?"

Jimmy was still, then he licked his lips, inhaled. "Much better, these last few years."

"Yeah, why is that."

"Hah." The spell was broken, and Jimmy turned to face Tuco, grinning. "Because he croaked, is why."

"What kinda guy was he?"

"He was all right, you know, to be around. But he had this gambling jones. He worked for the transit authority, made okay money, but it all went to the bookies. We were forever getting the lights cut off, the landlord would be coming around looking for the rent money, shit like that. I remember once, when I was about ten, some shylock he owed came to the house, had these two big goons with him. They beat the crap out of him right there in his own

kitchen, my mother's standing there not saying a word, just holding me and my sister. Had about as much sympathy as a rock. I
guess she was sick of it by then. Anyway, they finish up, they sit
him down at the kitchen table, he's holding his stomach, right,
blood's dripping out of his nose onto the table. One of the goons
walks into the living room, I thought he was gonna take the TV
set, we had one of those console TVs, you know, came in a big
wooden cabinet, but he didn't, he just picks it up, holds it about so
high off the floor, drops it. Picture tube goes, cabinet splits open.

"They leave, he's still sitting there, my mother doesn't say a
word, she just pushes us out the door, we went over my grand-
mother's for a week or so. After that, he was never the same."

"He straighten his act out?"

"Hell, no. But he stopped playing the horses. Stuck mostly to
the numbers after that."

"That was before Lotto."

"Yeah, but they still do it, there's a guy works in the steelyard
down the block still books the numbers. The one my old man used,
they used the track handle, meaning, in the paper, under results
they always print the handle, what the track took in. Last three
numbers of the handle was what they used. Say you wanna bet,
one two three, whatever your number is, you give the guy a buck.
Your number comes up the next day, he gives you fifty back. No
big deal, right? Play a buck a day, so you're out five, ten bucks a
week. No big deal, except when you're taking home ninety, hundred bucks a week, like back in those days. But my old man, he
has to put ten on this number, ten on that number, fifty cents on
these other four or five. What a mutt. It was the only thing he ever
cared about. He used to carry this spiral notebook in his pocket so
he could remember all the numbers he played."

"He ever win?"

"Shit, man, it didn't matter if he won, you got to know when to walk away, and he could never do that. I go to Atlantic City or up to Foxwood, right, I take a certain amount with me. Say it's five hundred. So if I'm down two hundred and I hit for a couple grand, I put the two grand away, and I'll only play the rest of the original five, you get me? I don't stand there and piss away the whole wad."

"I'm surprised you'd play at all, after . . ."

"Oh, I ain't like him, believe me." He took off his hat and rolled the bill carefully in his hand. He suddenly looked older, more vulnerable. "When my mother died, he borrowed eighty-five hundred bucks off me to bury her. Cost me another five when he went. I was gonna let them put him in Potter's Field, up on Hart Island with the bums and winos, but my sister pitched a fit, said she'd pay it out of her own pocket, so I relented. Five grand, and nobody even showed up." He looked over at Tuco, a tired look on his face. "You gonna lock up, I'm outta here."

"Hey, sweetheart."

Tuco jumped two feet in the air. He'd been in the act of closing the gate to the parking lot, which Stoney had yelled at him about before he'd left for home. He spun around, his heart beating wildly, and there she was, a foot or so away, regarding him with amusement. Tuco remembered what Tommy had told him.

"God, you scared me," he said, carefully maintaining eye contact.

"You so jumpy," she said, chuckling. To Tuco, it sounded like music. "Maybe I could help you to, you know, relax. You like to party?" She reached out a hand to Tuco's arm, and the touch of her gentle fingers hit him like an electric charge.

Tuco felt himself turning red. "Aaah," he croaked, "I'm, I'm not much of a partier."

"I can see that," she said. She put her hand on his chest and pushed, and he backed into the gate, which swung open behind him. A lifetime of conditioning kicked in and he started to put his hands up to fend her off, but she was too close, and when he inhaled, his head was filled with her indescribably intoxicating smell. She put her hands up under his shirt and rubbed his chest. A voice in his head was shouting for his attention, it might have been the voice of an elder in his mother's church, but hormones raged in his blood, and his body took over. She unzipped him and took him out, and at her feathery touch he felt a rolling shock wave, starting with his hands, his feet, and his scalp, gathering force as it went, building the momentum of a sudden thunderstorm, but then quickly the sun broke through, and it was all over.

She wiped him off with a Kleenex. "My," she said. "I'd say you was overdue. This your first time, sweetie?"

Tuco was panting, wondering how to feel. "Yeah," he said. "I guess it was."

"That's so sad," she said. "You ain't had no one to love you, put they arms around you and all that? You been scarin 'em away, or what?"

He was still watching her face. "I didn't scare you, did I?"

"No, honey, you sure didn't. You gonna give me something for my trouble?"

Tuco had a twenty in his pants pocket. He fished it out and handed it over.

"Oh, that's too much, honey," she said, but she folded the bill and tucked it away. "Let's say I owe you one." She tittered that laugh again, and laid her soft hand on his cheek. "You go straight home, now." And then she was gone, leaving him alone in the parking lot under a darkening sky, wondering if there really was a God, and would He make a big deal over this, would He really burn you in hell for it.

• • •

Driving home, Stoney felt exactly the way he had when he was twelve or thirteen, going to school without his homework. He knew she was pissed, knew she probably had every reason to be, but since he couldn't remember what he had done, he had no idea what to apologize for. How can you negotiate, he thought bitterly, when you don't even know what your own cards are? He badly wanted to stop somewhere for a short one, or even hit the bottle under the seat, but he knew there was no single better way to screw things up worse than they were already. The sweat on his hands grew clammy as he turned up his street, but a wave of relief hit him as he neared the house. Her car was not in the driveway. At least, he thought, I can get inside and sit down. A little peace, that's all he really wanted . . .

His twelve-year-old son, Dennis, was the only one home. "Hey, kid," Stoney said, "How— What happened to your face?" The kid had a black eye and a swollen lower lip.

"I got in a fight in the hockey game yesterday afternoon," came the sullen reply. In a flash it all came back to him. Of course! He had promised to go to Dennis's game on Sunday. Donna had made him swear to be back in time. "He worships you," she'd said. "He's really hurt when you're not there." Shit.

Dennis looked down at the rug, avoiding Stoney's gaze.

"Come into the back room," Stoney said, "and tell me what happened." The back room was almost where Stoney lived. They'd added it onto the rear of the house as a sort of enclosed sunporch, but Stoney had gradually taken it over, and he'd outfitted it with an easy chair, a TV, a VCR, some bookshelves, and so on. The kids called it the "spanking room." Most of the serious discussions in the household took place there.

Stoney sat down in his chair, the kid stood just outside the doorway, eyes downcast, hands shaking. Jesus, Stoney thought, what does he think I'm gonna do? He remembered quaking in fear before his own father, but what a mean old bastard he had been. I can't be that bad, can I? he thought. But the kid was terrified.

"So what happened?"

"Well . . ." The kid shifted from foot to foot, struggling mightily.

"Were you on the ice?"

"Yes."

"Did you have the puck?"

A big sigh. "I'm a defenseman, Dad."

Oh, shit. Should have known that. "Defensemen get the puck sometimes, don't they?" Why did it have to be hockey? Why couldn't he play basketball?

"They had the puck." Dennis looked up finally, away, out the window. "One of their forwards. He beat us all day, he skated right by me twice, and scored both times. So I tripped him, and he got mad, and we had a fight."

"You hit him?" He couldn't quite believe it.

"I tried to," Dennis said, loud, defiant. But he quickly turned his eyes down again.

Small for his age, Stoney thought, private school, nice neighborhood. Ah, Jesus, what do I do? "Okay," he said, "suppose you play these guys again tomorrow. What would you do?"

The kid stood there shaking, fists clenched, fighting the fear and the anger. The answer came to Stoney while Dennis struggled. Thank you, God, Stoney thought.

"You want to win the game or you want to beat this kid up? You probably can't do both."

"Win," Dennis said without hesitation. "Win the game."

"All right. We can do something about that," Stoney said, getting out of the chair. "Come with me."

Dennis looked doubtful. "Mom says I'm grounded."

"Don't worry about it. I'll leave Mom a note. I'll tell her you're with me." Now she's really gonna steam, he thought. He laughed in spite of himself. "Tomorrow we'll both be grounded."

Stoney drove up Route 17, mall central, New Jersey, and into the parking lot of one of the biggest sporting-goods stores in the country. It took a while, but he managed to find an in-line skate salesman who was really into his sport. He was tall and rail thin, with a wispy red goatee and a long ponytail. "Gordon," Stoney said, reading the name tag, "this here's Dennis. Dennis is an ice hockey defenseman who doesn't get enough rink time. Fix him up."

"Oh, boy," Gordon said. "He's gonna need skates, street pads, gloves, a helmet, the works. You okay with that?"

"Gordon," Stoney said with a wink, "hockey is his life. Fix him up."

"Dennis, you are in good hands. Come with me."

Forty minutes and several hundred dollars later, Dennis was zooming back and forth across the wood-floored section of the store reserved for trying out new skates. He kept forgetting how the brakes worked, even with shouted instructions from Gordon, and whaling into the waist-high fence that enclosed the practice area, but he never slowed down. At length everybody was happy with the various equipment selections, and Gordon stood next to Stoney while Dennis stripped off pads.

"He's either gonna be real good," Gordon said, "or he'll kill himself. He can't seem to go at half speed."

"I think it's a genetic thing," Stoney said. "I remember when he was three, we moved into the house we live in now, and I put up a basketball hoop over the garage. He stood in the driveway, right under the hoop, and he kept shooting the ball straight up in the air. Naturally, the ball stops like six feet short of the basket, comes back down and hits him in the puss. He blinks a few times, goes and gets the ball, does it all over again. Over and over. He winds up with his face all puffed up, redder than a baboon's ass. He screamed like hell when we made him stop."

"Desire that strong is impressive. You think he would benefit from a lesson or two?"

"You know somebody?"

"Let me give you my card . . ."

"Oh, sure," Donna hissed, darting a look over her shoulder. She stood in the same doorway that her son had, hours earlier. Stoney was back in his chair. "You can buy him off, but you're not buying me off. You can't keep pulling this shit and think everything will be all right the next day."

"I didn't buy anyone off." No way to win this, Stoney thought.

"What do you call all that stuff?"

Stoney inhaled, blew out a big sigh. "Why do you think he got into the fight?"

"I don't care why he got in the fight."

"Oh, come on."

"Because it's a stupid game, then," she snapped, her voice rising, "played by a bunch of knuckle-dragging Neanderthals who beat each other senseless. I never wanted Dennis to play this fucking game to begin with, but you and he both promised me there would be no fighting."

Oh, no, Stoney thought, she said the F-word. She must be really cranked. "He got into the fight," he said patiently, "because the other kid was better than him." She doesn't get it, he thought. "The other kid faked him out, scored on him. He was letting his teammates down."

"Is that what you think?"

Stoney shrugged. "Well, that's what usually happens when the other guy is better than you. He wins, you lose. What do you do when the other guy is smarter, or stronger, or makes more money than you?"

"Well, apparently, if you're from this family, you punch him in the face."

"No, no," Stoney said, laughing. "Not always. Sometimes you push your luck a little bit. You stretch the rules. You run your stick in between his legs, maybe he'll fall down, maybe he'll just lose the puck. You wait for your shot, and you take it."

"And that's what he's learning, playing hockey."

"No," Stoney said, a bit louder. "That's what's in him, already."

"And you're proud of that."

"I would prefer that he didn't—"

She cut him off. "I don't want my son growing up to be some asshole who's missing half his teeth and who goes around punching people in the face. I want him to be a real man, not a bum." She looked sorry as soon as she said it.

"Yeah, well." He was subdued. "Listen, lot of middle-aged guys go down to that rink early in the morning, still like to play. Doctors, lawyers. Intellectuals, even," he said, enunciating carefully.

"Stoney, what am I going to do with you?"

He heard fear in her voice, fear and desperation and longing. He waited before responding.

"Look, I'm right about the hockey thing. Let him practice on the street skates. When he gets faster, he'll be the one the other kids are chasing, he'll feel better about the whole thing, and there won't be any more fights."

She stood with her arms folded across her chest. After a moment, she spoke in a softer voice. "I really don't understand this booze thing."

"I don't know how to explain it," he said, not looking at her. "I'm doing the best I can, you have to know that."

"Yeah," she said. "Yeah, sure." She turned on her heel and headed for the linen closet to get sheets and a blanket. Stoney watched her go, thinking that she'd probably leave the couch made up from now on, wondering if he could ever find a way to turn the clock back, somehow, to go back to the way they had both been, back when they were young, but that was such a long time ago, it almost seemed like a dream.

Tuco went up Troutman Street in a fog, turned right and went up the hill on St. Nicholas. Such a simple thing, really, how could it make any difference? And yet it had changed everything. It was like the time he'd found the comic-book store on Grand Avenue, and had checked it out on impulse. They had everything in there— history comics, comic book novels, Bible comics . . . In that one morning, a door had been opened, and it had changed the world. Things he'd thought forever out of his reach were suddenly brought into the light, and he could see, and even read, if he worked at it, things that he'd only been hearing for his entire life. Even his opinion of himself was different, after that morning, he was not so stupid, after all, he just needed to find his own way. For whatever reason, the normal pathways did not work for him, but he had stumbled across an alternative. Who knew what others were out there?

And now, this had happened, this encounter with the girl in the parking lot. He didn't want to use the word "prostitute," not even in his mind. It had only taken minutes. He didn't even know her name. How could it mean anything? How could it make any difference? And yet he had the feeling that it had changed everything, that somehow he had taken a step that he couldn't take back, that from

now on, in some important way that he didn't completely understand, he would be different from who he had been, before. But then
he noticed where he was, and it was a quick knife to the guts to real-
ize he was on that block, right across the street from that building,
five-story red brick, front door forever ajar, first- and second-floor
windows broken, looked like what it was, you had to be a desperate
motherfucker, go in there. The spray paint on the front stoop looked
like graffiti, but if you knew how to read it, it was a declaration of
war. Fuck with one of us, you fuck with us all, and we'll kill you,
we'll kill your parents, your kids, your girlfriend, anyone else who
happens to be home at the time.

He had stuck his head in the lion's mouth one last time, counting on family ties, wanting to talk his cousin Miguel into coming
out, somehow. It had been stupid and rash, and he'd paid for it.
And worse, his chances for success had been exactly zero.

The memory of the beating he had taken, as well as the warning that went with it, made him shiver, and he quickened his steps,
feeling lucky that there was no one around.

His building, the one he and Rosa lived in, was in the middle
of a block of identical buildings, no stoops or stairways, no archi-
tectural flourishes of any kind, just a sheer, continuous rise of soul-
less red brick on both sides of the street, punctuated by doors and
windows. They were only five stories high, and they only went the
one block, but they always seemed much larger than they were,
monolithic, somehow, drearily eternal and eternally dreary. He
pushed open the front door and walked into a dim, urine-scented
hallway. He could feel his spirit leaching away as he trudged up the
same stairs he had climbed all his life, God what a place, God what
a place, God what a place, step by step.

He had a feeling, going down the hallway, that the guy was in
there. Have to knock on the front door of my own place, he
thought, and the realization dawned on him, once again, that it

was Rosa's home, and that lately he'd only slept here. He wanted to stick his key in the lock and barge in, surprise them, but he did not. Chickenshit, he said silently to himself, and he knocked.

Elder Thompson opened the door. What she sees in this guy, I'll never know, Tuco thought. He ain't smart, he ain't rich, he ain't good looking. Arrogant, too, guy's so holy, probably thinks his shit doesn't stick. And how's he get his hair to do that? He must go to Al Sharpton's barber.

I don't need this, he thought. I just want to eat something, watch TV, go to sleep.

"Your mother," Thompson was saying, "invited me over tonight because she's concerned about your spirituality." My ass, Tuco thought. She's concerned about your marital status, and I know what you're concerned with, you ain't even honest enough to admit it. Come mousing around here, Oh, Eddie, we so worried about you . . .

Thompson was going on about the prodigal son. "And you see, Eddie, he wouldn't listen to his father. He wouldn't listen to those who were trying to help him, trying to help him understand the right way for him to live. He thought he knew what was right for himself! He wanted to go his own way." Thompson leaned in earnestly, trying to make eye contact. "Do you understand what I'm trying to tell you, Eddie?"

This guy isn't gonna go away, Tuco thought. He's not gonna let me blow him off this time. He's gonna keep pushing until I push back, or cave in. The more he thought about it, the more irritated he got.

"What," he said, "you think I'm fucking retarded, is that what you think?"

Thompson retreated, blinking and looking hurt. "No, Eddie, no, I don't think you're retarded. I know you got your problems, but—"

"Everybody got their problems." Tuco's face was twisted into an angry scowl.

"I know that, Eddie, but I don't think you're retarded, and anyway, that's not what I want to talk to you about. And I don't want you to get mad and use foul language, I want you to listen to me with an open mind. Can you do that, Eddie? Because you can learn from the mistakes of others, Eddie, and by doing so, you can save yourself and your mother some serious pain. That's what the story of the prodigal son is all about."

Tuco had figured out the whole story in the comic-book store, and he could see it entire and complete in his mind. "Yeah, yeah," he said. "Kid goes and pisses his money away. Has to eat with the pigs."

Thompson stopped again, opening and closing his mouth several times as if uncertain as to how to proceed.

"What?" Tuco said. "You forget how it goes? Kid has to go back home, go back to his old man, right?"

"Edward," Thompson began, in a grave tone.

"Don't 'Edward' me," Tuco said, getting angrier by the minute. "Tell the truth. You think I'm so stupid that I don't get it, right? You think you need to come over here so you can tell me what I need to do, 'cause you think I'm too fucking retarded to think for myself, ain't that right."

"I never called you a retard!" Thompson was way too defensive, and Tuco could tell he was lying. "I never said that!"

You know, Tuco thought, you keep acting like Stoney, something bad's going to happen. You really want to wind up throwing this guy down the stairs? Why don't you try to figure what Tommy would do, he asked himself. He stared at Thompson, and slowly he began to grin.

"Let me ax you something," he said, finally. "You ever eat any pig food?"

"Aah . . ."

"No, for real." He turned and winked at Rosa, who was sitting on the couch, but she looked disgusted. "You don't have to tell, like, the details, but you musta ate a little pig food, am I right?"

"I'm not quite sure what you're getting at, Edward."

"You see?" Tuco was grinning broadly. "You thought you had to come explain this all to me, right, but you're the one doesn't understand the story. 'Cause the way you're telling it, it don't make no sense. I ain't got no money, for one thing." Not much, anyhow, he thought. "And I ain't got no father, either."

"Eddie, you have more than—"

"No," Tuco said, cutting him off, "don't get started up again. Listen to me, and I'll tell you what the story's about. 'Cause I know that you've ate pig food before."

"Why do you keep saying that?"

"You don't live at home with your mom, do you? You're a man, right? You think that you're a man?"

Thompson quivered with insult, and he stood up to his full height and tried to suck in his stomach. "My mother is dead," he said in a wounded tone, "and yes, yes, I am a man, I'm a man of God."

"How'd you get that way?"

"I attended Bible college—"

"Wrong answer, that came after. Think of the story. Kid's living at home, right, he's not a man yet. He's a boy. What happened?"

"All right, I get it."

"See? You did eat some pig food. Didn't you."

"I made some mistakes, but—"

"But nothing. It was the pig food that did it. He was a man when he came back."

"I just don't understand—"

In an instant, the smile was gone, and Tuco's voice got loud. "Because he made up his own fucking mind!"

"Eddie," Rosa said, startling them both, "come in the bedroom and talk to me one minute."

"You like this guy, right?"

"I'm worried about you."

"I know. Look, I'm going out, I'm gonna go get something to eat. I'll be gone a couple hours."

She looked over his shoulder, out into the other room where Thompson sat waiting. "It's not like that."

"None of my business," Tuco said, "it's your life, you got a right to it. Figure two hours, okay?"

4

WHEN BAGADONUTS GOT HOME TO THE LOFT, HE DIDN'T TURN ON
the lights, or the TV, or the radio. He shucked his suit jacket and
went over to sit in a chair by the front window. It was placed so
that he was sitting parallel to the window, looking down at the
floor, but the light, the street noises and the summer air came
through the window and washed over him. He sat without moving, his hands in his lap, counting his exhalations, one to ten,
one to ten, over and over. Sometimes when he did this a sense
of peace would settle over him, but other times the voices in his
head would start up, an accusatory chorus that exhumed his
past failures and humiliations and reviewed them one by one.
The first few times he'd tried it, the racket in his mind had driven him out on the street in search of distraction, and he'd gone
looking for conversation and human contact. At the time, he'd
thought of it as a weakness, a sort of running away from himself. He had progressed from there to justification, telling himself
he was the social sort, and he needed company to function.

Ultimately, though, he'd chosen to sit by the window and look inside.

So he sat, in the dark, alone, and his mind bounced from one thing to another in a seemingly random series of associations. He kept trying to bring it back, counting, feeling himself breathe, but on this night it was not to be.

My problem is that I let these things get to me, he thought. I can't be like these Americans, like Stoney. Seeing the girl on the street that morning had disturbed his balance, that along with all of the other stuff, poor, dead Marty, the two kids in the alley, the EPA and all the rest of it. Why? Why, with so much fruit on the tree, was there so much misery? Why so many beautiful women, and so few could dance?

Always back to that. The mind, when you let it go, that's where it goes.

Stupid, he thought, to torment yourself with these things when there's never an answer to why, but it is one thing to know that in your head, quite another to ignore your heart, which does not reason, but keeps asking why.

Ask Stoney about the girl, the streetwalker, and he might not even remember her, let alone torment himself with thoughts of what she could have been. Could still be, if only. Another casualty, he would say, and shrug his shoulders, another dead soldier. Tommy knew him so well, he knew exactly how Stoney would react. "Another name on the wall," he'd say, and go back to what he had been doing. "Hey, better her than you. No?"

Tommy was no longer confident he knew the answer. He thought back to younger days, when it had all seemed so much simpler. They'd had less money, but more fun, back then. He wondered what that younger Tommy Rosselli would think of this one. The name had hung strangely on him then, like another man's coat. Now it felt totally natural, and he hardly ever thought of those early, desperate years, and Stoney, Stoney had been a kick, back when, wild, sure, but nothing like now. He wondered what had happened out at Vittorio's, earlier that day. Stoney had handed him the money without comment. Tommy had tried to scope out what had happened by talking to Tuco, without being too transparent. Tuco had rolled his eyes. "You know Stoney," he'd said. "You know how he gets." Tommy figured to let some time pass before he tried mending any fences out on Staten Island.

He gave up, crossed his legs, and leaned on his elbow and looked out the window. Why do you do it, he asked himself. Why keep on, such a ridiculous predicament, like a bear dancing in the circus. Surely there must be something better. But Stoney kept on, he would be there in the morning, no matter what. If he can do it, I can, too, he told himself. Besides, it's a game, and everybody wants to beat the other guy, particularly here in this city that he had adopted.

Go to bed, Tommy, he thought. Go to sleep, you gotta get up early tomorrow.

Early in the morning, Stoney's car was the first one in the lot. He got out, went over to look at the guy in the corner.

"Hey, what you doing in here, bro?" It was the same guy as yesterday, looked like someone's grandfather, an emaciated Santa Claus.

"Shooting Dr. Jack." The old man was sitting on a milk crate in the corner of the lot.

"'Scuse me?"

The old man grinned and held up several tiny blue plastic bags for Stoney to see, each one carrying the image of a grinning skull wearing glasses and sporting a crew cut. "See, Dr. Jack is what passes for a brand name."

"Oh, I get it, the suicide guy."

"The very one."

"They name this shit after him?"

"Not exactly." Now it seemed clear the old man was not going to get rousted this morning, and he turned his attention back to business. "The street enterprise that handles retailing in this area is run by an intimidating young gentleman who acquired the nickname of Dr. Jack because he is very good at, aah, assisting people to, aah, cross over, you might say." He held up one of the bags by one end and tapped it with his finger to get all the powder in the bottom. "Clever bit of marketing, don't you think? Given the customer demographics."

"Cute. Don't die in here, okay?"

"I'll make every effort."

"So you buy from this guy, Dr. Jack?"

"Oh, no, good grief, no. Besides, I haven't seen him in ages. Lives right around the corner from here, though," He pointed with his chin. "Up on St. Nick. No, I buy from one of his, aah, authorized representatives."

"Why?"

"Are you joking? Anyone else trying to do business around here wouldn't last out the day."

"No, I mean why shoot up? You don't look that fucked up to me. You look like you got some intelligence. Why don't you get your shit together, get straight? Ain't you got a life, someplace? Grandkids, a little old lady you could schput once in a while?"

"Hah." The old man grinned, showing even, white teeth. "You think I'm some hapless fool, in the grip of some horrible addiction? Come on, grow up. You want to know why I do it? You already know."

"What are you talking about?"

"Why do you drink? Come on, man, I know you drink, I can see it in your face. Why do you do it?"

"You tell me."

"Because it gets you by."

"That's it?"

"Of course that's it. Why does anyone take any drug? Why do you take aspirin? When you feel poorly, you take it to feel better." He clicked a plastic cigarette lighter.

"It's gonna cost you."

"Everything has its price." He didn't look up. "Nothing is free. Bourbon costs you, cigarettes, women, your career, all of it. Most people never look at the price tags." He held the loaded syringe up to the light. "This stuff," he said, "has liberated me from all of those things I picked up without thinking of what they would cost me." Very carefully, he squeezed the air out of the end of the syringe. "I no longer care, at all, about tenure, or my ex-wives, or houses, cars, books, you name it." He leaned forward, studying his forearm. "I don't even think about that shit anymore." The tip of the needle dented, then pierced his skin. He pushed down on the plunger, then pulled it back, filling the syringe with blood, and pushed down on it again.

"Peace," he said. "You ever consider what it's really worth?"

Stoney watched him a minute longer. "I gotta lock the gate," he said, but the old man was past caring.

In the early hours of the morning, White Plains Road in the Bronx was deserted. Tommy sat in his car in the middle of the block, fifty yards away from the only two places open, a doughnut shop on the corner and a newspaper stand on the sidewalk outside. He munched contemplatively on an inferior cinnamon roll, listening to the occasional clatter of the trains on the el that ran down the center of the street. He figured they'd get to him toward the end of the shift, and sure enough, at seven-thirty, a blue-and-white patrol car rolled to a stop behind him. Two cops emerged unhurriedly. The older of the two, a tall gray-haired white guy opened the front passenger-side door of Tommy's car and got in. His partner got in the backseat behind him.

"Gentlemen."

"Nope," the cop said. "Just us."

Tommy Bagadonuts, unlike Stoney, was comfortable with cops. They played the game by their own rules, and as long as you knew what the rules were, and stayed within them, you would probably do okay. Gangsters, in Tommy's opinion, were much the same in that regard.

Tommy reached across the seat to shake hands, money passed smoothly, from one to the other. "I called a few of Marty's other customer," Tommy said. "Nobody wasa get the same bullshit as us. They call Marty's partner, 'Oh, yeah,' the guy says, 'come in, no problem, we take care.' Us, he'sa tell us, 'oh, I don't know, we gotta look, we don't finda the record,' and all that. You think this guy, he'sa try to shake us down?"

The cop pursed his lips, shook his head. "No. He's stalling you."

"Yeah?" Tommy was interested. "Why?"

"He ain't got your stuff." Amusement sparkled in the cop's eyes. "The DA's got it."

Part of Tommy's mind was screaming, but he was so quick that nothing showed on his face that he didn't want to be there. In a fraction of a second, he considered his options and settled on a calm puzzlement. He looked at the cop, who was watching him carefully. "Why?"

The cop looked into the backseat, at his partner. "Well," he said, "your accountant had all of your business records for the past two years with him in the room, in that roach palace where he got popped. They were spread out all over the bed." He glanced over at his partner again. "I'm told, by people who know about such things, that they make for interesting reading."

Again, Tommy ran through his options in a nanosecond, reached his decision, and was grinning broadly before the cop finished his sentence. "Our business is, what you call, complicate. You know what I mean?"

The cop laughed humorlessly. "Tommy, listen to me. You and I go back a long way. I know you got a real nose for a buck. That's okay with me, I admire you for it. But soon enough, they gonna put you and me together, they gonna ask questions. You and me, we goombahs, but you see this?" He took off his hat. "This is a cop hat. I can take it off, do a little something for you once in a while. But when they start asking me questions, I gotta be a cop. Do you understand me?"

"Honesty," Tommy said, "isa the best policy."

"Jesus Christ." He twisted to look out the side window in disgust, then twisted back. "Sometimes you really give me a pain in my ass, you know that?"

"No, serious. They aska you, tell the truth."

"Look, Bagadonuts, they ask me what you guys do, what do I say? You two guys can smell a dollar blowing down the street two blocks away, have it in your pocket before anybody knows it's missing. You want them looking up your ass?"

Tommy shrugged philosophically. "They wanna look, they gonna look. Whattaya gonna do?"

The cop in the backseat piped up. "Ain't you guys a criminal enterprise?"

"No more'n you." Tommy's stomach growled. "Let'sa say in this way. You crossa the George Washington Bridge, take the Palisades Parkway north. Drive a little ways, not far. You look up, you gonna see these bird, they soar, back and forth, back and forth. I thought they wasa eagle, but this lady friend of mine, she say, no. Turkey vulture. What they do, they wait, they watch. Down here, you, me, everybody else, we run up and down, working, driving, chasing. Bound to be some casualty, no? The vulture, he'sa see something sick, dying, maybe he'sa see somebody who'sa don't pay attention, he swoop down, he takes a bite. Me and Stoney, we watch, we see something, back door open, maybe, we swoop in, we take a bite, we fly away. We don't gotta kill nobody, we don't gotta robba no bank. We just take a little bite, and we fly away."

"Tommy, the DA's not going to buy this fairy tale you're selling. You guys run a lot of shit through that goddamn junkyard of yours. I seen paper on everything from wine to cigars, truck parts, fine-art prints, Japanese rubbers. Jesus. You guys must fence half the swag in New York, for Christ's sake."

Tommy looked rueful. "I know, isa don't look so good."

"You damn right it don't look good."

"Listen. We pay tax, just like everybody else. The rest, wasa just business. The condoma wasa come from Japan, but the distributor wasa go bust. Nobody want. They got little picture of Richard Nixon on the end, you wind up with a dick ona you dick. Little joke. Plus, they wasa little short, maybe don't cover the whole thing. In most cases. But we buy at the auction, got the invoice, okay? We wasa sell in Paris. Maybe Frenchmen," he said, "used to having women laugh when they got a hard-on. The wine, we buy from you guys. You dumb bastards, you run two auctions the same morning. Everybody wasa go to the other one, had twelve police motorcycle in it. We go to this one, at one Police Plaza, right on the steps. Wasa maybe six people there, me and Stoney, four Hasids. We got a whole tractor-trailer load, '74 Bordeaux. Wasa no too bad, you know, drinkable. Turns out, Stoney knows the guy writes a wine column. Guy's daughter goes to the same school with Stoney's son. So maybe one year before, Stoney's kid, he'sa walk to hockey practice, he sees the girl, she'sa getta bad time from these two guys. Kid goes to a house, calls the cops. Smarter than Stoney, Jesus, Stoney, he have the stick already, maybe he kill 'em both, we gotta go hide the bodies. Anyway, the old man says, 'Anything I can do for you,' you know. Stoney calls him up, says, 'Take this bottle, write something nice.'" Tommy looked up at the ceiling of the car. "From God, I'ma tell you, that was money from God."

"Okay, what about the cigars? What were they, Cubans?"

"Nah. Honduras. Look the same, though. Not many people know the difference."

"And the prints?"

"Ho-boy. What a scam. You wanna hear?"

The cop looked at his watch, glanced at his partner. "Okay, one more story."

"Okay. Artist, famous guy, does etching. Gonna make two hundred copies, no more. Each one, he'sa sign his name, number one, number two, number three, and so on. Of course, he don't tell, two hundred regular number, two hundred Roman numeral, two hundred in Europe, whatever. Anyway, back then, art market wasa very hot. He takes one print, puts in auction, now he's got one hundred ninety-nine. Three guys at the auction, they bid, thing goes for, say, thousand dollar. His money, you understand, all three guys worka for him. He gets his money back minus the vig for the auction house. Does this, two, three time. Okay? Then, he goes to the bank, says, 'Hey, I need a loan. Got alla these print, worth a grand a pop. You hold 'em.' Get it?"

"Sure. He walks away, they're stuck with a bunch of posters."

"Please, print, not poster. Whos'a give a thousand buck for poster?"

"So how did you two wind up with 'em?"

"Bank put 'em in a warehouse. Warehouse have a roof leak. Insurance company pays the bank, we buy from warehouse guy. Meantime, this artist, famous guy, I told you, he had a nose candy problem, have a heart attack, he croaks. Every piece of paper got his name on it worth a fortune."

"Did you know he was into the coke?"

"I see him at a party, here and there, ask a few question, shit, you the cop, you know how this works."

"So you bought the paper and he bought the farm."

"Oh, we hadda wait a year. He went to rehab, once. Scare us to death. But, he wasa don't make it."

"Lucky for you."

Tommy grinned. "Capitalism at work, baby. Free-market economy."

"So how come you guys didn't find another artist, run this scam again?"

Tommy considered it. "We just come in on the end. Besides, old saying, 'Pigs get fat, hogs get kill.' You remember what I told you about turkey vulture? Very important not to forget the part about flying away."

The two cops were laughing. "All right, Tommy. I'm gonna go tell the man my story. I just wanna know, is any of this shit true?"

Tommy winked at him. "Alla the best lies," he said, "about three quarters true."

"So what was in the records? Just normal business, tax shit," Stoney said. "Who cares?"

"Yeah, maybe." Tommy looked doubtful. "I just worry, somebody gonna take interest in us."

"Nothing we can do about that. Listen, Tommy, they're looking for whoever did Marty, and it wasn't us. After they come sniffing around, they're gonna go look somewhere else. I'm telling you, it ain't the cops we need to be worrying about, here."

Bagadonuts looked glum. "Marty."

"Yeah. Marty, in some hot-sheet house, up in the Bronx, with all our records. For what?"

"Meet somebody."

"Yeah. I wonder if he paid the day rate, or what."

Tommy shook his head. "Pay for all day."

"Okay, so he's planning to spend some time. He's got plenty of room to spread out, he's got privacy so he can talk. And the topic, apparently, is you and me. Then he comes down with lead poisoning. What's that tell you?"

"Somebody thinking about taking a run at us. We piss offa somebody, or maybe someone gonna try to set us up."

"Ahh, I dunno. We got nothing going on right now. We're almost like a regular business, at the moment. Besides, we been leaving everybody smiling, lately."

"Nobody gonna shoot Marty because they looka for us. Don't make sense."

"We piss off anybody you can think of?"

"Vittorio . . ."

"Ahh, Vittorio's a putz. He ain't gonna shoot anybody. Besides, he was just yesterday, Marty was already dead."

"You gonna bet Vittorio can't do it?"

"This don't feel like Vittorio, Tommy."

"No."

They sat silent in Tommy's office, listening to the traffic out in the street. "You think," Tommy said, "Marty would roll over on us?"

"He was there, and he did have all that stuff with him. No other reason for it to be there. But if you asked me that last week, I would have said no way. We knew Marty a long time. It would take a lot, I think."

"Money?"

"Nah. Marty made plenty, doing what he did. He was a bean counter, anyway, not a player."

"Something else, then. Maybe someone threaten him, tell his momma he'sa, you know, gay."

"Gimme a break, Tommy, that was no secret. Look at the way he dressed, for chrissake. No, it's gotta be something else. I would bet somebody was getting squeezed, maybe even Marty. We just have to sit tight. Wait and see if someone comes sniffing around, or gets indicted, or something. If we're the target, we don't have a move, not yet."

"No. You know, I told the cops the vulture story." Stoney rolled his eyes. "Well, it make'a me think. We know what the vulture is'a do."

Stoney waited.

"Who'sa try to eat'a the vulture?"

"Maybe we'll find out."

The sign over the office door read "TFG Freight Forwarding," but it was from a previous tenant, and it had the wrong phone number on it. The office itself was actually a small building, maybe twenty-five feet square. Walk through the front door and you were looking at the long counter where Jimmy the Hat worked. The counter was overcrowded with a computer, fax machine, copier, telephones. Behind the counter, along the back wall, was a row of closets and file cabinets. Two old wooden desks sat in the middle of the floor. To the right was the door to Tommy's office, which occupied one end of the building, and in the left-rear corner was a tiny bathroom. In the center of the back wall was the door leading into the yard.

The yard was about fifty feet by one hundred, a slab of poured concrete fenced in all the way around with galvanized metal sheets topped with razor wire. The office was on the Troutman Street side, next to the office was the parking lot, a box within a box, with the gate on the street providing the only egress. There was also a gate in the fence opening from the yard to the side street, and more often than not there was a container parked just inside it, the kind of container that went on a freighter for shipment overseas. The rest of the space in the yard was filled with scrap-metal hoppers, a trash Dumpster, and an old trailer on flat tires. There was a little wooden porch built onto the end of the trailer, and one of Tuco's never-ending jobs was to climb the wooden steps over and over, getting tools out or putting them away. He kept telling himself that someday he'd organize the trailer, run a string of lights inside so you could see what the hell you were doing, but there never seemed to be time for that.

Tuco and Commie Pete worked in the yard. Some days they spent their time cutting old trucks up into parts that went into containers for shipment to Colombia, and other days they would have to unload trucks that dropped off crates of God only knew what, could be anything from Korean televisions to women's coats, and usually a day or so later Tuco and Pete would relabel the crates with a new address and load them onto another truck. Jimmy the Hat spent his days inside the office on the telephone, together with whatever combination of Walter, Stoney, and Fat Tommy happened to be present.

"Tuco!"

Jimmy the Hat stood in the door that opened from the office to the yard in back. Jimmy had that weasely tone in his voice, an uncertain attempt at authority. Tuco had noted that both Tommy Bagadonuts and Stoney rarely ordered anyone around. He assumed that they had gotten beyond the need for it. Jimmy seemed to need it bad and Tuco held out on him, dissed him in subtle ways, made him call a few times.

"Tuco!"

Tuco could hear the phone ringing through the open door,

heard Jimmy curse and go inside to get it. Tuco had heard that Jimmy was connected, knew everybody in the truck-leasing business, wrote a lot of orders. Tuco had never met anyone, however, who claimed Jimmy as a friend. They all knew him, sure, but . . . It wasn't his business, Tommy and Stoney could look after their own interests, hire anyone they wanted to. You got no reason not to like the guy, Tuco told himself. Get off it.

He was walking across the yard, wiping his hands on a rag when Jimmy came back through the door. "Hey, Tuco," he said, this time without the phony undertones. "We got a pickup from that truck-rental place next to the impound yard, under the Kosciusko. You know the one I mean?"

"Yeah."

"You gotta take somebody with you. Is Commie Pete out here?"

"Yeah."

"Okay, take him. Walter's tied up." He glanced over his shoulder, lowered his voice. "Fat Tommy and Stoney are waiting on some kind of inspector, from the EPA, I heard. Big problems."

Tuco shrugged. "You got this all set up? These guys at the truck-rental place, they gonna be looking for money or anything?"

"No, no, they're gonna invoice us. Just see the guy that runs the garage down there. He's holding three big crates for us."

"You got it."

Commie Pete was this white-haired Lithuanian dude who worked in the yard a couple of days a week. Tuco wasn't real clear on where Lithuania was, but he knew that it had been run by the Russians, who had recently been kicked out. Tuco never used Pete's nickname, because he had the feeling that Pete sort of had a thing about Russians. He had told Tuco, one time, about how he'd brought his mother over once, years ago. She had stood in the middle of the Key Food supermarket, the one that used to be on Atlantic Avenue, and cried, looking around at all the food in the store. The old bird hadn't stayed, got homesick and went back. Pete shook his head after he told the story, and Tuco figured that Pete had plenty of reason to dislike commies.

Tuco loved to watch Pete work. Pete could cut freehand with a torch and have the cut come out looking like it had been done by a machine. Tuco's cuts always came out snaggle-toothed unless he used a straightedge. Pete always knew the easy way to do things. Give him a piece of chain and a come-along and he could move the whole building. The other thing was, he never minded showing you when he knew a slick way to do something. Tuco had always been a natural with a wrench, but Pete was an artist. Sometimes he had trouble explaining things, and Tuco had his own problems understanding, but if you were patient, it was amazing what you could learn from the guy. The two of them had worked on the ancient wreck of a truck that they used for pickups and deliveries. It was an International cabover from the late sixties. The cab didn't pivot up on springs the way the newer ones did, it weighed a ton, and if you needed to work on the diesel you had to unlatch the cab and then crank on the hydraulic jack that raised the cab until your arm was ready to fall off. Behind the cab was a flatbed body, metal rust-colored sides and a dry-rotted wooden deck. When Tuco had started working there the truck didn't run, and Pete had ripped into the old diesel like a twelve-year-old taking apart his mother's toaster. He'd had Tuco's head spinning, trying to remember how it all went back together, but Pete had paid him no mind, scattering parts everywhere. "Here's the difference," the old man told him, "between a mechanic and a shoemaker. Anybody can take old parts off and bolt new ones on. No parts for this engine anymore. Got to find the problem, make it work."

Commie Pete didn't really have an accent, just a little something with the v's and the w's, but he wore ill-fitting false teeth, and they made him spit when he talked, particularly when he got excited. Tuco had learned to stand off to one side, out of the line of fire, but Pete still got him once in a while. To Tuco, who had never learned much of anything in a school, it was just the cost of doing business. He was happy to take the occasional hit if it meant he could work with the old man. Once, when Pete had left his uppers home, Tuco hadn't been able to understand him at all. "Jedud," he'd said. "I lefth the houth topleth."

Tuco went looking for Pete.

"Hey, Pete, you wanna go for a ride? The Hat says we gotta go make a pickup."

Commie Pete straightened up from what he was doing. "I'm getting too old for this," he said, stretching his back. "I ain't humping no more heavy boxes up onto that truck."

"No, they got a forklift down there. All you gotta do is ride shotgun. Jimmy probably figures, he sends me out alone I'll stop off at OTB for an hour."

"What a crew," Pete muttered, and then he brightened. "Why? You got a horse?"

"I wouldn't know a good horse if he bit me on the ass. Get the gate for me, okay? And don't forget to lock it up after I pull out."

Tuco turned the key on, waited for the glow plug to heat up. When he kicked the engine over, it caught immediately, smoking a little at first. Ain't nothing for it, the old man had told him. Just be easy on her.

It was a twenty-minute ride down to the truck-rental yard. The garage foreman had three wooden crates in his back room, and he started up the forklift and loaded them on the truck himself.

"Do I hafta sign anything?" Tuco asked him.

"Yeah, right. Just get outta here, okay?" He was a tall guy, getting fat, who had once had orange-red hair. Now he sported an orange-red thing that sat on his head, looked like a thatched roof on an English cottage. "When is Bagadonuts gonna buy you guys a new truck? We junk trucks way better looking than that thing."

"You kidding? Pete loves this truck. He'd never let Tommy get rid of it."

The guy shook his head, turned to go back into the garage. "Go on, get outta here already."

They pulled out of the truck-rental yard, past the gate, where the security guard did not look up from reading his newspaper. Probably knows us from the sound, Tuco thought.

"You know," Pete said, as they pulled away, "I've known that guy for a long time."

"Who? The guy with the rug? Why doesn't someone tell him about that?"

"You gotta let people have these things, you know. Rubbing his face in it don't serve no purpose. But the reason I bring him up, I know they're looking for a good mechanic, somebody smart, somebody that works hard. I could put in a word for you, they'd hire you in a second."

Tuco's face flamed red as he thought about filling out employment applications. "Why would I want to work there? Stoney and Tommy treat me good, and I like working with you. Why would I want to leave?"

"Tuco, you got a gift. I never seen a kid pick up things as fast as you. If you went to work in a big company like that, you'd be making real money in no time at all. Stoney and Tommy, I know you think they're nice guys . . ." His voice trailed off and he seemed to reconsider what he'd been about to say. "Okay, I know they treat you right, and all, but they got nothing to teach you, Tuco. And I'll tell you something else too. Stoney would be the first guy to tell you to go, if you got an opportunity to do better. He'd never stand in your way."

"Maybe so. But I fit in with you guys, Pete. I feel like, you know, comfortable. I don't care about the money. I don't wanna go to some new place where I don't know nobody."

"I understand. Just keep it in mind, okay, what I said, because I hate to see you get stuck someplace you don't belong. Sometimes these guys get into things that ain't good, and like I said, you got a gift."

"Maybe I got more than one."

"Ah." Pete looked out the window. "Could be. You're the one has to figure that out. Just be careful, what you get into, you understand what I'm saying? And if I can help, just give me the word. Incidentally, I hear you may be looking for a place to stay."

"Looks that way."

"Turn left here. No, left, don't worry about what the sign says. Now right. Pull over." They were on a short block, a tiny residential oasis in a desert of industrial buildings. One side of the street was a huge dilapidated church with rectory attached, surrounded by a jungle of sumac bushes, waist-high grass, and pages from last year's newspapers. On the other side of the street was a row of four-story brownstone apartment houses, one of which was in far better shape than its neighbors. "This is my building," he said. "There's space here."

"They got an empty apartment here?"

"Not they. Me. It's my building. Bagadonuts talked me into buying it, years ago."

Tuco looked at him in wonder. "You bought the building?"

"Tommy said it was too good a deal to pass up. I think he just did it for the fun of it. I figure he liked getting over on the bank. He made me pretend I didn't speak any English. He told them he was my nephew. It was a bank that owned the place. Did I say that? I'm telling you, son, by the time he got done with them I think they'd have given me the place just to get rid of him." He chuckled, reminiscing. "He starts out arguing about the contract, then after it's all signed, he threatened to sue them for stealing an old man's life savings, the certificate of occupancy was wrong, the boiler's gonna blow up, you name it. He got Walter all dressed up like a reporter, sent him down to ask the bank manager for a statement, 'Is this true and is that true, we want your side of it, too,' you wouldn't believe the stuff he pulled. Anyway, it's mine. I live on the first floor. Couple nice ladies live on the second floor, friends of Tommy." He gave Tuco a sidelong glance. "Ahem. Top floor's empty, we don't know anyone we wanted moving in. You wanna go look at it?"

"I dunno, Pete. That place across the street kinda creeps me out. Nobody uses that place?"

"Nope. Bagadonuts says not to worry, the Koreans gonna buy it, turn this whole block around."

"Unh. Well, thanks for the offer. I don't know what's going to happen yet. I'll let you know, okay?"

"Anytime, kid."

The cat, a smallish black-and-white shorthair who thought his name was getthefuckoutahere arched his back and spit at Stoney, who was in a foul mood because he hated meetings, bureaucrats, lawyers, and threats, and he and Bagadonuts were dealing with all four wrapped up in the personage of one C. Maxwell Hunt.

"Stoney, easy, you scare him," Tommy said, rising out of his chair. "Just open the door, he gonna go out. Watch me." He went over and opened the office door, but the cat stayed where he was, under the desk eyeing Stoney. Tommy knelt down, made kissy noises, and the cat, with one last, baleful look at Stoney, ran out.

"Jesus," Stoney said. "I wouldn't mind him if he didn't piss everywhere. We should get one of those traps."

"You catch that cat, Walter never gonna forgive you. You know he'sa love that cat."

"Well, if he loves the cat, how come he can't teach him to piss in the box?"

"Gentlemen." C. Maxwell Hunt had had enough. "I don't know how to impress upon you the seriousness of this situation." He was a doughy, pasty-white, middle-aged, receding-hairline, no-chin bean counter who indulged in an improbable combover and dressed like Joe Friday. "We are talking about significant poundage, here. If I chose, I could have this entire office impounded, and the front door of your enterprise padlocked shut until we have gone over every piece of paper in this building. We at the EPA like to hold that option in reserve, but if we don't get what we need, we will not hesitate to do what needs to be done. And what I need right now is cooperation."

Tommy returned to his chair behind the desk. "Well, Mr. Hunt, like I try to tell you over the phone, we got a small problem. Maybe not so small. You don't gonna find what you look for over here. Mosta the kinda record you look for wasa take care by our accountant, Marty Cohen, up inna Bronx. Last weekend, some-time, he wasa get shot. Policeman told me, crime scene, no disturb, you know what I mean?"

"He got shot in his office?"

"No. Isa long story. Look, I gonna give you phone number, policeman inna Bronx. You talka to him, he explain everything. Okay?" Tommy wrote the number on the back of a business card and thought, Another favor we gotta pay for.

"Very unusual," C. Maxwell said. "Very unusual."

"It ain't every day your accountant gets shot," Stoney said sourly. "Usually they last a couple years, anyway."

"Marty wasa like family," Tommy said, glaring at Stoney. "He wasa take good care of us. We don't know whatta we gonna do without him."

"Very unusual." C. Maxwell sat in his chair, looking at Tommy Bagadonuts and at Stoney, his eyes going from one to the other as though he were following a tennis match. "All right," he finally said, standing and snatching up his briefcase. "I'll touch base with the police, and I'll forestall any action for the time being. But I want you gentlemen to understand me. This case is not going to go away."

C. Maxwell stepped through the door out onto the sidewalk, squinting in the bright sunshine. He turned to where his car was parked, just down the block. She was coming up the sidewalk, just past his car. A smile played on her lips as she watched him. She paused, turning away from him to bend over and brush some imaginary something from her shoe, and then she straightened up again and turned to face him once more, smiling a little more broadly. She knows, Maxwell thought, she can feel her power, she knows exactly what she's doing to me. The problem was, he knew a little bit about street girls, and a little bit more about addiction. He had lived through the sixties, after all, gone off to college in the seventies. He had cleaned up his act after seeing some of his contemporaries fall by the wayside. One of the casualties had been his wife's younger sister.

He had watched cocaine turn her life inside out. In college she had been urbane, sophisticated beyond her years, and she had breezed her way through school, on her way to something exceptional, he had been sure. Then, in her junior year, she had become erratic, and had only attended classes sporadically. Soon after, she'd dropped out altogether, and no one saw her for over a year.

Her first rehab had come after a family intervention. He had gone along to lend his wife emotional support, and he'd witnessed the whole scene. It had been ugly at first, with shouting, curses, accusations, and counteraccusations, but as the evidence piled up, including stories of her climbing into cars with strange men in order to support her habit, she had begun to break down, and ultimately she had tearfully agreed to go off to rehab.

Her return a month later had been greeted with optimism on all sides, and he remembered seeing in her the girl she had been when he'd first met her in school. Unfortunately, it was not to be. The worst thing about dying from addiction, he thought, was that the process took such an excruciatingly long time. By the time hepatitis C had taken her liver and her life, it was almost a relief to see her go.

It had been a wrenching experience for his wife, and she, too, had suffered in the process, slowly turning into a pale image of what she had been when he'd married her. He had adjusted. What else could he do? But it was a cold and joyless life.

So it was with no illusions that he stood on the sidewalk watching the girl close in on him. He knew what she saw when she looked at him; not a man who she felt an attraction to, not even an out-of-shape, balding, middle-aged schlump. She saw the price of her next few hits, and no more. But Lord, it had been so long. And she really was something.

"Hey, baby," she said, taking another slow step, overloading his senses. His desire hung in the air between them, an invisible cloud, smoke from a fire you could smell but not quite see. Oh, no, he thought, if she gets any closer, if she lays a finger on me, Jesus, I'm lost . . .

He looked around wildly, remembering himself, himself and his whole goddam life, and he felt, even as he backed away from her, an unfamiliar whiff of testosterone, a hardening and a quick sweat.

"Woof," he said, exhaling heavily, swinging out around her on the sidewalk. "Whew. Excuse me."

She pouted. "Awooo . . ."

"Sorry, darlin'." He stopped a safe distance away. "I, ah, ahem. Whew. I'm on a tight schedule, here."

"Well, okay, baby." Even her voice had the power to draw him closer, like the pull of a distant sun. "But you know, you gonna be sorry tonight, layin' cold up in your bed."

It was too much. C. Maxwell turned and fled for the safety of his car, a big, unmarked government sedan just like the ones real cops used, and locked himself inside. "C'mon, Max," he said to himself. "Let's get the hell out of here."

Tuco had seen her from way down the street, but Pete wasn't looking her way at all. "Hole up, hole up. Park over here, over on this side."

Tuco pulled the truck over to the curb opposite the gate to the parking lot. A white guy wearing a trench coat had just come out of the office door. A gust of wind lifted some of the long sprigs of hair that grew from the side of his head, exposing the skin underneath.

"At's him," Pete said. "Gotta be the guy." They watched as he came up the sidewalk, obviously drawn to the girl, and then backed off and evaded her.

"Be useful, you suppose, see where this guy goes?"

Commie Pete looked over at Tuco in alarm. "I told you, you hafta be careful with these guys. Much simpler life, just being a mechanic. Nothing wrong with that."

"I just wanna see where he goes, is all. What if he ain't who he says he is? What if he's some guy running a hustle, like those guys that dress up like cops, walk into a bank with a gun and rob the place? He goes back to a building says EPA on it, at least we're sure."

"Yeah, all right." Pete couldn't keep the disappointment out of his voice. "Let me out, I'm going back to work. I'll tell 'em where you went."

Tuco thought he'd lost him. C. Maxwell had taken off like he was on fire, buzzed the red light at the end of the block and vanished from sight, but Tuco guessed that he'd head straight up Flushing to get to the Long Island Expressway, and Tuco knew a quicker way to get there. The old truck had just pulled out onto the service road when C. Maxwell went smoking by, and Tuco watched him roar up the ramp and grind to a halt in the traffic. Tuco stayed on the service road, and even though he had to work his way through local streets, he was there when C. Maxwell got off on 108th Street, and it was easy enough to follow him from there back to his office building off Queens Boulevard. Tuco went and looked at the building directory, and sure enough, the EPA had the top three floors.

Jimmy the Hat was in the parking lot when Tuco parked the truck.

"Lemme ax you something."

"Yeah, what," Jimmy said.

"You had a chance to make more money somewhere else, would you go?"

"What do you mean, more money? How much more?"

Tuco hadn't thought of that. "I don't know. More."

"What happened? Those guys I sent you to make you an offer?"

"Not exactly."

"I'll bet. I used to work there, and I'll tell you something, money ain't the whole story. You might think it is, but it ain't. You like working here?"

"I guess so," Tuco said.

"You only say that because you never worked for a giant corporation. If you had, you'd know for sure how much better it is here. Place like that lease company, they hire you, right, they might pay you okay, maybe better than here, but once they get you, it's like they put you in a box. Say they want you to change oil, they put you down in the pit, you could work there ten years, nobody gives a fuck if you know how to do other things, or that you want to learn. I knew this one guy, for fourteen years, what he did every night, he drove this oiler around a fleet-parking lot, filling up diesel tanks on tractors. Fourteen years! Nobody to talk to, nothing to think about, same shit, night after night. Who wants that? I'll tell you a story. I know a guy has a little scrap yard up in Hunts Point. You know where that is?"

"Yeah, up off the Bruckner Expressway."

"Right. Matter-of-fact, you could see his place from there, right across the railroad tracks from the Bruckner. Anyway, he was taking old busses, pulling the engines and rears and whatnot, packing it all up and sending it off to South America. Some of the best mechanics and body guys in the world come from down there. You know why?"

"Yeah. No parts."

"You damn right. You need a set of points for an old Willys sedan, you better know how to make 'em. So anyway, they got a lot of old busses down there, still running, he figures he can make a buck, sending down stuff that we'd just throw away. Turns out the dude is making a nice living. So I figure, leasing company has all this old crap coming in off lease, ain't worth much, why not hook up with someone down there, turn it all into cash? You think

I could get anyone to listen to me? Hell, no. I hadda go though these three guys, every one of 'em over sixty, they were like the old-fart committee. You can't tell 'em shit, they already know it all. You make one mistake and they beat your head in with it for the next year. You do something right, they get the credit. I'll tell you, man, you stay in a place like that too long, all your juices leak out and you turn into an old fart yourself."

"So you'd rather work for Stoney."

"Unnnh. I didn't say that. Him and Tommy, they're both crazy. I first interviewed with them, if you could call it that, we were in this restaurant on Queens Boulevard. Tommy keeps sending his food back. He sent the salad back twice! First it has too much iceberg, and the leaves are brown, and the next time the bacon bits are too gooey, they gotta be crunchy, and the radishes are limp, or some shit. And when his food comes, and he's finally eating it, right, he's making all these little grunting noises while he's going at it, I feel like I'm watching a porno movie, for chrissake. And Stoney ain't eating at all, he's drinking a vodka martini, he's looking at me like I'm a cockroach walking across the tablecloth. I'm thinking, I can't believe I wanna quit my job and come work for these two bananas. And Stoney says to me, 'Why the fuck would you wanna quit your job and work for us?' I swear he did."

"What'd you tell him?"

Jimmy shrugged. "Told him I was bored. Underemployed. Told him my idea about truck parts, and a few other things I wanted to try, and here I am."

"And you wouldn't go back, even after the way they break your balls?"

"No way. And you can keep the profit sharing and the tuition reimbursement and all that shit. I ain't been bored one time since I got here. You gotta do what you think is right for you, but I'm gonna tell you something. We might all be nuts for working here, but you'll learn more shit in one year with these guys than you will in five years anywhere else. Maybe about half of it, you'd be happier not knowing, but still. Neither one of us is gonna make any real money working by the hour, don't matter if it's here or there. Me and you, we both have the same problem: We gotta find a way to make money for ourselves, and not just keep working to make money for someone else. These two guys really know how to turn a buck. I'm hoping some of that will rub off on me, maybe I can learn how they think. Good luck, anyway."

"Yeah, thanks. Don't say anything, okay?"

"Course not."

He was already home when she got there, sitting out back in his little room, drinking beer, laughing. He could hear her unlock the front door and walk through the house to find him sitting there reading the local weekly paper. It was free, every week the van drove up the block throwing them on everyone's lawn. Usually Stoney cursed the paper and whoever had delivered it, threatening to lie in wait and throw something back, but he'd never gotten up early enough to do it. It didn't bother him to the point where he would actually set the alarm and get dressed an hour ahead. Still, it was a good thing the guy never came by when Stoney was leaving for work.

"Your son hurt himself today."

"Uh-oh."

"Oh, he's all right. He just kept forgetting how to stop on those skates you bought him. He got a couple of big bruises on his thighs, and another one on his behind."

He could tell she was trying hard to keep the amusement out of her voice. "Bet he remembers how they work next time."

"You think so? I must say, they were a great move. He worships the ground you walk on, this week."

Stoney mulled over several possible responses but chose to remain silent.

"Have you ever thought," she said, "about taking Dennis to work with you someday? Show him what you do? He'd think he died and went to heaven."

He turned in his chair to look over at her. "Are you nuts? The last place I want to take him is to work with me."

"Really? It can't be that bad."

Stoney turned to look out the window. "Yesterday," he said, "Tuco, the kid that works for us, found two dead kids around the corner, maybe seventy-five feet from our front door. They looked, I dunno, maybe sixteen or so."

"I didn't see anything on the news," she said, in a voice suddenly small and quiet.

"Please," he said. "Two more dead kids, wearing their gang colors, nobody gives a shit. But even without that," he said, waving his hand. "Even discounting that. You get close to our street, you start thinking you're in a different country. Everything is so different, if you look. In Jersey, dog gets sick, someone takes it to the vet, either fixes him or gives him the needle. Troutman Street, the dog dies right there on the sidewalk. Had one just last month, Tommy's out there trying to feed the goddam thing, it's got distemper, back legs don't work anymore, can't even drag itself around. Took a few days to die. I wanted to put the thing out of its misery but Tommy kept hoping it would get better. Kept looking at me with those eyes, Jesus, God, what a fucking world. But we don't see it out here in the burbs. Out here, everybody goes to the dentist every year. Even me. I got caps and bridges and root canals and every goddamn thing else. But on Troutman Street, people smile at you, you don't see side-to-side teeth like you do here. Tooth comes out, it stays out, whether it fell out or someone knocked it out. Whores hanging down on the corner, doing their business wherever. I got to keep the gate locked on the parking lot all the time or we'd have people living in there. Got these little plastic crack bottles all over the sidewalk, little smack Baggies . . . The other day, this car stops, bitch gets out, washes a needle off in the water from the hydrant. Jesus. Maybe God is dead, after all, and you could call it natural selection, and dead is dead, but I am goddamn tired of looking at it."

She opened her mouth to reply, but he cut her off.

"You know what Tommy says? He says that he and I are like vultures. We sit in the tree and wait, we perform a service. We weed out the sick and the dying, the ones not smart enough or quick enough to survive. We live off the bones." He lapsed into silence.

"No," he said finally. "Keep him out here. Let him grow up to be a doctor or something. Maybe even a hockey player." He twisted in his chair, winked at her. In spite of the beer, in spite of herself, she took him to her bed that night.

The streets were clean, even though it hadn't rained in some time, and every available parking spot was taken. The sidewalks were slate, somewhat uneven from lying in place for two centuries, studded with trees. It was purely a residential neighborhood, no factories or industrial buildings of any kind. Pedestrians stopping in the deli on their way home, talking to each other under the street-lights. The buildings were all old, just like in Tuco's neighborhood, but without graffiti, and little gardens sprouted here and there, green and well tended, fenced, for the most part, to keep the dogs out. A lot of small differences added up to an enormous difference in aura. There was no feeling of menace, nobody bunched up on the stoops or hanging on the corners, just people, mostly prosperous-looking white ones, walking home from work.

Tommy Bagadonuts pulled the car over in a no-standing zone

in front of a building on Clark Street. Tuco got out and looked up, counting the stories, came up with eight. "Man, this place is huge."

"Don't worry," Tommy told him. "This isa no Bushwick. Four apartment, each floor, not sixteen. Believe me, this is a beautiful thing, you gonna like." They waited out front. Residents came and went through the bleached-maple front doors. A few held the door open for them. "Thank you," Tommy told each one. "We waita for someone."

After some time she clicked down the sidewalk in her high heels, tall and blonde, linen suit, white blouse with the top three buttons open, thin gold chain around her neck, hanging down inside. "Hi, Tommy!" Half a block away, she was waving and calling his name. "Tommy!"

Tuco watched Bagadonuts light up as she came closer. He could see the fine lines in her face when she got up close, but she was beautiful in her own way as she smiled, closed her eyes, and kissed Tommy full on the lips. She folded herself in his arms, and he beamed down at her. And then just as quickly she detached herself and took three short steps to Tuco, holding out her hand. "You must be Eddie," she said, and he was surprised once again, how Tommy never forgot a thing, as they stepped inside.

The lobby was almost as big as Rosa's apartment, cool, green marble floor, cream-colored walls and high ceiling with plaster lion heads and a big, round medallion in the center. There were some Chinese food menus piled up on a radiator near the mailboxes against the far wall. Absentmindedly she gathered them up and then pushed the button for the elevator. Tuco was struck by the fact that he could not hear it coming, in fact, he couldn't hear anything at all, no radios, no televisions, no human noises other than the three of them breathing. There was a single clunk when the elevator door opened.

They got in and she pushed the button for the basement.

•   •   •

"The trash has to go out twice a week." She sat in the kitchen with Tommy, talking loudly to Tuco as he walked around the apartment. It was the only one in the basement, facing the narrow alley that ran around behind the building. Access to the alley was through a wrought-iron gate, which was kept closed and locked. The floor-to-ceiling windows looked out at brick walls eight feet away, but let in plenty of light.

"The halls have to be mopped twice a week too." Tuco marveled at the size of the bathroom, twice the size of Rosa's, without the steam pipe running up in the corner, you bend over wrong, you wind up with a big burn on your ass. "In the winter, you have to keep an eye on the boiler." In a quieter voice, she asked Tommy, "Is he mechanical? Can he fix things?"

Tommy was incapable of talking quietly. "You joking? Fix anything. In his first life, he was builda the pyramid." Tuco walked down the hallway, past the kitchen. Tommy winked at him on his way by. Tuco shook his head as he looked around the living room. Better keep them out of the bedroom, he thought.

"Nice boy," Tommy continued. "I told you, you gonna like."

5

STONEY WOKE UP ALONE IN SWEATY DARKNESS, THE BEDSHEETS
soaked. It seemed that his whole body trembled, his hands and
feet, his stomach, his brain even. He rolled over, trying to ignore
the thunder in his head and the ashen, thirsty feeling in his
mouth, wanting, really, just to go back to sleep, but he knew it was
no use even as he lay there fighting the whole body-shaking,
mind-ripping need for a drink, not an urge but a fire raging for a
lack of water. He didn't want to get up and go down to the kitchen,
what he wanted was just to sleep, and to get up in the morning
like a normal person, but it was no contest, just a rolling, sweaty,
aching delay, until finally he gave in, as he had to, and sat up on
the edge of the bed.

She was gone.

He could see her shape in the lay of the sheets on the dry side
of the bed, and he hoped that it was only his restlessness that had
driven her away, and tried to ignore the gnawing inner conviction
that something bad had happened. It hung in the air about him

like a cloud, Jesus, what happened this time, what did I do now? He hoped to God that it was nothing too horrible, and he reviled himself for his weakness as he padded down the stairs to the kitchen.

There was no need to turn on the light. There was a quart of vodka in the cabinet over the broom closet, and another one on the floor in the back of the broom closet itself, and a half gallon of Canadian Club out in the garage, just in case. Donna probably knew about the quarts of vodka, and never in all their years together had she ever tried to hide or pour out his liquor, but there were some things you couldn't take chances with. He wondered for one panicky moment what on earth he would ever do if they were all gone. By morning he would surely be driven mad. He remembered, though, there was Nyquil in the medicine cabinet, two big, green bottles. They would do in a pinch.

Vodka was made for nights like this, he thought, filling a tumbler halfway and splashing a little water on top. He swilled the first one down hungrily, feeling the familiar burn as it went down, then the comforting, spreading warmth. The effect was immediate, and miraculous. The shaking went away, the headache abated, confidence returned, and he quit worrying quite so much about Donna, whatever he had done, he'd make up for it, it couldn't be that bad.

Why couldn't life just be like this, he wondered. He was not so unrealistic as to wish that his problems would vanish, just that he could keep them at a comfortable distance, the way they seemed at this ethereal and fleeting moment. All I want is this, he thought, this slippery promised land, this elusive magical distance, this perspective, this wisdom, this peaceful oasis one step removed from the day-to-day, never-ending, pointless grind.

He poured himself another hit and put the bottle away. He drank down about half of it, then left the glass on the counter and opened the refrigerator. The light inside was burned out, had been for years, but they were always in the same place, Miller High Life long necks, champagne of beers.

From long experience he could sense the approaching blackness, and he cracked the beer open and headed for the stairs, drunken optimism flaring briefly in his mind, everything would be okay, somehow or other things would work out, they always did. The water glass, one quarter full, stood forgotten on the countertop behind him, a land mine buried in the sand.

He came to a few hours later with the conviction strong in his mind that he was in deep shit. He couldn't remember what had happened, but he was sure that he had crossed the line again. It seemed prudent to get up and get out. Donna was generally easier to face at the end of a day, with honest fatigue and a workingman's dirt on his hands. It had to count for something, that he was spending his life to purchase theirs, going in to Troutman Street every day, whatever dreams he'd had long dead and buried in his subconscious, with just the bones left to jab and prick him from time to time.

Dennis was in the kitchen when Stoney got down there, he was making a breakfast of some slices of ham and cheese, drinking orange juice from the carton. Stoney looked at him.

"Hi, Pops." Dennis was grinning broadly.

I wonder if he knows how bad I'm hurting, Stoney thought. "Breakfast of champions," he said, trying to remember if he had any aspirins in the glove box of his car. He didn't want to go back upstairs to get some out of the medicine cabinet, it would be just his luck to wake Donna in the process.

"Gotta go, Dad." He still had that stupid grin on his face. "Gotta go practice." He put his skates around his neck, suspended from laces tied together, knapsack holding his pads in one hand.

Stoney waved him away. "Have fun," he said, preparing to depart himself, but then he noticed the empty water glass in the sink. Was that where he'd left it? A terrible thought crossed his mind, and he tried to think through an ocean of pain, tried to remember. Had the kid been a little unsteady, walking out the door? He couldn't go by the stupid grin, not all by itself. He remembered his own initial experiences with alcohol, how the stuff had made him feel like a real human being for the first time in his life. Oh, Dennis, he thought, don't do it, please God.

He thought he heard someone stirring upstairs. Go now, go, he told himself. Get away while you can.

Tall, walks with that tucked-in butt so common among gay men, brownish hair with platinum streaks, but cut in an acceptable Republican manner. Straight back, one unbroken line from his shoulders to his heels, but almond shaped in front, virtually no muscle tone, thin, hairless arms. He seems prematurely old, as he smokes a long, thin old woman's cigarette, wears an old woman's slippers, blue shorts and a dark, oddly hued muscle shirt that hides none of his imperfections. Even the dog he walks is an old woman's dog, tiny, sickly, limping, wearing an old, smelly dog sweater, fussy about where to shit. What would make a young man abandon his youth in such a way and adopt this frumpish, middle-aged, suicidal housewife persona? Perhaps he was paired off with an old man, and took refuge in this repressed old woman's head.

It was Tommy Bagadonuts's favorite pastime, and he sat at a table by himself at a sidewalk cafe on West Houston and indulged. People fascinated him, particularly city people, free as they are from the constraints of a village or a small town where everybody knows you, you and your family as well, where your history sticks to you and colors peoples' perceptions for your entire lifetime. Tommy could imagine the kid snapping out of it when the old boy died, diving furiously into the Lower West Side musclehead culture, strangling the dog, perhaps. And a year from then, who would remember, who would care, would anyone even wonder what had become of that prematurely old womanish young man?

He caught the waiter's eye and ordered another Turkish coffee. It reminded him of his own youth, long ago and far away, and who ever wondered about that young man? What ever happened to that kid who . . . He turned away from the thought, uncomfortable with it.

He had the sensation again and looked around, but it was impossible to tell in this great, flowing crush of humanity. Eyes on him, though, he was sure of it. He paid the check and moved off down the sidewalk, debating with himself. Catch a cab or take his chances on foot? It's very hard to pick up a tail, impossible, really, if there's a team of good people working on you. Easy enough to lose them, but you wind up giving yourself away, and learning nothing at all. A tiny edge of fear itched in the back of his consciousness, but he ignored it and considered his options rationally.

He turned down Varick Street and paused in front of a store that sold cartoon animation cels and watched the reflections in the glass window. He had no idea what he was looking for, so he just watched, sidetracked, presently, wondering at all the young ladies, bikini tops were in this season, thank God for hot summer nights. But there it was again, shivering up his spine, warping him swiftly back to the problem at hand. He turned away and walked quickly back up the avenue, watching for anyone reversing direction, turning suddenly from view. Impossible, he thought. Impossible. He stepped off the sidewalk and hailed a cab, passed up the yellow car that stopped at his signal and hopped into the gypsy cab that had been trailing hopefully behind. He gave the driver Madam

Cho's address, Third Avenue just north of Fourteenth Street. He didn't really want to see her, he'd have to listen to her complaints about the police for the umpteenth time. There wasn't much he could do for her, the cops would much rather take the money than keep raiding her, but with the mayor's much-publicized campaign to make the city safe for visitors from Omaha, or wherever, they were under increasing pressure to shut her down. Things ain't like they used to be, Tommy, they'd say, and he would agree with them and make bail again.

He didn't go up the stairs to Madam Cho's, choosing instead to scoot through the long corridor on the first floor, out the back door into the stinking alley, past the Dumpster, through the door that led into the kitchen of the coffee shop that fronted on Fifteenth. He held a cautionary finger to his lips at the startled Spanish kids working in the kitchen, tossed two fives to the one who looked like the senior cook, and kept going, out through the front door and west, hurrying, eyeing the door to see who followed, jumping into the first cab he saw.

He tossed a twenty over the seat, telling the driver to keep his flag up, and slithering down in the back, he gave the address of his loft. The driver pulled away, raising a questioning eyebrow in the mirror. Tommy tried to shrug, hunched down in the seat. "Cabron," he said, using the Spanish pejorative term for a cuckolded husband. "Wants to shoot me." The cabdriver laughed and buzzed the red light at Third.

Tommy's building had been a factory once, and it still had the look: concrete, exterior of peeling paint, big metal-framed windows with small panels of opaque or painted glass, small street-level platform entrance that had once been a loading dock. Tommy took a seat on its edge, with his feet hanging down, and began, once again, to watch the people going by in the night. The uncomfortable sensation of being observed was gone. He kept seeing tall, broad-shouldered men who reminded him of his brother. Blond Americans, not just overweight but large, with round faces that seemed to be lit from within by some rosy happiness. Very American looking, his brother had been. From that memory it was all too easy to succumb to the chorus of inner critics, those voices that reminded him of errors in judgment made long ago. He made an effort to silence them, thinking about who it could have been, watching him. He never questioned his conviction that it had been so, his survivor's paranoia automatically linking his observer to Marty's death and then to most of his other current difficulties. He thought again, in spite of his efforts, of his long-dead brother and the trusting, naive nature he'd had. It must be true, he thought, this idea that the sins of your past lives live on to haunt you.

It was in this sad mood that he got up and went into his building, using his key to what had, long ago, been a freight elevator. Turning the key and pushing the correct button sent it clanking and lurching up to his floor, where the elevator door opened up in the corner of his kitchen.

He saw him right away, sitting at the kitchen counter in the dark. He couldn't make out any facial features, but he recognized the man from his outline. His mind automatically cataloged all the possible reasons this man could have for being here and summarily rejected them all, leaving only the one his paranoid nature had given to him first. Another error in judgment.

"Ah," he said sadly. "It was you."

The darkened figure at the counter shrugged elaborately, arms raised to the sides, pistol in one hand.

"Why you hadda shoot poor Marty? He wasa never hurt nobody."

A long, deep breath in the dark, a short, heavy sigh. "I mousetrapped him good, Tommy. I tricked him into coming to that motel with all your papers. I told him you guys needed to go over some stuff about the business and he should bring everything there. I figured I could leave him there, you know, all tied up, while I cleaned out a few of your accounts and deposit boxes. I thought for sure you guys would have, like, an emergency stash, you know, that there would be enough there for me to take off, start over again someplace new. I was all ready, Tommy, I thought I'd be gone that day. I figured I could get it from Marty, or find out from him where it was, and just take off. I can't believe I'm still here, I can't believe I'm still alive to talk to you."

"You don't gonna find anything from him."

"He didn't know anything! Nothing! He kept telling me that you like to keep fully invested. No cash. Look, Tommy, I know you and that asshole Stoney have to have a war chest salted away somewhere, running-away money." He fidgeted on the stool, pointing the gun more directly at Tommy. "I'm running out of time, and I've gotta have it."

"Listen to me," Tommy said. "You don't gotta shoot nobody, you don't gotta steal nothing. Why don't you let me help you?"

"It's no good, Tommy, it's too late for that. Come on, you used to be a player, you and that fucking Stoney. What do you do when the wheels come off and everything has gone bad? I've gotta run, Tommy, and I've gotta run now."

He didn't want to tell the story, but Tommy got it out of him.

Tommy shook his head when he'd heard it all. "You shoulda come to me with this, maybe we coulda did something good with it. But now look! Poor Marty's dead, and for nothing. And what about those two kids in the alley? That wasa you too?"

"No, Tommy, it wasn't me, I swear it! I got into the yard through the gate on the side, over by the container, but I couldn't go back out that way, there was a bunch of kids hanging out in the alley. The front door had the gate down over it and it was locked from the outside, and it was getting late. Then I heard some shots outside, and I got scared. So I climbed up and jumped over the fence, and they were there, they were already dead."

"Ah, Jesus. This isa terrible. First of all, the way you ran this, you gonna be the first guy they think of. You gotta makea the back door, so nobody knows what happen, you can walk away. But now you wind uppa screwing the wrong people, and they never gonna get tire, looking for you. Ah, Christ. Why didn't you come to me? Now we gotta big mess, I can't believe you. Poor Marty, for nothing."

"Will you get offa that?" His voice got louder. "I didn't wanna do it, Tommy, but I had to. If Marty had tipped you off, I'd have never gotten this close to you. He woulda gave me up in a second, and you woulda, too, Tommy, don't fucking tell me you wouldn't. So stop screwing around, you know I need the money, you know I've gotta run."

Tommy shook his head, wondering how he could explain to this kid who thought he was so smart why he had to stay and try to pull it out. "It'sa no good. You can't—"

"Goddammit, Tommy, it's only money!" His voice was loud and strident, with a touch of panic. "You can make more! Everybody says you got the touch. It's my life we're talking about here, otherwise—"

Just then somebody pushed the button for the elevator, Tommy could hear the ancient relays clacking in the motor room, and the elevator doors started to lurch closed. He turned to dive through into the car, moving on his toes with a fat man's grace, but he was a bit too far away, and of course, too slow and too heavy.

"Tommy, no!"

He heard the scream behind him, and the boom of the shots, and he felt something slam into him, knocking him to the floor of the car.

"Tomeeeee—" Plaintively. "Shit!"

And then he was lying in the grass, back in Courmayeur, in the Italian Alps, on the hill that overlooked the town, watching his brother climbing up to him calling his name, and then the disconcerting realization that his brother would never call him Tommy, and then, darkness, and quiet.

"YOU CAME FROM THE OPPOSITE DIRECTION," THE COP SAID. "Normally you would come down Cypress, no?"

Tuco was surprised to see him there in the early morning, before anyone had even opened up. Tuco himself was earlier than usual because he was still just getting a feel for how long the train ride was going to be. The cop looked like he was ending his day, not beginning it. He looked a little ruffled, and he had tired lines in his face.

"I moved," Tuco told him. "I'm over in Brooklyn Heights now."

The cop whistled. "The Heights, no shit. How the hell can you afford the Heights, Eddie? Business must be good."

"Not that good. I took a super job in a building there." Tuco wondered why it was that he was willing to talk to this guy.

"Smart," the cop said. "Very smart. Young guy like you, little work, you get a free place to stay. Whattaya do, sweep the floors and whatnot?"

"That's pretty much it, so far."

"That's good thinking, Eddie, that's a smart move. Anything going on here that I should know about? Any new competition for our friends up on St. Nick?"

Tuco shrugged. "Same faces," he said. "And it's been quiet. Anybody was moving in on them, we'd have a war down here. I ain't heard anybody say anything about those two kids, either. You find out anything?"

The cop thought for a minute before answering, eyeing Tuco, considering. "Not a lot," he said, finally. "Boy was in and out of juvie, the last few years. Shame about the girl, though. She was still in school, up until June. Good student, on track to graduate. You gotta be careful who you hang with."

"I meant, you know who did it?"

"Whoever it was," the cop said, "came over your fence. Two big heel prints in the dirt, where he landed."

Ain't my fence, Tuco thought, but he listened carefully.

"I figure, guy's in your yard, he's ready to leave, he's afraid to use the front door, that metal grate is bound to make a racket, someone's gonna wake up, maybe they'd notice him."

"You think anyone around here's gonna call the cops? In this neighborhood?"

"Probably not. But they might tell your boss, Stoney. I'm told that the guy is a real hard case."

Tuco's radar went up. Careful what you tell this guy, he thought. He doesn't miss much. "Stoney," he said, "is a good guy, generally. Sometimes he flies up the handle."

"That sounds painful," the cop said, suppressing a grin. "Anyway, you guys notice anything missing, broken maybe, out of place?"

"Hard to say. We're kind of disorganized. You probably should ask Tommy about that, or Walter. Even Jimmy the Hat would know better than me."

"Yeah, okay. Still, one question keeps rattling around in my mind. What's the guy doing in your yard?"

Ain't my yard, Tuco thought, but did not say. "Stealing something, maybe."

"Somebody steals, they make a mess. Rip drawers open, throw shit on the floor, break shit up, you know that. You guys might not even call it in. But if two kids get shot right outside your place of business, you'd say, 'Hey, Officer, somebody was in here, stealing shit,' am I right?"

"Probably."

"So I figure, that ain't it. Plus, how did he get in? No broken windows, got metal doors and grates and razor wire, place looks like the state pen."

"Maybe they picked the lock."

The cop gave him a look. "What do I look like, some kind of moron? Nobody picks locks down here, either they break the lock off with a rock or they drive a fucking car through the door. Am I right? No. You know what I think, Eddie?" He leaned a little closer. "I think," he said, "whoever was in there had a key. And I keep coming back to the same question. What was he doing? What was he doing in there?"

Jesus, Tuco thought. He thinks it was one of us.

"Plenty of people," he said, trying hard to sound calm and reasonable, "worked here the past few years. Stoney gives somebody a key, they have to come in on Saturday or something, he forgets, he don't ask for it back."

"You got a key, Eddie?"

"Walter opens up, not me."

"Hnh. Yeah, okay." He stepped back, away from Tuco, looked around for his car. "You see, Eddie," he said, turning back, "I'm spoiled. I ain't used to spending this much time trying to figure out who did what. You work this precinct, you get used to things being simple and straightforward. I show up at a crime scene, I look around, I can tell you exactly what happened, almost every time. You know what I mean? Very seldom do I have a lot of questions in my mind. Say I get a domestic violence call, I get there, the guy's drunk, the woman's all covered with bruises, maybe one of them's dead. Even if we don't get to lock up the bad guy, I know what happened. Bing, boom, that's the story. Am I right? But this one here, this one is way too complicated. Some part of this," he said, tapping his forehead with a finger, "something here I don't have scoped out yet." He gave Tuco another card. "Something comes to mind, you call me."

"Yeah," Tuco said. "Sure."

Stoney pulled his car into the parking lot. He took a quick hit off the bottle under the seat, just to clear the cobwebs. He looked at his watch. Seven-thirty. God, he thought. How am I going to get through this one? Tuco came out to help him with the gate and to tell him about the cop's early morning visit.

"Over the fence, huh?"

Tuco could see the wheels spinning, but as usual, he could not read Stoney. "Said he could tell by the heel marks."

"Makes sense." Stoney stood motionless outside the gate with the lock in his hand, his mind racing. "Could be someone with a key," he said. "But the cops only know two ways to get past a lock, unless they're crooks themselves. One is to break it, two is to get someone with a key. Tell me. You wanted to get inside, how would you do it?"

Tuco shrugged. "The fence, probably. Gotta be a piece of metal loose, somewhere. Or else, throw some rags over the razor wire and go over. Or get up on the office roof, maybe . . ."

"Yeah, yeah," Stoney said. "Okay, go take a look. Take your time, see if you can figure how they did it."

"All right. You think anything will happen with this?"

"You mean, are the cops gonna find out who did it and put him in jail? Maybe. They'll want to clear the case, one way or another. They might get lucky, trip over the guy. More likely, next gangbanger needs to cop a plea, they'll hang it on him. If he's gonna be doing time for something anyway, it'll give him a bigger rep. He might find it easier to defend his honor, if you get what I mean. They get to put another one in the win column, bad guy went to jail, even if he was going there anyway on account of something else. Keeps the numbers down."

"And whoever did it walks away."

"Yeah, well. It's the perfect solution, though. Everybody's happy."

"Don't seem fair."

"Fair? What planet you from? Listen, go around, look at the fence, see if you can tell if someone's been getting in, but don't look too obvious about it. You understand what I mean? Take your time, mix in some actual work."

At nine in the morning, Stoney passed by as Walter made another cup of tea. "Happen to Fat Tommy, Boss?"

Something else to worry about, Stoney thought. "He didn't call you?"

"Ain't heard nothing."

Stoney rubbed his face with both hands, feeling the throbbing within. "He wasn't taking a day, was he? He say anything to you?" Tommy would normally tell Stoney and Walter both when something was up, knowing that Stoney would usually forget.

"Nope."

Stoney looked at his watch. "Give him an hour."

He hated it when Tommy Bagadonuts wasn't around. It meant he had to talk on the phone, listen to complaints, answer questions, take messages, use muscles he wasn't used to using. For a while he thought he was doing okay, but then he realized that he hadn't written down who called, or what he'd told them. Jesus. His head hurt worse than ever.

Tuco opened the office door, looked inside.

"I need a vacation," Stoney told him.

"You came back worse than you left, last time."

"Is there something you want?"

"Nah-ah. But there's two sheets of metal loose, one on the outside past the gate, and the other one in the corner of the parking lot. Somebody could squeeze through the outside one, into the lot, then through the other, into the yard."

"Son of a bitch." Stoney's face flushed dark red.

"You think that's how they got in?"

The muscles in Stoney's jaw flexed. "Maybe. There's more than one way in and out of here."

"You want me to fix 'em?"

"No. I want . . . Come in, shut the door." He waited until Tuco shut the door behind him, and then continued in a lower voice. "I want you to stay late tonight. After everybody's gone, I want you to take a tube of that infrared dye that Commie Pete uses to look for Freon leaks, and I want you to rub it on those two sheets of metal and on the posts they used to be screwed to. You understand what I mean?"

"Yeah."

"Wash your hands good when you're done. And listen. Don't wear those clothes to work again. Throw 'em out when you get home. Just replace 'em, tell me what you spent, I'll pay you back. Okay?"

Tuco nodded. "Sure."

Kid catches on fast, Stoney thought. Maybe we're wasting his talents. "I don't have to tell you—"

Tuco held up his hands, palms out, and closed his eyes. "I don't know nothing," he said. "I don't even speak English."

"Been a hour and a half," Walter said the next time Stoney passed through the outer office.

"You try calling his house?"

"Just get de rasshole machine," Walter said sourly.

"All right. Tell Einstein over there," he said, pointing at Jimmy the Hat, "that he's in charge here. You take a ride into Manhattan, make the rounds, see if you can scare him up. Make sure you lock the gate when you leave."

Walter drove around behind the big cemetery that was under the Brooklyn-Queens Expressway and headed for the Midtown Tunnel. Be nice, he thought, to get away from that place, forget his troubles for a few hours. Stop someplace for a few Red Stripes, maybe get a decent lunch for a change. He knew a Jamaican restaurant on Twenty-third, you could get good flying fish with yellow hot sauce, fried bananas . . . This whole nine-to-five thing was getting to be a pain in his ass. He wanted to be a clerk, he would have gone to school. They had asked him if he wanted in, back when Bagadonuts had this junkyard brainstorm. Sure, he'd said. He hadn't counted on it going on this long, though. Who would have thought these two crazy white boys would want to have real jobs for this long?

He dumped the car at Tommy's parking garage, slipped two bucks to the Haitian who ran the place. "Seen Fat Tommy?"

"Not today."

"All right," he said. "Back soon."

"Be right up front," the Haitian said, grinning. Walter strolled the few blocks between the garage and Tommy's building, amused by all the people hurrying by. This Bajun, he thought, ain't going to die from a heart attack. Save hurrying for when hurrying was wanted. No reason to die, running to get somewhere. Besides, there were too many sights to enjoy on a Manhattan summer morning. He smiled at the girls in their short skirts, winked at a lady pushing two babies in a stroller, gave a buck to a bag lady panhandling for her breakfast. His mood changed abruptly when he got to Tommy's building.

Cops everywhere.

He went on by without stopping, crossed the street, and went into a deli and considered his options. Call in now, the way Stoney felt about cops, he'd call him off, and Walter would go back without having learned a thing. He looked at the cops milling around. He couldn't remember doing anything actionable recently. It would take a whole lot of digging to come up with paper on him. He decided to take the chance.

He crossed the street again, picked out a blue suit with an Italian-looking face, little bit of gray hair. "Officer," he said. "My fren' live in dis buildin', 'ere. Could I go on up, see if 'im home?" He laid the accent on a little thick. Most people take you a little easier, he found, when they can hear the islands in your voice.

"What's your friend's name," the cop said.

"Rosselli. Fat Tommy Rosselli."

"Do you mind telling me how you know Mr. Rosselli, sir, and what the nature of your business with him might be?"

Cops always say "sir" when they mean "asshole," Walter thought. It was his policy, in situations like this one, never to tell the truth when a lie would do as well. "I suppose to meet 'im, down by 'im garage. But 'e don't come, so I come by to see, 'im still sleeping, maybe."

The cop's expression never changed. "Come with me."

• • •

It was another hour before they let him make a phone call. He'd had to tell his story to three different cops, while someone else took his ID and went off to check him out. Finally one of the cops came back, gave him back his license, asked him a lot of questions about Thomas Rosselli, aka Fat Tommy, aka Tommy Bagadonuts.

Used to work for him, at the garage, Walter told them, over and over. Finally they let him go. He looked for the first cop on his way out.

"They took him to Beth Israel," the cop told him. "Last I heard, he was still under the knife."

Jimmy held the phone out at arm's length. "It's Walter," he said, his face grave. Stoney took it from him.

"What'd you find?"

"Stoney, Tommy's in the hospital. Been shot, three times. Two in the lower back, one up high in the shoulder. I going over now to see what I find."

Stoney felt suddenly dizzy, as though the whole world had lurched under his feet. "Walter," he said, "call me as soon as you know anything."

He went into Tommy's office and sat down heavily in Tommy's chair. The wheels in his head began to grind in spite of the hangover that continued to intensify. Now you're fucked, he thought. Now you don't have Tommy to figure things out for you. Now you actually have to think. He got up unsteadily and went over and filled a coffee cup from the water cooler. His whole body cried out for alcohol, but he shook it off and drank the water instead. That tears it, he told himself. There's no question, someone's coming after you, and you've either gotta run or you have to fight back. He filled the cup again and as he drank the water he decided on a mantra and repeated it to himself several times. Think, be smart. Think, be smart.

All right, he thought, first smart thing today. He picked up the phone, dialed his home number. "Hello," she said, and in that one word he could hear the stress and anger in her voice.

"Tommy's been shot."

"Oh, no, oh, God . . . Poor Tommy. Is he all right? Is he going to be okay? What's happening?"

"I don't know," he said. "I'm trying to find out right now. But I want you to listen to me carefully. I want you to pack up the kids and go up to visit your sister . . ."

"Oh, my God—"

"Listen to me. Stay with me, now. Okay?"

"What's going on?"

"I really don't know, but I can't function if I'm worrying about you. Pack up the kids, plan on at least a couple of weeks. Close up the house, stop by the post office and stop the mail. You got it?"

"Mm-hmm." Her answer was almost a moan.

"Donna," he said, his voice firmer, "everything will work out, but you have to do this, it's important. I want you out of that house, today, this afternoon. You can get in touch with me here," he said. "Walter will know how to find me."

"All right," she said. "All right, we're going." She really wanted to unload on him, he could hear it in her voice. What a tough broad, he thought. I really have to make it up to her somehow.

"You call me, you bastard," she said. "You let me know what's going on."

"As soon as I figure it out myself," he said. "I promise."

Walter headed for Beth Israel, moving much faster this time. As he went, he remembered a nurse he'd gone out with, back when he'd been in his twenties. She'd been an island girl about ten years his senior, and she'd had a refreshingly earthy approach to life in general and to sex in particular. The very thought of her made him smile fondly. She had been something . . . Didn't like hustlers, though, or con artists, gangsters, drunks, or bums. Didn't have much use for men, in other words.

The lady behind the desk was middle-aged and Jewish looking, and very firm. "All I can tell you is that Mr. Rosselli is in the operating room. From there he will go to the ICU. No visitors. If you leave your number, someone will call you as soon as we have any information."

Walter wandered off to look around in the gift shop. When the information lady left her desk for something, he went on back to the elevators and went up. When he was relatively sure he was on the right floor, he looked around for a nurse, maybe a nice island girl who didn't take too much shit from doctors, or from cops.

She was a vision. Tall, with honey-brown skin and a rich, dark voice that she was using to fuss out a hapless porter, a poor Hispanic kid who was trying to mop the hallway, and who had apparently left it too wet for Miss Thing. Walter watched her with admiration. Oh, I could make you so happy . . .

She spied him watching her, and when she finished with the porter she turned on him. "What you hanging around up here for? You got business up here?"

"Yes, ma'am," he said, in his most resonant baritone. "My sister call me at work, all upset. She work for this man, Mr. Rosselli, keep the house and all that, and she told me that 'e was in the hospital, and that no one would tell her anything at all. Now she very worried, for she says that 'e is a very nice man, and she would never want for anything bad to happen to 'im, that she could never find such a nice person to work for as 'e. I told her I come after work to check, but she keep calling and calling, so I had to say that I would come to see what I could find out."

She straightened up to her full height, a study in brown and white, with attitude. "You come here from work," she said. "What work you do?"

"Oh," he said, "I have an auto-body shop on Woodhaven Boulevard. Mostly paint antique cars."

"All right," she said. "You stay here, I go see what I can find." He watched her sail majestically down the corridor, wishing her white dress were tighter. Spirited woman like that, he thought, got to be alone. Maybe married once, probably throw the old boy out years ago. I come back, I bring flowers for Tommy, chocolates for the nurse, or maybe chocolates for Tommy, flowers for the nurse. Oh, hell, flowers and chocolates for the nurse, Fat Tommy don't need the chocolates, can't eat the flowers.

Walter skipped lunch.

He picked up the car and drove hastily crosstown and through the Midtown Tunnel. He kept shaking his head, having a hard time comprehending Tommy in a coma, Fat Tommy in some strange land between life and death. Fat Tommy being fed through a tube! Surely it was an omen. This should tell me the answer, he thought, stay or go, this should tell the story. He hurried through the local traffic back to Troutman Street, and he didn't know why. No need to rush, really.

Walter calmed himself down before he got to the yard, put his car back into the lot, locked the gate behind him. He pondered how, exactly, to impart his news. He decided, on his way through the front door, just to hit him with it. Stoney could take a punch. It was the best way.

Jimmy the Hat was trying to explain something to Stoney. They were both looking at Jimmy's computer screen, but Jimmy could barely get a word in. Stoney was the kind of guy, sometimes you had to slap him to get his attention. They both went silent when they saw Walter.

"He's still alive," he said. "Just barely."

"Oh, shit," Jimmy said. Stoney said nothing, but his face went pasty white. Walter told the story that his nurse had told him. Tommy Bagadonuts was in limbo, clinging to life. Only quick action by his downstairs neighbor had gotten him this far. She'd heard the shots, heard somebody yelling, heard the elevator. She had called the police immediately, and like all seasoned New Yorkers, she had told the dispatcher that she thought a policeman had been shot. Then she'd gone looking, found Tommy unconscious on the floor of the elevator, and had begun CPR. He was bleeding profusely from the shoulder wound, and it had been very difficult for her to hold pressure on it while she breathed for him, but she'd done the best she could. She did not recoil, the way she thought she might, taking the classes, because it was Tommy B., whom she held in such high regard.

Stoney interrupted. "Doctors tell you all this?"

"Doctors tell you shit," Walter replied. "You got to know who to ask." He continued his story. The shooter had been waiting inside the loft. After shooting Tommy, he'd gone down the fire escape. The cops, in Walter's opinion, were doing the full-court press, dusting the scene for fingerprints, interviewing the neighbors, trying to backtrack Tommy Bagadonuts's movements that night. There were even cops in the hospital, off duty, apparently, friends of Tommy, watching his back.

And nobody knew if he would live. The emergency-room residents had thought he was done for when he'd first come in, Walter's nurse had said, and they had more than a passing acquaintance with gunshot victims. And if he did live, there was no guarantee that Tommy would ever walk again, or even speak, for that matter.

Stoney turned and paced to the door to Tommy's office, and then slowly back. There was no emotion on his face, nothing to indicate what was going on inside as he groped for a way to deal with this new information. He turned and paced away again, over to the window this time, and stood there looking out. I know you want to get him, he told himself, but think, be smart. He repressed the growing bubble of rage.

"Well," he said, still looking out the window, "I gotta go to the hospital and see Tommy." His voice was subdued. Be smart, he told himself. What would be the easiest way to put Stoney in a box? A simple phone call, Hey, Officer, there's this guy, drives to work every day, and I know he lost his license.

"Jimmy, call me up a car-service guy. Call that four-eights guy that Tommy used to use."

"Okay."

"Walter," he said, "we need some muscle. Not just some mutt to stand around looking bad, either. We need someone hard enough and smart enough to take someone out if they show up here with a gun. You know anybody?"

"Yeah, man. Some ex-cops got a security thing going, over to Hunts Point. Couple of bad mothers, very cold. Laugh at you while they shooting your ass."

"Get on the phone. Set it up."

"How much you want to spend, boss?"

"I don't want anyone else getting shot. Tell your guy what we're up against, see what he says. Jimmy, forget the car service, I can't wait. Get Tuco up here to drive me. And listen, both of you. Nobody goes anywhere until you hear from me, got it?"

Be smart, he told himself again. Think, be smart.

7

TUCO REALLY WANTED TO PRAY FOR TOMMY BAGADONUTS.

Sitting behind the wheel of Stoney's Lexus on Eighteenth Street with the window rolled down, he started and stopped in his mind, over and over, but he had to keep looking in the mirrors for cops, because Stoney had made him park the car by a fire hydrant. "Don't worry about it," he'd said. "If the cops roust you, just go around the block." But they did not. The few cops who cruised by paid him no attention.

God, he thought, starting up again in his mind, but he could not continue. He wasn't sure if it was because he felt dishonest asking for favors, even if they weren't for himself, after he'd already decided that it was all a crock, and that he was really and truly on his own, or if it was just that he'd lost the knack, that confidence that comes when you really believe, when you have that strong image in your mind. But after you recognize that it's just an image, just a synthesis of all the words, all the stories, all the things taught by the ministers of your mother's church, then what? It had seemed a reasonable enough picture, at the time, and he had felt comfortable talking to that image, asking it for help, leaning on it. It was gone now, though, and he could not talk himself into imagining it back into reality. He could not talk to a black hole, could not lean on a figment of his imagination. How he had gotten to this point, he did not understand.

Well, it had been his cousin Miguel who had started it. They had been standing in front of a funeral parlor off Broadway, in Brooklyn, down by the Williamsburg Bridge. Tuco had been wearing his Sunday clothes, suit and tie, polished shoes. He'd been just a little surprised to see Miguel there, dressed in his street clothes, complete with the colored beads that identified his affiliation. He'd been fidgety, nervous, twitchy, which Tuco had never known him to be, a gas engine running on nitro, eating itself up from the inside, but right now, right now, way stronger than it had a right to be, hot. Tuco had felt Miguel's eyes on him, during the second half of the service, and he'd wondered if Miguel was watching for fear, and if they would get him again on his way home. He was past caring, by this point, but he did want to know. But when he caught Miguel's eyes, he saw only amusement.

"You think you're better than me," Miguel had said, afterward, out on the sidewalk. Even his voice was different than Tuco remembered it. It seemed darker, less human, like the rest of him. "But you know what's the funny thing? God loves me better than you, and I can prove it."

Tuco hadn't wanted to hear it. "Hey, listen—"

"No, serious," Miguel said. "It's right in the Bible. I know you ain't readin' it, but tha's no excuse. You don't even listen to the stories when they tell 'em. You just close your eyes and follow along, because you too goddamn lazy to figure out wha's what. You remember the stories about David and Solomon? Which one you think God love better?"

Tuco was silent.

Miguel shouted his question, his face a mask of anger, inches from Tuco's. "C'mon! Which one!"

Tuco stayed outwardly calm. "David."

"Why? Why is that?" Miguel was seemingly back to something like normal, grinning, bouncing in one spot.

"I don't know."

Miguel puffed up and seemed almost to strut, standing still. "Because," he said, "David was like me. He was a ass kicker. What things was he good at?" He ticked them off on his fingers. "Music, drinking wine, fighting, fucking." He was laughing, enjoying what he could read of Tuco's expression. "What did Solomon do? What you do. He pissed and moaned about how much his life sucked."

"So you're happy now. You're satisfied with what you are."

Miguel's expression went dark. No one had dared to talk to him like that in some time. "Tha's right," he said, his face twisting into a sneer. "I got everything."

"What about Angelito, inside? What's he got? He didn't even make twenty."

"No." Miguel cocked his head slightly, shrugging.

"You don't even care."

"The ones that did this to him will pay, very soon. Angelito will be at rest."

"That's for you, not for Angel. He still gonna be dead, either way."

"I used to believe that you could think, you know that, Eddie? I knew you wasn't very good in school, but I still thought you was pretty smart, but you're not. You're stupid." Miguel shoved Tuco with sudden violence, knocking him back several feet. His voice got loud, and he started shouting. People coming down the sidewalk began to give the two of them a wide berth. "Only reason you say that is because you're stupid. All this time, you been going to church, Sunday school, all of that, but you don't pay no attention, you don't even fucking listen. You too lazy to think. Now listen to me, I gonna tell you something. Angelito, you, me, all of us, we die tomorrow, it don't make no difference." He was up close again, blowing fetid breath in Tuco's face. "Don't mean shit. It's just God, cutting the fucking grass, that's all it is." He was almost whispering. "Listen to me, now, 'cause they never gonna tell you this in that church. You, me, all of us together, we only have one life. Between us all. Angel is dead, but his sister gonna have a baby. It don't matter. Don't mean shit." He leaned back, pleased with himself. "Still, God loves the ass kickers. Always did."

A small kernel of doubt had grown into a question, and that only led to more questions, and Tuco had eventually been forced out of his comfort zone into a nether world of gray fog and uncertainty. Something in his mind had changed, and in time that something had forced him to admit, if only to himself, that the only thing he was sure of was that he was alive, and he held to that more because he needed it than because he knew it, it was just a supposition, really. Other than that, he felt completely ignorant. He didn't even trust his own senses anymore, because, after all, what he saw with his eyes was really caused by the chemicals in his brain, he had seen that on the Discovery channel. And who could he talk to about it? Not Miguel, that was certain, and his mother was just as adamant, in her way, as Miguel was, wrapped so tightly around those things that she wanted to be true. And there had been no one else. He was alone.

Not so bad, anyhow, he told himself. Ignorance must surely be the place of all beginnings. But it would have been so nice if there had been some string he could pull for Fat Tommy, if somehow, he could put in a good word . . . But even there, he doubted his own judgment. What made him think that he knew how things should

turn out? All he had was his own pinched, small life, his own narrow experience and desire.

Stoney rapped on the window, ending Tuco's reverie and taking a year or so off his life span. He thumbed the button that
unlocked the door, and Stoney flopped into the passenger seat.

"What did you find out?"

"Not too much," Stoney said. "He could go either way. Three
nine-millimeter slugs can do a lot of damage." He could still see
him, behind the glass wall, an unrecognizable half-moon shape
under the sheet, hooked to a confusing array of machinery with
wires and tubes.

Tuco noticed Stoney's hands trembling. "You feel okay, boss?"

"No. Fucking hospital, I probably caught something in there."
He felt weak and shaky, all of a sudden. Sweaty, with his hangover
still lurking in the background. Couple nice big gin and tonics, he
knew, would fix him right up, but he clamped down on that
thought angrily. Think, he told himself. Be smart. "Let's go downtown," he said. "There's a big electronics store on Chambers. We
gotta pick up a few things."

Stoney came out of the store carrying a bag. He looks worse than
ever, Tuco thought. "Boss," he said, "you want me to drive you
home?"

"No. Head back uptown, around Union Square someplace.
Wake me when we get there." Tuco drove off as Stoney reclined
his seat back, sweating and shaking. Jesus, he thought. Maybe I
did catch something in that place. He couldn't get comfortable, so
after a few blocks he sat back up again and looked out the window.
He felt confined in the car, stressed by the presence of this kid who
expected so much of him. He ran out of patience when they got to
Twelfth Street.

"Pull over. Park right in front of that deli."

"That's a bus stop."

"I don't give a shit," he said irritably. "Just pull over here." He dumped the bag out on the console between the front seats.

"What's this stuff?"

"Cell phones. One for me, one for you, one for Walter. Here, this one is yours. Take a piece of paper, write down the other numbers, put it in your wallet. I want you to carry this thing everywhere. It's got voice mail, see that button that looks like an envelope? Why am I trying to explain this to you, you figure it out. Listen to me now. I want you to drive back to the shop, drop this on Walter, but don't hang around. Just drop it off and go home. Take the car, find some-place to park it in your neighborhood, but out of sight, you get me? Don't leave it out in front of your building."

"I get it, boss."

"Smart kid. Now listen to me. Stay home tomorrow, okay? I'll call you sometime during the day, but don't go anywhere until you hear from me. Got it?"

"Yeah. You sure you don't want me to take you home? You look terrible."

"Yeah, well, I feel terrible. Don't worry, I'll get over it. Just do like I told you." Stoney opened the door and got out, slammed the door behind him and walked off down Twelfth Street without looking back.

He felt buoyed up, drifting like a balloon floating away, cut from the anchors that had held him in place, Donna, the kids, the house, Tommy, even Tuco and the car. He walked aimlessly through the twisted streets of Greenwich Village, balancing the pull of the wind against the tug of the cell phone in his pocket. He came to rest on a bench at the edge of Washington Square Park, watching the flat-bottomed clouds drifting overhead, seeming so close, if you had a stepladder you could climb right on up inside and sail away, rain down in some other place, feel yourself soaking down into the dirt of some faraway mountainside.

He wondered where this spacey feeling was coming from. His head felt like it was being squeezed, and he was unsteady, and he wondered how it was that he could be covered in sweat and yet chilled through to the bone, both at once. Across the park to his left, two cops sat in a blue-and-white car, and to his right, on the other side of the square, the dope sellers sat, impalas taking a drink, knowing that they could outrun the lions, not nervous but alert, watchful. And their customers, desperation overruling their fear, made their slow approach, eye contact, hey, got anything? And a slow, easy walk for half a block . . .

Stoney knew he needed a drink, needed it bad, and when he'd had this feeling in the past he had always listened to his body, every time. But this time he knew he could not. Think, he told himself. Be smart.

He shifted his weight on the bench, wiped the sweat from his forehead. A wino was making a circuit around the edge of the park, quick, jerky, uneven steps, altering course uncertainly around the benches and other obstacles in his path, talking in a monotone. Stoney could hear his voice, as he came around, and then he could make out the words when he got close. He was reciting Bible verses, words pouring out into the air, working his way through the begats, this one begat that one who begat the other one, over and over, on and on. Stoney watched him go by, briefly forgetting himself. He watched, rapt, as the man made his stumbling progress around the square, all the way around, almost out of sight, back again, within range, the mumbling first, then the words, still on the same book, grandfathers, fathers, sons, children, all three thousand years dead.

"You watching Arthur?"

The voice came from right behind Stoney's ear, and Stoney flinched from it, startled. He turned to see a short, thin man with white hair and an unlit, half-smoked cigar clamped in his teeth. He was wearing green work clothes with the name "Benny" written on the shirt pocket. "Jesus, buddy," the guy said. "Sorry, didn't mean to scare you."

Stoney deflated back down onto the bench. "S'all right," he said. "My nerves are shot. Yeah, I was watching that guy. Friend of yours?"

"Brother-in-law." The little man stepped around to the front of the bench, walking in that way that short guys do, in energetic, choppy movements. He sat down next to Stoney.

"How does your sister put up with him?"

"Oh, she don't. She's dead." There was a trace of sadness in his voice.

"Sorry." Stoney crossed his arms and shivered. Arthur continued around on his circuit. He had given up chanting and now was singing tunelessly. The two of them watched silently as Arthur came around and passed by their bench without noticing them, still singing.

"It's the wrong way, to tickle Mareeee . . . It's the wrong way, to go . . ."

They watched him go. Stoney wiped off his forehead again, then wiped his hand on his pants leg. "So," he said. "What happened to Arthur?"

Benny shifted his weight, getting comfortable on the bench. "Well," he said, "Arthur was the kinda guy always drank heavy. Put my sister through a lot. Four, five years ago, he quit. I won't say he got sober, he didn't go to AA or nothing, but he did stop. They had two years together, Jesus, two years out of a whole life . . . Anyway, she died. Just like that, she's gone. I seen Arthur at her funeral, he wasn't drinking or nothing, but he's not saying anything, either, not crying, nothing. He walks up to the box, after the service, looks inside for a while. Then he turns around and walks out. I don't see him once in the next two years. Then, six months ago, maybe, I get a call. People that took over the apartment say Arthur is there, he's banging on the door, making a ruckus. I got there just after the cops, Arthur was like this here." He waved at Arthur, who was on the far edge of the square, still moving.

"They let me take him. What was I supposed to do? He don't drink no more, at least. He goes to AA with me, which he'd never do before."

Stoney wiped his brow again. "Sort of late, ain't it? What's the point, stopping now?"

"Beats the shit outta me. I ain't in charge. Maybe the man upstairs has a use for him."

Arthur changed his course and headed straight across the square to where they were sitting. He stared hard at Stoney. "Detox," he said. "Detox, detox." Busted, Stoney thought. Can't fool a pro.

Benny looked at Stoney in alarm. "Oh, shit."

"What's he talking about? I just got the flu."

"Detox," Arthur said.

"How long has it been?"

"Twenty-five years," Stoney said, "on and off. Mostly on."

"How long has it been since your last drink?" Benny talked slower, patiently.

"Oh. Yesterday."

"Oh, hey," Benny said. "You gotta go to the hospital."

"If I'm bleeding. Not until."

"You could die, doing this." Benny's voice was getting higher and louder. "You've been on this drug for twenty-five years, you think you just put it down and walk away? You ever hear the word 'withdrawal'? You ever hear of the DTs?"

"Bugs," Arthur said, and he did a whole body shiver, almost a little dance. "Whoo-oo."

"Jesus," Stoney said. "What are you guys, out on patrol or what? You go trolling the park, looking for some poor asshole you figure needs your help?"

Benny was laughing. "I'm just out watching Arthur take his daily constitutional. I didn't come here looking for you."

"You figure I just got lucky?"

"Well, I don't know. There's an old saying, 'When the student is ready, the teacher appears.'"

"Oh, God."

Benny shrugged. "What could I tell you? There's drunks everywhere, current and former. How much do you drink, on an average day?"

Stoney thought about the question before he replied. Maybe it was Arthur, maybe it was the bench and the dope sellers and the cops, maybe it was Benny. Whatever it was, he tried to tell the truth. "Coupla beers," he said, "in the morning. Coupla hits off a bottle under my seat, on the way in. Then I go get breakfast, ten or ten-thirty, to a Dominicano joint up the street, they always have something to drink in there. Couple of El Presidentes or some *aguardiente*. Sometimes just a few screwdrivers. After that, who knows? Sometimes nothing, sometimes a lot, depends on what's happening. You know what I mean? Like, if I stop in a bar, forget it. I can't go into bars anymore, especially the low-rent joints. I go into one of those, I wind up doing lineups. You ever do those? A beer, a joint, a line of coke, a shot, and a cigarette. Your brain don't know what to do." They were both staring at him, their mouths open.

"Figure a fifth," Stoney said, still trying to answer the question. "Maybe a quart, average day. Oh, hell, I don't know."

"You sure you don't wanna go see a doctor?"

Stoney shook his head. "Nah, I'll be okay."

"Sure you will. Look, I'm gonna give you my number. You can call me anytime, day or night. Specially if you feel like drinking, call me first, not after. You don't have to live like this. You wanna do something about it, I can take you to a meeting . . ."

"Oh, here we go."

"All right, all right. Take my number. Call me anytime."

Tuco surveyed the damage while the sanitation cop wrote out the ticket.

The previous afternoon he'd sat in his apartment, in silence so deep that all he could hear was the ringing in his own ears. After an hour or so he'd gone out and mopped all the hallways. He was surprised by how little time it had taken. He was also surprised that in the process he'd met no one. It was if the entire building was deserted. That done, he went downstairs and out into the alley behind the building, where the garbage cans were kept. They were ancient-looking galvanized-metal cans, each lined with a black plastic bag. The tenants in the building brought their own stuff down and dumped it in the cans, so he was told. He hadn't seen anyone yet. All he had to do was tie up the bags and carry them to the street, and then reline the cans. Forty minutes, he thought, and my job for the week is half done. Now all he needed to do was find a way to keep from going stir-crazy. Go buy a TV, he told himself, and a radio. It struck him for the first time that it was all up to him, from now on.

What he felt was loneliness.

"Probably street kids," the cop said, handing him the ticket. "I'm really sorry about this, but I got no choice. My supervisor is up my ass, particularly about this neighborhood."

Tuco surveyed the broken bags, garbage all over the street and sidewalk. "Sixty bucks," he said. "First day on the job, and already I'm losing money. How can there be street kids around here? All I see is yuppies. This happen very often?"

"Yuppie street kids," the cop said, shrugging. "What can I tell you? It happens now and then. What you can do, leave the bags behind the gate, then get up early and put 'em out."

I'll get up early, all right, Tuco thought, but not to put bags out. He started cleaning up the mess. "People throw away some weird shit," he said, looking.

"You don't know the half of it."

It was the sound that got you first, more than the smell. Men's voices, shoes and boots clomping, mumbling, phones ringing, shouted conversations, constant, unending, gaining and then losing volume, toning down but never going away, coming back louder again, waves hissing up the beach, soaking in, receding.

Stoney had been a little worried that they wouldn't let him in, since Arthur had pegged him right away. "Detox, detox." Stoney could still hear him saying it. Even so, he'd stood in line, shambled up to the desk, handed over his eight bucks, got the same speech that everyone else had.

"No drugs, no booze." A fat man handed him a colored piece of paper without looking at him. It had a number written on it. "No radios, no weapons, no fighting. No trouble, everybody's happy. Make trouble, you'll be sleeping in the Tombs, or Riker's Island. Next." Stoney took his piece of paper and stepped away from the desk. The guy in line behind him recited the speech along with the guy behind the desk. "No drugs, no booze. No radios, no weapons, no fighting . . ."

It was an enormous room, like a gymnasium, long and wide

and open to an impossibly high ceiling, somewhat warm in the winter, sweltering in the summer. It was divided into rows of small cubicles; each cubicle had a cot, a small desk, and a chair. It was the Royal, downtown, a few blocks off the Bowery. It was both safer and cleaner than a city-run shelter or jail. There was a certain level of civility in the place, because everyone there had ponied up his eight dollars, and no one wanted to get tossed. For one thing, you didn't get your eight bucks back, and for another, management at the Royal had a long memory, and some cold night you might not get back in.

The neighborhood had been full of places like the Royal, back in the days before shelters, rent-control laws, and lawyers. They had provided an affordable haven for transients, immigrants, and workingmen who sent their money back home. Along with a cot and a blanket you were allowed a measure of dignity, because you were a man; you paid your own way. Times had changed, and most of the old flophouses had long since shut down. The Royal and a few others soldiered on under the grandfather clause, bearing noisy witness to a bygone age of reason and common sense.

Stoney wandered down the rows of cubicles until he found the one with his number on it. He lay down on his cot and stared at the far-off ceiling, his eyes playing tricks on him, showing him spinning, shadowy, dancing shapes way up high in the gloomy distance. I'll go to the hospital, he told himself, if they come down here and start talking to me. He felt oddly comfortable at the Royal, at home, surrounded by fellow unfortunates, almost as if he'd really been playing house with Donna in the suburbs, pretending. Most likely he'd never seen any of the other men staying here before, but they were his people, his brothers, and he felt as though he belonged among them. He knew their stories and they knew his, enough, at least, for one night's coexistence. And they all knew the rules. No drugs, no booze. No radios, no weapons, no fighting.

• • •

*"Not in here!" the bartender said loudly, "Don't bring that shit in here!"
But they kept coming, ignoring him, and he gave up. "Down in the back,
then, pick a booth down in the back, for chrissake," he said, disgust heavy
in his voice.*

*Stoney waved the dealer on back into the darkness and stopped at the
bar. "To start out," he said, "we're gonna need two drafts and two double
shots of Jim Beam. And one ashtray."*

*"Ashtray's on the table," the bartender mumbled, looking around as
he fished for the glasses.*

*The table was clean enough. In the dark, Stoney could not see much
dirt. The dealer sat across from him in the booth, white guy way past whatever prime he'd had, dirty blond ponytail, rheumy eyes, scraggly growth of
beard on his face, blurred tattoos on his forearms. Money passed over the
table, and they were almost ready by the time the bartender brought the
shots and the beers. There was a large plastic ashtray centered on the table.
Stoney paid the bartender and arranged everything in order while the dealer
chopped the coke into two lines the old-fashioned way and laid two plastic
straws next to it. Stoney lit two cigarettes and left them smoldering in the
ashtray, then he lit a joint, puffing on it just enough to get it going. God, he
thought with a pang, I have really fucked it up now. Can't even stay straight
for a few days, my best friend in the ICU, Donna wants to hang me, somebody's taking out people all around me, and I'm going on a tear, Jesus,
what a fucking loser. But then just as quickly he was past caring, fuck it,
fuck it all, they were ready, no reason to wait. Jim Beam first, the two of
them together, Stoney could feel it burn its way down, down through his
arms and legs and then back up to his head, and before it subsided the
dealer was passing him the joint in a shaking hand, and he sucked in a
big chestful of sweet smoke. He could feel it hit the bourbon, amping it up,
and he held it in as long as he could. His head was throbbing, waves of
something, not pain or pleasure. It was his blood, he realized, roaring in his*

ears, and in the next heartbeat he was snorting the coke off the table, and he could feel himself inflating, growing, morphing into some primitive, animal, prehistoric version of himself, bulletproof, suddenly strong enough and fearless enough to stand against anyone or anything, but as he put the beer to his lips, a tiny voice in his head was saying, This is it, this is how you're gonna go, maybe next time, maybe now. Fuck it, he thought, I don't care, but his conviction was gone, and the voice kept on. No need to shoot you, just buy you some lines and watch you die. At that very moment the dealer reached inside his green jacket and pulled out a Colt semiautomatic and held it out, one hand wrapped around the other trying to hold it steady, but before he could pull the trigger Stoney felt something inside him rending apart, catastrophic failure, they called it, literally going to pieces, he didn't know if it was his heart, his liver, his throat, or what, but he could feel a hot tide welling up inside him, and he thought, This is it, this is how it feels to drown in your own blood, and he fell off the bench as he doubled over in pain, and as he hit the floor it flashed on him, how meaningless it is to be sorry to have hurt everyone who's ever loved you . . .

Papery-dry hands pulled at his shoulders, rolling him over on his side. An old man, down on one knee, no teeth, dry and whispery voice. "Hey, boy, you got the heebie-jeebies, you shook your ass right out of your bunk. You all right?"

It was the Royal, the big, dark room, other voices hushing the two of them. Stoney, slick with sweat, rolled over and sat up weakly. "Yeah, I'm okay," he said, and for a tiny fraction of time he knew what bullshit that really was, but he pushed it back down, pulled himself back from it. "Just a bad dream," he said. "I'll be fine."

The old man helped him back to his cot. "Yeah, them night horrors," he said. "Ain't they a bitch."

8

TUCO HAD NEARLY FORGOTTEN ABOUT THE CELL PHONE. HE'D LEFT IT
on his kitchen counter in its recharger stand, and from the living
room he could hardly hear the tinkling noise it made when it rang.
He hadn't heard it ring before, but he'd surmised what it must be
before he'd gotten to the kitchen to answer it.

"Stoney?"

"Good morning." Stoney's voice was subdued. Tuco found that
odd, because in his experience, Stoney was always loud and bois-
terous in the mornings, hung over or not. "Come on in and pick
me up," he said. "We have to go in to the shop for a while."

"Okay, sure. Same place, up by Union Square?"

"No," Stoney said. "Houston Street, on the eastbound side,
corner of First Avenue."

Tuco picked up Houston at its eastern extremity, off FDR Drive. He
made a U-turn and pulled over to a bus stop on the corner. There

were three winos on the stoop of the nearest building. One of them was Stoney. He handed his half-smoked cigarette to the man next to him and ambled over to the car and got in.

"Damn," Tuco said. "If I wasn't looking for you here, I wouldn't have recognized you at all. I couldn't tell you apart from those other two bums." He looked at Stoney's unshaven face. "You okay?"

"Yeah, I'm fine," Stoney said, in the same uncharacteristically subdued tone he'd used on the phone.

"You find a place to stay last night?"

"Oh, yeah. I took a room at the Plaza. I only came down here because you can't get a good bottle of T-bird anywhere uptown. We gonna go, we gonna sit here?"

"I just wanted to see if you're okay," Tuco said, pulling away from the curb, "because you look like shit."

"Yeah, I know. It's all part of the plan."

"We got a plan?"

"Aaargh." Tuco didn't know if that was a yes or a no, and kept silent. "We got the beginnings of one. Tommy was always the planner. We're going in today, thrash around a little bit, look a little desperate. Nervous, you know, disheveled."

"You should have told me," Tuco said, "'cause I look good."

"Yeah, you do," Stoney said, looking over at him. "You can be the guy, don't know what's going on, too dumb to be afraid. Swing by the hospital, you can take a run in and check on Tommy, make sure they're still watching him. I'll wait in the car."

Tommy's condition had not changed. Tuco sat with him long enough for the cop who'd been watching him to go have a cigarette. Something told him that Stoney, who normally had no patience at all, was different, at least for now. He was right. When he got back to the car, he found Stoney had reclined his seat all the way back and had gone to sleep. He didn't wake, even when Tuco got in, shut his door, and started the engine. Tuco sat for a minute, listening to Stoney mumbling in his sleep, but when he drove off, Stoney went silent, and Tuco knew he was awake, but by the time they hit the Midtown Tunnel, Stoney was asleep again.

Tuco pulled up on the sidewalk in front of the parking lot, got out, and opened the gate. Stoney was sitting up when he got back to the car. Tuco got in, prepared to drive the car inside and park. "Hold up, hold up," Stoney said. Think, he was telling himself. Be smart.

"I should have set this up ahead of time," he said.

"Set what up?"

"I want to rig that black light, the one that goes with the dye that you put on the fence the other night. You did that, right? Put dye on that section of fence that's loose?"

"Yeah, I did it."

"What's it look like?"

"It don't look like anything. A little oily, is all."

"Well, can you rig that black light up in the ceiling somewhere, somewhere up where no one will notice it?"

"Of course. You want it in Fat Tommy's office, or outside in the front? You want it on all the time, or you want a switch? Better have it on a switch, it's on all the time, it's gonna get too hot. Plus . . ."

"Plus what?"

"Well . . ." He didn't want to say it. "Say the light's on all the time. If it's someone who's in there a lot, he'll notice himself being bright green, you know what I'm saying? That might not be a good thing."

"If it's one of us, you mean." Assuming it ain't you, he added silently. "Can you rig it in the office? Where would you put the switch?"

"Aah." Tuco thought for a minute. "You remember how Tommy bitched, after we finished building his office, how the power to the clock on his desk would go off when you shut the lights off? Because we wired the lights through the outlet."

"Yeah, I remember. I thought you fixed that."

"Well, not really. We just hot-wired a new outlet from the outside, out in the shop. If we tap into the original outlet behind the desk . . ." He was thinking as he talked. "Yeah, I can do it. I'll do it from the outside, on the shop side of the wall. I just hafta get inside long enough to mount a toggle switch someplace. Need a handi-box and a switch, some wire and whatnot. You want me to run up to the hardware store on Grand?" He waited for Stoney to curse the guy who owned the store for a thief, like always.

"Yeah. Yeah, all right. Here, let me give you a twenty. That cover it? Oh, I still owe you for your clothes. You throw them out like I told you?"

"Yes, boss."

"Good. Here's two more twenties. Now listen to me. When you're at the store, before you come back down here, there's a brown leather briefcase in the trunk, get it out. Put your stuff in the bag. When you get back here, take the bag with you and go out in the back. Put the light in the bag, whatever else you need for what you've gotta do in the office. If the bag isn't full, put some other shit in it, rags or whatever. I want it to look full, I mean packed. Bulging out. Understand? Then find a couple of cardboard boxes, good size, but they have to fit in the trunk, and fill them up too. Then go into the office, do what you've gotta do. Wait, lemme think about this a minute." Tommy is so good at this shit, he thought.

"Okay, here's the sequence. First, the hardware store. You put the stuff in the bag. Second, you come back, take the bag inside. Fill it up with rags, fill two boxes with rags too. I won't be there, I'll be up to the corner, getting breakfast. Hang around, wait for me. When I come back, I'll make some noise, get everybody else out into the street for something, you go into the office, rig the light. How much time you need?"

Tuco thought about it. "Ten minutes."

"Okay. When you're done, leave the light off, okay? Go back into the yard, take the bag with you. Stash it out there until I tell you it's time to drive me home. Then go get it, take it right through the front, I'll take the two boxes, and we throw it all in the trunk. Got it?"

"Yeah, no sweat."

"Okay. Be cool, but remember the first rule: Watch your back."

I am beginning to think like a crook, Tuco thought. Maybe Commie Pete was right. "Yeah, okay."

Stoney got out of the car. "You take off," he said. "I'll get the gate."

He got one side of the gate closed, was walking to get the other side when he saw the two white legs on the ground, sticking out from behind Walter's car. Oh, shit, he thought, not another one, please, God, I can't handle another dead guy . . . He went over and looked, but it was just the old junkie. He watched for a minute, saw the slow rise and fall of the old man's chest. He's breathing, anyway, Stoney thought, and then he saw the works on the ground beside the car. All right, he thought. Whatever. I wonder what planet he's on right now. I wonder what he's seeing, or feeling. He thought of the feeling of release he'd gotten when he'd called Donna, knowing he wasn't going home, didn't have to face her that night. Probably multiply that by a hundred, or a thousand, to get to where this guy's head is at. I wonder if I could take it, he thought. Oh, you could take it all right, the inner voice came back. The question is could you ever let it go. Could you ever live without it, after.

There was a brown minivan parked across the street from the front door. A middle-aged white guy was leaning against the front of the minivan, watching Stoney close and lock the gate. He was wearing blue jeans, a black T-shirt, running shoes. Even without the pistol strapped to his belt, he would have looked formidable. He watched Stoney come up the sidewalk the way a snake watches a mouse. Stoney nodded to him, got one back, very slight movement, down, up. No lapse of attention, not even an eye blink. Inside the office, in the far corner, stood his negative image, black instead of white, white T-shirt instead of black, otherwise much the same, leaning against the wall, arms folded.

Walter was the only one glad to see Stoney. "Hey, whitey! How we doing? You see Tommy?"

"Yeah, me and Tuco stopped in this morning. Nothing to report."

Walter gestured to the black ex-cop in the corner. "Say hello to half of our new security team."

Stoney walked over to shake his hand. "I saw your partner outside," he said.

"He got the nice job, out in the sun."

"Hey, Jimmy, you feel better now?" Walter said. "Stoney's here, you ain't a minority anymore." Jimmy the Hat, on the phone, looked up but did not speak.

"Yes, he is," Stoney said.

Jimmy hung up the phone. "Could I speak to you?"

Stoney shrugged. "Yeah, sure. Step into Tommy's office."

•   •   •

"Are we bait?"

Jimmy was visibly afraid. His hands shook, and he appeared nervous and unsteady. Stoney thought that, for once, it was something other than him that Jimmy was afraid of.

"Bait? Who we trying to catch?"

"Come on, man. First there was Marty, then there was those two kids, now Tommy. And now we got these two jamokes with guns standing around, you're off someplace, calling in on the phone. Who's gonna be the next guy to get it? I figure somebody's gonna show up, looking to shoot you, maybe they'll shoot me or Walter instead. Maybe one of those guys outside gets him, and what good does that do me if I'm dead already? I feel like the worm on the hook, man. I'm right out front, behind the counter, you ain't even anywhere around. I'd feel a whole lot better if I had a gun."

"A gun?"

"I don't wanna have to depend on someone else to fight for me."

"You got any felony convictions, Jimmy?"

"Stoney, come on, man! You got access to firearms, don't tell me you don't. You have to be carrying, after all this. Don't tell me you don't have a piece."

Stoney was silent.

"So why don't I get one?"

"Jimmy, in this city, guns are for cops and bad guys. You and me, right at this point in time, we ain't either one of those. I promise you right now, you carry a piece, you'll be in hot water before the week is out. That's why we hired security. Those gentlemen outside are pros. You're much safer just letting them do the dirty work. You shoot someone, even in self-defense, the cops take you to jail. They do it, the cops show up, say, 'Hey, it's you guys again,' and that's that. I tell you what. I understand your nerves. I'll get another guy, off hours, he'll stay with you, you'll be the safest guy in New York."

Jimmy seemed to think it over. "No," he said, after a minute, "no, I don't want that. Just get them to, like, follow me home. Once I get home, I'll be okay."

"Fine. We'll get them to cover you both ways, coming to work and going home. You satisfied with that?"

"Yeah. Yeah, I guess. For now. I mean, providing nothing else happens. What about Walter?"

"What about him?"

"You gonna cover him too?"

"I don't know how well you know Walter, but he's the last guy you need to worry about protecting. I thought I had to shoot Walter, I'd go back and reexamine my objectives, find some other way to do whatever it was I was doing. Okay? Are we done with this?"

"I guess so."

"All right. Now, I want it to at least look like we're back to business as usual. Did you order the next container?"

"No. After Tommy, I didn't know what you wanted me to do, you didn't say."

"True enough. Go ahead and order it, and let's get on with it."

Jimmy squared his shoulders, nodded, turned and went out, but to Stoney, he still looked very frightened. Maybe he's right, Stoney thought. Maybe I should be carrying. Tommy never needed a gun, though. His thing was to get everyone else to shoot each other. Think, he told himself. Be smart.

"Hello, my fren." The Dominicano cook scraped his grill clean. "What can I get you today? Nice frie' *plátano*, couple frie' eggs wit' bacon? We got El Presidente and we got Budweiser."

"Yes, to everything," Stoney told him, "but no to *cerveza*. Today, I gotta be good."

"*Sí*, my fren. *Daily News*," he said, handing the paper over. Stoney took it and went to sit at his usual seat by the window. A few minutes later the cook came out from behind the counter with Stoney's breakfast. Stoney was a little surprised, usually the girl who worked the cash register brought the food out. The cook didn't go to Stoney's table, he went to one in the corner, away from the windows. "Over here," he said. "Over here, out of da sun." Stoney picked up his paper and moved over, sat down at the new table, and the cook sat down across from him.

"How's business?" the cook asked. "You do okay?"

They had never had this sort of conversation before, not in the whole time Stoney had been going there. Stoney shrugged. "We been having a few problems."

"I hear, you know, dis an dat."

"At right?"

"*Sí*. My business, berry good. We been doing, you know, lotta deliveries." The cook looked around, lowered his voice. "Home cooking, you know, people miss da food from dere home. Steak, South American style, you like it, too, da way I make it."

Sliced thin, cooked thoroughly, with a spicy brown sauce, some of those South American roots, take hours to cook, on the side. "Yeah, I do."

"Yeah, I made, last night. Lucita had to make delivery after I finish. Food for tree men. Missing home, you know what I mean? Down da block, other end, dis side, four' floor. Front of da building, look out on da street." He pushed his chair back from the table, looked around again. Stoney looked over behind the counter where Lucita was studiously ignoring them, looking out the window. "I was in Panama," the cook continued, "few years back, before da troubles, you know, before Reagan. Dey used to have teams dere, to, you know, take care of little problems. I forget da word, in English." He turned, spoke in rapid-fire Spanish to Lucita. She answered him almost inaudibly.

"Trauma," she said.

"Yeah, trauma team," he said, turning back. "Two shooters, one t'inker. Da's what she say dey look like. My fren, please be berry careful."

"Always," Stoney said. "Thank you, amigo." He ate his breakfast slowly, wondering if this acquaintance, who had put himself at some risk by imparting his news, would be insulted by a big tip. That was not, after all, why he had done it, Stoney felt sure. Still, he had to work hard to make it, cooking for whores, steelworkers, and the occasional white guy from down the street, not, as a group, very good tippers. He could use the money, Stoney decided. He left a hundred on the table and went out.

Stoney walked back down the sidewalk, staying close to the buildings, so that an observer in a window in one of the apartments above would have difficulty following his movements. He told himself it was stupid, they already knew where he was going, if they were watching at all. They could pop him at any time, for that matter, if they chose, without showing their faces on the street. But to what end? Who would gain from his death? There had to be a reason for it all, something he didn't know about. He crossed the street, lost in thought, no longer wondering if there was a gun pointed at his back.

South Americans, he thought. What possible connection could there be? The first thing that came to his mind was Tommy's truck parts, containerized and shipped to Colombia, but he dismissed it immediately. No money there, he thought. We only do it to keep the door open, really. Who gives a shit about truck parts? Nobody.

You could contract for a hit, he knew, in South America, Ecuador in particular. Cheaper than homegrown, safer, generally, too. You work through a broker, a cutout man, you never see the shooters, they never see you. They just get a plane ticket and a picture of the target. Terrible thing, Stoney thought, America is really losing its edge, all the manufacturing going overseas, now the hit men are facing foreign competition too. What's next?

He walked through the front door to find Walter all by himself behind the counter. "What happened to the troops?"

"Jimmy wanted to go down to Greenpoint, look at some trucks. I send the blackie with him, leave the whitey out in the street."

"Ain't you afraid of getting shot?" The two of them laughed together at that one. "Seriously. You ever get the feeling you're in the crosshairs, Walter?"

Walter looked at him. "I ain't seen nothing," he said, "make me want to duck, not lately. But if you know something, man, you tell me now."

"I'm getting paranoid in my old age. Let's go sit in my car, have a private conversation." The two of them went out the front door.

Tuco watched them leave, waited two minutes longer, then came through the back door and let himself into Tommy's office. He went around behind the desk and pulled it away from the wall, and working quickly, changed one of the receptacles there, connecting the new one to some wires he had shoved into the electrical box from the rear. When he was done, one of the outlets looked like it always had, with two places to plug things into, and the other one had the outlet on the bottom and an on/off switch on the top. The wires from the switch went up the outside of the wall, out in the shop, and into the space between the ceiling tile and the actual office roof. He pushed the opaque cover under the fluorescent ceiling fixture to one side, slid the blacklight up inside, clipped it to the support wires holding up the ceiling, and wired it to the leads from the switch. When he was done, he slid the cover back in place and pushed the desk back into its original position. He sat in the chair and flipped the switch with his knee. Perfect, he thought. There was a slight bluish cast to the light coming through the plastic panel covering the lights, but no one would notice it unless they were looking straight up at it. He went over under the light and held his hand out, and a pale green stripe lit up the back of his hand where he'd rubbed a tiny bit of dye on it. The numbers on his watch glowed a ghostly green too. Hurriedly he went back and flipped the switch down, turning off the black light, and taking a quick look around to make sure he hadn't left anything behind, he went out.

Walter settled into the passenger seat. "Leather," he said, rubbing the door panels. "Very nice. Looks good. You starting to let go of some of your money. Wha' happen, the pile getting too big?"

"Donna made me get it." I don't know why, Stoney thought, I keep feeling like I have to apologize for this car. "She got it off lease."

Walter, who was very good at voices, dropped the Bajun accent. "You could afford," he said, "any damn car you want."

"Yeah," Stoney said unhappily.

"Any house, almost."

"Almost. You ain't doing so bad yourself. You could buy half of Barbados, you wanted to."

"I got a nice piece of it. House up on top of a hill in St. James parish. Big damned breadfruit tree. Hot, you know, but the trades blow every day. I could sit on the porch, watch the sun go down behind the sea. Drink Bajun rum."

"So why are we here?"

"In this junkyard? You got me, Stoney. I do think, from time to time, that maybe I ought to go back home. Marry a fat girl, have some babies. The thing is, after you're done watching the sun go down, that's it. It's all over. Nothing else to do but watch the soaps on television. Hanging around with you and Tommy has gotten me accustomed to a certain rate of pulse, you know. Keeps me interested."

"So you ain't ready to go sit on your front porch yet, is that what I hear?"

"Yeah, well I ain't ready to get shot, either."

"Me neither." They sat in silence for a minute. "Well, this junkyard ain't exactly a thrill a minute. But we did make some nice money here."

"That we did."

"And I don't feel too good about having someone run me off it."

"Got to be something going on here," Walter said. "Why go to the trouble, otherwise. The only question is, what is it? You been hosing the mayor's girlfriend again? Something like that?"

"Not me."

"Well, it's a money problem, then. Somebody's wallet laying here, and we don't see it. Got to be. Either that, or we got something somebody else thinks belongs to them, and they want it back."

"Plus, we ain't the only dogs sniffing around." He told Walter what he'd heard up the street.

"Ah." Walter considered for a moment. "So now what?"

"It has to be them. They popped Marty and Tommy, trying to

collect. We don't know what it is they want, they don't know where we're hiding it, that's how I figure it."

"Question is," Walter said, "better to be the mouse or the cheese?"

"It ain't like we got a choice, right at the moment."

"Yeah, but this is stupid. Got to be something here, Stoney. Something right under our noses."

"Remember the first rule."

"I'm gonna die of old age. What happens next?"

"Me and Tuco are gonna load up some boxes and a briefcase, walk them out to the car, take off. See if anybody comes out to play."

"You think they'll figure you got their property, they'll come after you?"

"Either that or they'll try coming inside to get you."

"They do, I'll send every one of them to meet God." Walter scratched his chin. "Nah, they won't come for me. Too public, too soon. They got the guy in the street to consider, plus the guy inside, and it would be a war. And if you're right, they don't know if what they're looking for is in here anyway. Nah, they'll come out after you and Tuco." He looked over at Stoney. "You like this kid?"

"He's got possibilities."

"You know he don't read."

"I know. He compensates pretty well for it, though. I don't think it was the school, I think there's something wrong with his wiring. He's very visual. You only have to show him something once, and he doesn't forget much. Got quick hands too. Doesn't scare."

"Angry about something, though. I never seen him smile."

"Yeah, well, things are tough all over. What do you think of Jimmy?"

"Aah." Walter dismissed Jimmy with a wave of his hand. "I don't put a stone in he way, I don't take a stone out he way."

"You got one of these gorillas watching this place at night?"

"You pretty smart for a white boy. Oh, before I forget, that EPA turd called. He wants to stop by tomorrow afternoon."

"Fuck him. Whoever you've got coming here at night, I hope they're less obvious than these two."

"Street like this, people always watching, anyway. All you got to do is tap the network."

"You been corrupting morals again?"

"Half the grandmothers on this block," Walter said, grinning, "on your payroll."

9

TUCO COULDN'T DECIDE IF IT HAD BEEN FUN OR JUST NERVE-RACKING. He was still jittery from adrenaline, safely back out in the shop where nothing was happening. The part of the exercise that he'd enjoyed the most, he decided, was thinking of everything beforehand, and then having it all come together the way he'd thought it out. What must it be like to be a burglar, he wondered, where you're going into unknown territory, coping with the unexpected, like dogs, alarms, or people who came home early. Or course, he was thinking of television burglars, *Masterpiece Theater* and all that. Most burglars that he knew were junkies, driven by the fires of addiction, on the watch for opportunity. Kick the door in or break the window in an insane, frenzied rush of fear and excitement, grab something and run before somebody came looking.

Still, it had been fun.

It wasn't too hard to figure where Stoney was going with all of this. Tuco knew all too well what it felt like to have someone stalking you, waiting for the right time. He thought back, remembering the last year he'd attended high school, the year his cousin Miguel had joined the gang and begun going around with a string of colored beads hanging out of his pocket. Miguel had tried hard to win him over, get him to join too. He'd tried reason, at first, and when that didn't work, he had changed tactics and made Tuco the focus of the gang's attention from then on. Walking down the school hallways, going home, in the entryway to his building, Tuco had been knocked down, stomped, ass kicked, eyes blacked, nose broken, spit on, derided, again and again. He'd never known when it was coming, sometimes days would go by, or a week, until he'd begin to think they'd forgotten him, and then they'd get him again.

Finally he'd reached his breaking point. In a quick flash of anger his paper-thin mask of civilized expectations had been burned off, and the ism's he'd learned in church, his ideas about the ways that people should behave, and his own squeamishness when it had come to inflicting physical pain had fallen away, luxuries he could no longer afford. He'd wondered, at the time, what God thought of him caving in to the pressure, resorting to things he'd believed morally wrong. Shaking His head, maybe, marking it down on Tuco's scorecard. Or driving home a lesson, perhaps. It was Stoney's first rule. Take care of your own self.

He couldn't remember consciously deciding to do it. Confronted in the high school hallway once too often, he'd walked over and put a fist through the glass door on the box that held a fire extinguisher and had attacked his chief tormentor with it. He could remember swinging it wildly in a fit of rage, felt the shock of a heavy projectile in his hands connecting with bone and skin. Tuco had hit him twice more before he went down. The others had scattered, leaving just the one writhing on the floor.

So he hadn't gotten his diploma. Hard to see what good a diploma is when you can't read it anyway. He'd been relieved, in a way, once the charade was over. His only regret had been that Miguel had not been with the group that had confronted him that day. Maybe things would have turned out different. He'd expected them to repay him, to ratchet the pressure up higher, to see how far he would go. They didn't, though; after that they left him alone.

Stoney, however, did not seem to have Tuco's self-imposed limitations. All he's doing, Tuco thought, is baiting them, waiting for one of them to stick his head up.

They all trickled back in, Stoney and Walter first, Jimmy and the big ex-cop just before lunch. Stoney caught Tuco's eye, pointed to his watch, held out three fingers. Tuco nodded. Three o'clock, he's telling me. Get lost until then.

It didn't make any sense to Tuco to start doing some work, get all dirty, and then get called off it to take Stoney someplace, so he found a comfortable corner to sit in where he could see through the fence to the street. After a while, Jimmy the Hat came through the door from the office. He didn't notice Tuco at first, and he wandered around the yard, lighting up a cigarette as he went. Tuco waited until Jimmy was just a few feet away, and he cleared his throat. Jimmy dropped the cigarette and jumped.

Tuco regarded him with amusement. "What is it," he said. "Why do you do that?"

"I don't know what you're talking about."

"Get real, man. Every time you see me, you do this thing, it's like you think I'm gonna smack you in the head. What'd I ever do to you?"

Jimmy took off his hat and rolled the bill in his hand. He's thinking about it, Tuco thought, he does that thing with his hat every time he's trying to make up his mind to tell the truth.

"It's nothing," Jimmy finally said, "it ain't you. It's just that, you look so much like this guy I know, whenever I see you, for a second I think you're him."

"My cousin," Tuco said. "My cousin Miguel."

"I don't know any Miguel."

"How about Dr. Jack? That ring any bells?" Jimmy's eyes went wide and fear showed in his face, but he didn't say anything. "You hanging with bad people," Tuco told him. "How the hell you know him? You been buying crack from the yo boys?"

"No." Jimmy looked away, down at his hat. "No, I might blow a little reefer now and then, but I don't touch that other shit. No, see, what happened . . ." He heaved a sigh. "My girlfriend had me arrested. My ex-girlfriend. She had a order of protection on me, and the bitch set me up. I had moved out, you know, and she sued me for support and whatnot, for my son."

"I didn't know you had a son."

"Yeah. I don't get to see him much. But anyway, what happened, I had some stuff still over there in the apartment, she said, 'Oh, come and get it,' but when I did she called the cops and had me arrested for menacing."

"She must really hate you."

"No, it's this weird thing, I mean, I feel it myself. When I see her, I'm, like, still attracted to her, but as soon as she opens that mouth, Jesus. I don't know how we got that way. Like, if we weren't fighting about something already, she'd start one, just for recreation. And after we split up, I was, like, her main focus, like all she could think about was sticking it to me. So, anyway, she set me up, and when I went over there, the cops bagged me. I couldn't believe it."

"Friggin' cops."

"No, they were actually pretty nice about it. They wanted to let me go, but she wanted me up on charges, so they arrested me. We go to the precinct house, right, fill out a bunch of papers, and it turns out I gotta go to central booking. So I sit in a cage for, like, six hours, and they finally put me and this one other guy on a bus. 'Riker's Island Express,' I used to call them, you know, those corrections department buses you see everywhere, wire mesh on the windows and all that. Never thought I'd be riding in one. Anyway, the other guy was the one, looked just like you."

"My cousin."

"Yeah, I guess. He seemed okay, I was raving about my girlfriend, he thought it was funny. Told me I was a idiot, I shoulda seen it coming. 'You gotta look out after yourself,' he told me. 'Bitch had you all wrapped in flypaper, she don't wanna see you get loose.' Told me I screwed up moving in with her in the first place. Anyway, he says he's gonna do me a favor. 'We get to central,' he says, 'there's gonna be a bunch of dirtbag lawyers around. Bleed 'em and plead 'em, that's their game. Suck whatever money outta you that you got, go see the DA and plead you down, which you can do without a lawyer's help, and then turn you loose.' So he says his lawyer is already there, waiting, he'll tell him to take care of me. I'm in this roach-palace holding cell for about an hour, I'm scared shit, I don't mind telling you. What goes through your mind, time like that, you know, I shoulda took karate lessons, Jesus, help me, I'll be so good after this . . . So anyway, they come and let me out. This guy is waiting, wearing a suit had to cost a grand, easy, he's Dr. Jack's lawyer. I had no idea what was going on, you know, I was just trying to act brave, like I wasn't ready to crap in my pants. 'What's happening,' I ask the guy, 'how much is this costing me,' and he gives me this look, like, Shut up, you moron, and he says, 'My client instructed me to help you out. Help you out does not mean send you a bill.' I couldn't believe it. 'Is he still around?' I ask the guy, 'I should say thanks, at least.' He gives me that look again. 'Mr. O'Brian,' he says, meaning me, 'don't take this the wrong way, but you should not seek any further contact with my client. You should go back to your life and thank your guardian angel that you caught my client in a magnanimous mood.' And that was it. The guy got me out, got the charges dropped, and that was the end of it. But I'll tell you something. Even the lawyer was afraid of him. Your cousin." Jimmy shaped the hat carefully in his hands, put it back on his head.

That's not it, Tuco thought, that's only half the story, Miguel scared this guy so bad he still shits every time he sees me. "You're lucky," he said. "He musta did something bad, earlier in the day. Probably treated someone worse than he needed to, so he was nice to you to even things out. He's weird that way. Someone else's bad luck was your good luck."

The idea came to him whole and entire, all at once in all its perverted glory, just the way the solution to Stoney's wiring problem had. All of the main elements were already in place. All it would take would be a bit of manipulation, a little technology, some luck. And some money.

Well, he had the money. Even paying his mother room and board, since he'd started working for Stoney and Tommy he'd always had plenty left over. He'd never found much of anything to spend it on. He'd been keeping it in some envelopes in his bedroom, in pockets here and there. More than once some of it had gotten laundered with his jeans. But why spend it on a scheme like this? And why go to all the trouble? He didn't really know, but he thought it might be interesting to see if he could pull it off, see if he could do something with his mind and not just his hands.

• • •

"Hello, schveetie." Tuco made his voice sound like Eddie Murphy imitating an old Jewish guy. She turned slowly, and seeing him leaning against the gate, she laughed her tinkling laugh. She was wearing stretch pants; as she very slowly walked in his direction he could see every muscle in her legs flex, carrying her closer. It was very hard to keep his eyes on her face, the way Tommy had told him women liked. He did the best he could.

"Hey, baby."

He could see, when she got up close, that maybe she hadn't showered recently. It didn't really matter. God, she was beautiful.

"You wanna have some fun?"

"Nah," he said. "I can't. I'm working."

"That's too bad," she said, turning slowly to eye a car making its way down the street, leaving her in profile. It was almost too much to bear.

"Can I ask you a question?" The car kept going. She turned back to Tuco.

"Sure," she said, absently.

"This is a bad place," he said. "Why are you down here?"

"Oh, honey," she said, laying her fingers on his arm. "I got expenses . . ."

"You ever think about a rehab?"

"I been," she said. "Tha's where I found out about Dr. Jack. 'Oh,' they told me, 'you ain't never had nothing like Dr. Jack,' and that was no lie."

"You don't think you could get off it?"

"Oh, maybe I could. See, I owe . . . You know, there's a real Dr. Jack. And I gotta work off this debt. Means I gotta stay out on the street. If I could get away from here . . . But I can't. So I just keep going back to it." She shrugged.

He started to reply but she turned away, wiping her eyes. "It ain't even my fault," she said. Another car came down the street, and she took a step away from him to follow its progress. It didn't stop.

"So what happened?" he asked when she turned back again.

"My husband," she said, "started bringing it home." She turned back to the street, but continued her story. "I married him when I was seventeen, he was in the police academy." Her voice got a little harder. A little more real, Tuco thought. "We were okay for about a year. Then he got assigned to a buy-and-bust unit. He was so excited to get out of the uniform. But they don't tell you, see, you make a buy, you gotta take a hit. If you won't take a hit, they know you're a cop. Bang, bang, you're dead."

"He started bringing a little something home. 'What's the difference,' he said. 'Just like drinking a little wine.' We did have fun. Yes, we did.

"But." She stood, staring out into nothing.

"But what," Tuco said.

"Drip test," she said. "He came up dirty. They put both of us in a twenty-eight-day program. Some place upstate. After we got out, we did okay for a while. Went to NA meetings and all that. But, see, he had to keep taking the tests. I didn't."

"First time I relapsed, I wound up down here. Two days before I ran out of money. Then he found me and took me back home. Second time, same thing. But after a while, I guess he got tired of it. Finding me, I mean. And by then, I owed him big time. Dr. Jack, I mean. Did you know there's a real Dr. Jack?"

"Oh, yeah. You see him often?"

"Not anymore. He stays mostly on the top floor, don't go out much. The rest of them, they ain't nothing. But Jack, he's for real, honey. I will never try to run away from him. Never."

"What if I told you," Tuco said slowly, "that I could make Dr. Jack forget all about you?"

She turned her full attention on him. He could see fear and doubt in the shadows on her face. "Don't you play with me," she said. "Don't you."

It was the point of no return. Do I have the right, he wondered, to mess with what's left of her life? And do I really want to go through with this? Shouldn't I think about it some more? Yeah, sure, he thought. And talk yourself out of it. "Oh, I can do it," he said. "But you've got to do something for me."

"Oh, baby," she said, trying to pull that persona back up over herself, but the fear and the pain were too strong. "Honey, I still owe you a little bit—"

"Oh, no," he said. "It's something way sicker than that."

She said she was okay with it.

It still felt touch and go to Tuco. The timing had to be just right, for one thing, and how could he count on her to be on the block when he needed her? She had, after all, no address, no telephone, and was in the habit of disappearing for a day or so at a time, depending on how much dope she could buy.

She didn't see the problem. "Uh-uh," she said. "I'll be around. Where am I gonna go? Besides, I can stay straight for as long as I want. It's just that rest-of-your-life shit that gets me. If I start thinking about forever, then I lose it. But just for this job, yeah, baby, I'll be fine. I promise." The doubt crept back into her voice. "And anyway," she said, "you're gonna, you know . . ." She couldn't say it.

"Don't you worry. You pull this off, I'll make sure they cut you loose."

So it began.

It left him feeling grimy, even as he watched her saunter off down the block, her stretch pants serving to color but not disguise. He could feel his desire, but he was remorseful at the same time, using another human being in such a way, even if she didn't seem to care, herself. Did it balance out, he wondered, using her to do one bad thing, if it gave her a chance to be free? And he hadn't even given a thought to how he was going to get them to let her go. He felt himself sinking into a morass of second thoughts. Screw it, he thought. If it doesn't work out, I lose some money, that's all. If we can pull it off, everything changes.

He was sure of it.

They met in Tommy's office at three.

"All right," Stoney said. "You carry the briefcase, I'm gonna get the boxes." It was a brown leather bag, the kind that expands to hold files and such, and it was filled to bursting. "I want you to go out ahead of me, pretend you're looking for someone. I'll come out behind you, you stay in front of me. Open the gate, then open the trunk of the car. We're gonna toss everything in the trunk, and take off like a bat outta hell. I'm gonna take the rearview mirror. Leave the gate open, Walter's gonna get it when we go. The thing is, I want you to drive like your ass is on fire. Can you do that?"

"You mean you want me to drive like you. Of course I can do it."

Stoney shot him a look. "All right. Wait a minute, show me the switch you put in." Tuco demonstrated for him, showed him the dye on the back of his hand. "Son of a bitch, it works. Okay, you ready?"

"Yep." Tuco took the keys out and held them in his left hand, kept his right hand in his pocket, pretending to have a gun. "Like this?"

"Don't overdo it. We ain't making a movie."

Tuco went out the front door, peered up and down the street, then Stoney came out behind him. Seconds later they were roaring up Troutman Street, going the wrong way. Tuco held his hand on the horn as they got to the end of the block, jerked the car left onto St. Nicholas and accelerated down to Flushing. Two cars were waiting at the stop sign. Tuco went out around them and cut into traffic on Flushing to the blare of horns. He watched Stoney out of the corner of his eye. Stoney was braced in the passenger seat, his eyes glued to the rearview mirror. Tuco ran the red light at Cypress, weaving past slower cars. Stoney pulled out his cell phone and dialed. It was a short conversation.

"Yeah, okay, I got it." He snapped the phone closed. "Walter says they're in a burgundy Marquis, Virginia plates. That was a nifty move, going up a down street. All right, chill out a little bit, I want them to see us."

Tuco stopped for the light at Metropolitan. It was a big intersection with banks on two corners, too busy to run the light, anyway. From half a block back came the sounds of furious honking. A dark red Mercury was trying to pass a tow truck, but cars were double-parked on both sides of the road, and they had to wait. The light turned green.

"What now, boss?"

"Go on, but normal, like."

Tuco waited for the cars in front of him to move and then drove through the intersection. The red Mercury got to the corner just after the light turned red. The driver tried to bull his way through, but he didn't make it. They were stuck in the middle of the intersection, being honked at and cursed by drivers on all sides. Stoney was laughing as he watched in the mirror. "Keep going."

He used his cell phone again. "Good job, Walter. Nah, they didn't stay with us. Yeah, that was pretty slick. Listen, watch your ass, if they come back your way, they might be pissed off. No, I know that. All right, all right. Listen, tomorrow, just go in and hang out. Talk to you later." He clicked the phone off. "Good job, kid."

"Thanks. Where we going?"

"Midtown Tunnel, back to Manhattan."

"Did you want them to follow us?"

"I wanted to see if they would try, but I didn't want them to succeed at it."

"Why not?"

"We ain't set up for them yet. I had to know if they would stay and watch the office, maybe follow Walter or Jimmy home. Now we know, and we can set up the next step."

"Next time we just watch for a red car."

"Nah, they'll have a driver next time, they won't make that mistake twice. Use a car service, if they're smart. Those guys drive like lunatics, nobody looks twice. Okay, here's the deal. Stay home tomorrow. Take the day off, I mean. I'll call you tomorrow night and fill you in. Day after tomorrow, eat your Wheaties in the morning."

There was a white girl working behind the counter at the coffee shop on Henry Street. Tuco stopped in on the way home from the lot where he'd parked Stoney's car. She was striking, she had a face like the girls he saw on TV, pale, with freckles, long yellow hair. He couldn't really tell her age. Just out of high school, he guessed.

"I'm sorry?"

She smiled briefly. "Help you?"

"Oh, yeah. I, ah, I need to stay up late tonight. You got something that can keep me up?"

"Oh, sure. How 'bout a triple espresso?"

SHOOTING DR. JACK   161

He thanked Fat Tommy silently for getting him the job, for getting him out of Rosa's house and out of Rosa's neighborhood. What a place to get coffee, he thought, wondering if she worked there in the mornings. Woof. Stop in there every day if she does. Eight bucks, though, is a little steep for a cup of coffee. Maybe just tomorrow, to see if she's there.

A few of the people who lived in the building came down while Tuco was wrapping up the garbage and introduced themselves. They all seemed friendly enough, inquiring after his "uncle," the former superintendent, telling him their names and apartment numbers, and who had the best pizza in the neighborhood. One older woman asked him where he'd gotten the name, was it from that Clint Eastwood movie. "I don't know," he told her, "my boss just started calling me that, now everyone does." She began to tell him about the movie, then thought better of it. She did tell him about a dripping faucet in her bathroom, and wanted to know if he'd come and fix it for, say, twenty bucks. Sure, he told her. How about tomorrow. How about Saturday, she said. Here's my number.

He carried all the plastic bags around the alley, up the stairs and to the gate. There was a lot of it, and it took him seven or eight trips. He unlocked the gate and went out, locking it behind him. It was still light out. He figured he had a couple of hours to kill, so he went down the block to sit on the promenade that overlooked the Upper New York Bay. From his bench, he could see all the way up the East River to the Brooklyn and Manhattan Bridges, and in the other direction he could see the Statue of Liberty out over the water, with New Jersey behind her, and Staten Island in the south, off in the distance. Cars roared underneath him on the Brooklyn-Queens Expressway, which was cantilevered between the promenade where he sat and Furman Street, far below. People of all persuasions streamed by, walking, jogging, roller-skating, riding bikes, walking dogs. Once, a police car rolled slowly by, the cop in the passenger seat giving him the eye on the way past. Tuco had to smile. Up yours, buddy, he thought. I live here.

Once again he silently thanked Tommy Bagadonuts. God, he thought, forgetting his earlier difficulties, how about taking care of Fat Tommy? I know you might be mad at me for not, you know, believing like I used to, but Tommy didn't deserve what he got. But then the doubts began to crowd in on him, as if he really knew who deserved what, and maybe Tommy had done something rotten that he didn't know about, and so on. He got up and headed back.

He went over to the wrought-iron fence next to his building and unlocked the gate. He pushed it slightly open, then crossed the street and went to sit on the stoop of a building across the street, somewhat down from his, closer to the promenade.

I live here, he said to himself again, turning the words over in his mind. It was still hard for him to believe it. Everything here seemed a world away from where he'd lived his whole life, even if it was within the same borough. He ran the route in his mind: straight to the end of Clark Street, right on Court, over to Atlantic. Once you hit Atlantic you were out of the neighborhood, as Brooklyn Heights turned to Cobble Hill. The whole bottom of Atlantic, from Court all the way down to the BQE, was populated by Arabs. Most of the stores on both sides of the street, Middle Eastern groceries, bakeries, and restaurants, looked like they'd been lifted right out of a movie, some old black and white with Errol Flynn and the French Foreign Legion. Or Casablanca, maybe. Even the air smelled different. Tuco promised himself a trip down there someday. Go sightseeing.

But you had to turn the other way, left, to head toward

Troutman and the other part of his life. In that first block you passed the Brooklyn House of Detention, and then it comes, hard to believe how far it stretches, block after desolate block, mile after mile. Even though he'd only been on Clark Street a few days, those places had already begun to feel alien to him, Flatbush and Bedford and Bushwick Avenues, Jesus, why did it have to be like that? What a world, he thought. He could walk down Clark Street, almost like a tourist, but on St. Nick he could feel the hairs rising up on the back of his neck, attitude in every step, and he'd be thinking, come on, motherfucker, I'll even go slow so you can catch up, Come on, baby. It was either that or run, and you get tired of that.

It started to get dark and he began to think of his bed in spite of the coffee. He thought of the coffee shop up on Henry, and of the yellow-haired girl who worked there. Another one of those big espressos, that's what he needed, that and the short walk up to get it and he'd feel much better, but he didn't think he had the time.

He was right. The streetlights came on and cast their hard blue light down on the street, leaving the stoop where Tuco sat in deepening shadow. Be nice, he thought, if I'd planned it this way, but it was just the way the light fell. Then he saw them, four of them, two blocks up, boisterously making their way in his direction.

They walked four abreast, taking up the whole sidewalk, and the few other pedestrians either crossed the street or stepped into the gutter to avoid them. They quieted down when they got closer to his block. He couldn't make out what they were saying but he thought they seemed disappointed to see his garbage bags stacked in the alley behind the fence. Then they got close enough to see the gate was unlocked, and there was a sudden exhilaration, subdued quickly as they hissed each other quiet. They ran over and pushed their way into the alley.

To Tuco they seemed like children, sixteen, maybe, cartoon

caricatures of the real thing, white boys aping the yo-boy style, baggy jeans too long, worn low on the hips, jackets, jewelry, the whole production. What a joke, he thought. He stood up and stretched.

He took his time. He was right in the middle of the street, in the center of the pool of light from the streetlight, when the first black bag came flying out. He noted that it didn't split open when it landed. Don't pay to buy those cheap bags. When he got to the sidewalk, they saw him and stopped to look, smirking. Two of them began to look a little doubtful when he walked up to the gate so that the only way out of the alley was through him.

"Hello, children," he said.

The one who had thrown the bag took a step in Tuco's direction, stuck a hand in his coat pocket, and sneered. "You better just keep—"

Tuco didn't give him time to finish. In one quick motion he pivoted on his right foot and threw a stiff left. The heel of his left hand hit the kid on his nose and upper lip, and even though Tuco's hand had only traveled about fourteen inches, the kid flew back and went down hard. Tuco could see blood blooming across the kid's face as he sprawled the concrete of the alley.

The other three stood there stupidly, motionless. No one had ever touched them, he realized. Not their teachers, not their parents, probably not even the other kids who went to whatever schools they had gone to. The two who had looked doubtful began to flinch away, but the other one stood with an affronted look on his face, as though someone had just demanded that he hand over his lunch money instead of the other way around. Tuco reached out and grabbed him with both hands and slung him stumbling out through the open gate, and the kid flew backward into the streetlight hard enough to make the metal post ring. Tuco stepped out, ready to catch him rebounding off the light post but he pulled the right back, the one he'd been ready to stuff just over the kid's belt. It wasn't necessary, the kid was stunned from his impact with the streetlight, and he took a couple of groggy steps before collapsing to the sidewalk.

This is no fun, Tuco thought, maybe I should have spanked them instead, but as he turned back to the alleyway he saw the kid on the ground struggling to pull something out of his pocket. The other two kids bolted through the gate and went tearing off up Clark Street without even a glance back over their shoulders. Tuco ignored them and went for the first one, the one he'd hit first, the one with the gun. The kid tried to roll away as he saw Tuco coming, but Tuco was on him in a flash, grabbing him from behind by his elbows, yanking him to his feet and ramming him chest first into the side of the building. He pinned him there with a shoulder and reached around and ripped the pocket out of the kid's jacket. The kid gave up the gun without much of a struggle.

Tuco looked at it quickly before he stuffed it into his own pocket, hoping the safety was on. He leaned over to growl into the kid's ear.

"You pull a gun on me, you little shit? A thirty-two, for chrissake? What is this, your mother's gun? You steal this outta your mother's underwear drawer?" The kid was crying, and his lower face was red from the blood that was still streaming out of his nose, and his upper lip was swelling. Tuco eased his shoulder back, taking some of the pressure off the kid's chest.

He felt bad. He almost wished that they had been tougher, meaner. Wrap it up, he told himself. Get it over with.

"You listen to me now. Can you hear me?"

The kid nodded his head.

"You fucked with the wrong guy. This block is off limits to you now. I catch any one of you little assholes on this block, I'll fuck you up good. You see me coming down the sidewalk, you better cross over. You see me walk into a store, you better walk out. You understand me?"

The kid nodded silently. Tuco let go of him and backed away. "One a your friends is still outside," he said. "Get him outta here." The kid darted away, wiping his face on his jacket sleeve as he went. Tuco watched him drag the other kid to his feet and hustle him up the block. He watched until they turned the corner up on Henry. When they were out of sight, he carried out the rest of the garbage bags and stacked them next to the first one, next to the streetlight pole. So much for all that, he thought, still feeling bad about it all, even if they had only been a few years younger than he, one of them carrying, besides. Stupid kids, he thought. Shoot you for nothing at all. He went in, locking the gate behind him.

At his kitchen counter he unloaded the pistol and took it apart. Now it was just another mechanism, and its pieces told him how they all worked.

He began to regret the espresso after a while, because, as tired as he was, he couldn't sleep. He got up and began to wander around the darkened, empty apartment, which still carried the dirt and fingerprints of the previous super, the one who had died at Woodhull. Divine intervention, he thought sourly. If they had taken the guy to Wyckoff Heights, he would be sleeping in a room on the third floor of Commie Pete's brownstone instead of sitting in the dark feeling guilty over slapping some kids around. He debated the whole issue with himself again. You don't have to justify it, he told himself, nobody cares anyway, but the bad feelings would not go away, and when he couldn't sit in the dark with them any longer, he got up and went out. Gotta buy a TV, he told himself. Add it to the list.

He took the elevator up to the first floor and went out through the front door, pausing to hear it click shut behind him. He turned left. Columbia Heights was the last street before the promenade, and he turned left on it and began to walk.

It was fully dark, now, as dark as Brooklyn Heights ever got, but there were still people out. He noticed a woman a block away, walking her dog, following along unhurriedly as the dog made its rounds. Tuco couldn't tell if she'd seen him or not, but if she had she took no notice. He had expected her to cross over to the other side of the street, at the very least, or, more likely, seek shelter inside one of the buildings, but she paid him no attention, and neither did her dog, not until he got up to where she was, and then she looked up and smiled.

"Good evening."

It was the strangest thing.

He half-turned as went by, mumbling something in return, not wanting to appear churlish. In his experience, when you got home without anything happening, you stayed there, or if you did need to venture out, you didn't leave the limited area where you felt safe. Why tempt fate?

He walked past the quiet brownstones. A new feeling, something he couldn't identify, filtered into his mind as he went beyond the few blocks in this neighborhood that he'd been down before. Around Rosa's building on De Kalb, there were maybe a dozen blocks where he knew all the players and all the pitfalls, every building and every dark alleyway, everybody who belonged and everybody who did not. I was like a cat, he thought, because a cat only wants to go where he's already been, so that he can never be surprised. So many places he had never seen, so many things he did not know. The Discovery channel can show you only so much. You have to get out, go yourself and look, feel the wind coming off the bay, blowing past you up a street you've never walked down before, past buildings and trees you're seeing for the first time.

He turned left when he got to Montague.

Montague was less residential. It went four long blocks from the promenade up to Court, lined on both sides with the sorts of places that people who lived in this strange neighborhood might frequent: a piano bar, banks, restaurants with food from different parts of the world, antique stores, ice cream, fancy men's suits, jewelry, old books. He stopped and looked in the window of the bookstore, feeling that old, familiar swirl in his guts, man, you're a idiot, Eddie's a retard, the unspeakable dread that some teacher would make him stand up and reveal his ignorance. He stood there and he calmed himself. No teachers anymore, he told himself. Now you have to teach yourself the best way you can. The feeling ebbed away, leaving him strangely empty. The store was still open, and he was tempted to go in but he resisted. This place, he told himself, is not for you. You are made to punch out street rats, and to help guys like Stoney shake money out of fat Italian assholes that make ice cream, and to fix old diesel engines. Hell of a thing, he thought, to live in a world of machines that you understand and people that you do not. Not what I wanted, he said silently to someone or something out in the dark night air. This is not what I started out to be, I don't know how I wound up this way.

He crossed the street and went into McDonald's, where they had a picture menu, and ordered a number three, some kind of burger with fries and a Coke, no, regular size is okay. He sat by a window and ate, thinking of Stoney and of the girl from Troutman Street. A policeman's wife! He thought again of his latest brainstorm, ran through it in his mind. What an ugly thing to do, he thought. No real reason to take the risk, other than the fact that he wanted to do it, wanted to see Miguel again, ask him one last favor. Maybe they will shoot you this time, he thought. Maybe they won't get the chance.

Back out on the street, he wandered farther away from Clark Street, conscious of the changes in the auras of the places he passed. The neighborhood turned back into something more like the sort of environment he understood, not anything like Troutman Street, not really, but not pleasant, not at this time of night. The park on the far side of Court seemed ominous and dark. Tuco was turning back when he heard it.

The sound came from the direction of Pacific Avenue, down by the projects, and it rose up above the normal background rumble of the Brooklyn night, busses running up and down Atlantic, planes on an approach to La Guardia, gypsy cabs dueling for a fare, sirens off in the distance. It was an ungodly wail that started out as merely sorrowful but rose steadily in pitch and intensity as if in response to fingernails being pulled out. It was a sound impossible to ignore or tune out. He stopped to listen, mouth open.

Someone coming up the sidewalk behind him was laughing at him.

"What the hell is that?"

"The screamer," the man told him without stopping.

"Should I call the cops?"

"Nah." The man turned and backpedaled. "They're sick of dealing with her, they've got better things to do." He turned and continued on his way. "Easier for them," he called back over his shoulder, "to bust you than to deal with her."

But it really did sound like someone was shoving pencils in a woman's ears. It turned out that she was easy enough to find, four blocks down on Pacific, standing in a pool of darkness between two streetlights. She was a short and stocky woman with dark hair and rough features, and she stood staring straight out into nothing. He stood back, watching her, and after a few minutes she started back in again, breathing rapidly at first, and then the hands held rigidly at her sides began to shake. She contorted her face into a rictus of fear, and the sound came up, awesomely loud for such a compact person. He started over, thinking to ask her why, and he heard another voice, a soft one, from the shadows.

"No, *señor*, please."

Tuco turned to see an older, gray-haired version of the screaming woman. "What's wrong with her?" he asked. "Why does she do this?"

The old lady shook her head. "She sick, up here." Her hand fluttered uncertainly up next to her ear. "She get escare, in the nighttime. If I can keep her insye, itsa no too bad, but when she come outsye, she start looking, I don't know what she see, but she start the screaming, Jesu Christo . . ." The old lady crossed herself. "Soon she gonna stop, I thin'." She crossed herself again. "Soon, she come back insye."

"How long she like this?"

"Many year, many year."

"Your daughter?" The old lady nodded. "What's her name?"

"Margherita."

At the sound of her name, the screaming woman flinched back farther into the shadows. The old lady gabbled at her maternally in Spanish. Tuco turned to go home.

"You never get escare, *señor*?"

"Oh, yes," he said, "I do. Tell you something, though. Screaming don't help."

He could still hear her as he crossed over Atlantic on his way back. How do they deal with that, he wondered, those people living over there? That sound cuts right through you. How can they sleep?

Stupid question, he told himself. They get used to it, of course. Just another lost person. Another car alarm whooping. Another dog barking.

So what.

10

STONEY PUSHED OPEN THE DOOR TO MADAM CHO'S, WONDERING how in the world Tommy got involved in all of these strange enterprises. He trudged up the stairs and went through the gray metal door at the top. On the other side of the door there was a small room painted white, with a single desk and chair in the corner opposite the entry. The dark-haired woman seated behind the desk was easily ten years his senior. For the first time in days, Stoney really smiled. How do you come in here and tell a lady, looks like your mother, that you want a blow job?

She smiled sweetly. "Help you, dear?"

"Mrs. Cho in tonight?"

She looked doubtful. "Oh, I don't know. If you'll wait here, I'll go and check." She got up and went over to a door in the back wall. Stoney watched her punch numbers on a keypad on the wall next to the door to let herself through.

•   •   •

"He looks like a policeman," she said. "You know, one of the crooked ones. He's a little shaky, and he don't have a nice color. You know, he's just got that look . . ."

Madam Cho turned to a monitor on one side of her desk, pushed a button, and looked at Stoney through the security camera. "Crooked, maybe," she said. "No policeman, though. Bring him on back."

She stood to greet him, a small woman, five foot nothing, straight black hair going to salt and pepper, with a round face as gray and wrinkled as a circus elephant's backside.

She inclined her cheek to be kissed. As he did so he caught the faintest whiff of flowers and spice, with just a hint of black tea, but then she stood back and it was gone.

"Hello, Stoney," she said, waving him to a chair. "It's so good to see you. It has been such a long time." She sat back down behind her desk. "I haven't seen Thomas for quite a while, either. I'm afraid I've been getting on his nerves, harping about our problems with the police."

"Having cop troubles?"

"They've been very persistent. I don't know what we're going to do, and neither, I suspect, does Thomas."

"Yeah, well," Stoney said, rolling his eyes. "You gotta change with the times, Mrs. Cho. City's turning into Boy Scout central, you can't have a big sign on the avenue, says, 'Hand Jobs, Second Floor.' And those pictures in the doorway, gimme a break. Of course the cops are gonna hassle you."

"But we have to have a sign, Stoney. No one will know we're here."

"Please. Every pervert in New York," he said, "including me, has a computer. We don't need a sign, we need a website."

"Dammit." It was such an obvious solution, she didn't know whether to be overjoyed or irritated because neither she nor Tommy had thought of it. Maybe Stoney was smarter than she'd always assumed. "You think?"

"Absolutely. Believe me, your customers will know where you are. Take the sign down, get rid of those pictures. Hang out a sign, dance lessons, or something. You could even open a dance studio, you got the room. Get someone to knock you out a good website, could even have live coverage on it. Virtual hand jobs, right on the Web. I bet you'd make more money than you do now, and the cops would never bother you again. Except for the ones that are already customers."

"God, we are idiots," she said. "I'll have to ask my grandson to set it up for us."

"You have a grandson into computers?"

"Certainly."

"And he knows about this place?"

She gave him a wry smile. "Oh, he's been here many times, Stoney. We don't come from as childish a culture as you Americans."

"I guess some of us do get a bit overwrought."

She waited for him to get to the point of his visit. She'd always known him to be very direct, and here they were, sitting down and having an actual conversation. She didn't know what to make of it. Maybe, she thought, he needs a little help. "So," she said. "How is Thomas, and why haven't I seen him in so long?"

He looked out her office window to the alley in the rear of the building. There was nothing to see, it was too dark, but Mrs. Cho looked at the side of his face, and she thought she could sense a deep, yawning weariness inside him. He is too young, she thought, to be this dark.

"Tommy," he said slowly, "ain't doing that great, right at the moment." She folded her hands and waited, and by degrees he told her the whole story.

When he was done they sat in silence. Stoney listened to the ringing in his ears, and Mrs. Cho sat thinking of her friend Tommy. It was Stoney's turn to wait, and he sat without moving. Eventually she stirred, and looked over at him.

"So what will you do now?"

He shrugged. "Counterpunch, I guess. I'm trying to think of what Tommy would do, but I ain't as smart as him. I've always been more of the bulldozer type."

"Hah," she said. "Thomas is very bright, it's true. So am I, in point of fact, but neither of us could come up with the solution to our problems with the police, and when you walked through the door it was obvious to you."

"Well, I—"

"Each of us," she said, overriding his interruption, "is limited by that which we think we know. Thomas and myself, we thought we knew all there was to know about this particular situation, and so we could not see what should have been plain to us. You think now that you know that you can best these men in a fight, so you seek to provoke one. Yes?"

"Well, yeah."

"We have a saying. 'The world is ruled by allowing events to run their course.'"

He thought about that for a minute. "I don't get it."

"These are violent men, criminals, are they not?"

"They are."

"Violent men will meet with violence. If you allow events to follow their natural course . . ."

This really was the way Bagadonuts thought. "I just need to

manipulate, a little bit. Get 'em to do what comes natural." Another piece fell into place. This is how he does it, Stoney thought. This is why he winds up standing over to one side and never gets any blood on his shirt while the rest of us do it to each other.

She watched his face. After a few minutes, he looked over at her. "Have I been helpful?" she asked him.

"Aah, I think so. I think so. I didn't know you had such a fine sense of strategy. I'll have to consult with you more often from now on."

"Well, that would be nice. Perhaps you could have told me about the sign a year ago. Think of the aggravation I could have spared myself. Is there something else I can do for you?"

"Now that you mention it. What I came here looking for is a place to crash for a few days. I just need a room with a bed. I thought maybe I could stay here for a while."

"Oh, no," she said, horrified. "You don't want to sleep here. Besides, it's going to be very noisy around here. I'll have carpenters in here tomorrow." She opened a desk drawer and fished around inside. "'Madam Cho's Tai Chi Parlor,'" she said, laughing, "before you know it." She found a key in the drawer and handed it to Stoney. "I have a small studio over in the East Village. We use it when we get a new girl who has nowhere to live, or who needs to hide, for whatever reason. Or if a customer requests particular privacy. No one is using it now. It's very small, but I think it will suffice." She told him the address and the security code.

Stoney thought of his night at the Royal. "Mrs. Cho, I can't thank you enough."

Tuco could feel the butterflies in his stomach begin to flutter as soon as he dug out the Brooklyn Yellow Pages. This is an ugly business, he thought to himself. You start feeling sticky before you even begin.

Plus, in the cold light of morning, he could see the cracks in his plan. The timing, for example, had to be exactly right. Just this one day for a window, the necessity of getting everything together right now, this morning, and in place before his target showed . . . He'd already begun to think of him that way, no longer a human being, not another person, but just a target.

Yeah, well. Too late to wuss out now. He'd made his deal with the girl, and what she had agreed to do was considerably worse than what he was going to do, in his mind. If she were able to keep up her end, he ought to be able to do his part. Besides, what would she think of him if he turned chicken now? Then would it be his fault that she continued to be stuck out there on the street corner? He opened the phone book to the car-rental pages.

He recognized the outline, the exterior shape of the name of a prominent car-rental company. He'd seen their ads a hundred times on television, heard their name pronounced as the shape of the word was displayed on the tube, so even if the individual letters appeared in their normal indecipherable swim, he knew what he needed to know.

Numbers were much less of a problem. He made the call, heard the voice on the other end of the line, and he explained what he wanted. Sure, the voice said. And what credit card will you be using? I'm paying cash, he told her. Yes, but, she explained, we still need a major credit card number . . .

Shit.

He put the phone back down in its cradle.

So close and still out of reach.

He went back to the Yellow Pages again and looked at all the tiny combinations dancing on the page. There's gotta be, he thought, somebody here sleazy enough to just take the money.

There was a picture ad in one corner. He didn't recognize the name, but there was a lot of poorly done graphics in the ad, cars with toothy smiles and floating dollar signs. He dialed the number and explained what he wanted, and his intention to deal strictly in cash.

"Well," the man said. "Hmm. Normally we need a credit card to protect ourselves, if you get what I mean. We don't know you, right? You could take the vehicle, claim it was stolen . . ." But he didn't hang up, and he didn't say no. "I may be able to help you. My cousin has an older van on his lot. I think he's asking fourteen hundred for it. It's got a lot of miles on it, but it's in decent shape. Got a working fridge, seats that fold back into a bed, tinted windows. How about this. I'll borrow the van and throw some plates on it. You give me a thou for a security deposit, four hundred to rent it for, say, a week. Where did you say you were taking it?"

"No place. Queens Boulevard."

"Ah. Got a special date?"

Pig, Tuco thought. But I am doing something piggish with it. "Something like that."

"When do you need it?"

An extra hundred persuaded him to drop what he was doing and go for the van immediately.

Tuco looked at the pile of bills in the kitchen drawer. For two years he hadn't had much to spend it on, hadn't been able to think of much of anything he really wanted. He didn't feel much of anything about blowing it now. He slid the drawer closed. Stupid to keep it there, he thought. I ought to get a bank account.

He walked up Clark Street toward the subway stop in the old St. George Hotel. Feeling the weight of the money in his pocket, he reconsidered. Too much at stake to take the train, he thought, and he walked on past the hotel and out to Court Street and hailed a cab.

"Northern Boulevard," he said, getting into the backseat. "Right off the BQE."

It had to be the one. Ford van, eleven or twelve years old, a few dents, paint chipped and peeling here and there, but no Bondo and not much rust. The inside looked clean enough, the driver's seat was the only thing that showed any real wear. The clock showed sixty-seven thousand miles, but the only real question was, how many times had it been around?

A tall, gray-haired man walked out of the office trailer that was parked at the rear of the lot. He was thin except for a basketball-size paunch just above his belt line.

"You the gentleman I talked to on the phone?"

"'At's me," Tuco said. The two of them got in the van and Tuco took it around the block, listening to the ticking of the six cylinder, feeling the transmission slide from gear to gear. The suspension soaked up the potholes with only minor complaints. Guy didn't lie about the van, Tuco thought, still in good shape, regardless of the miles. They went back to the lot to do the paperwork.

He really did drive the van to Queen's Boulevard, to an electronics place that he knew about across from Macy's. He went inside and spent more money than he had renting the van, on a video camera with a tiny remote lens, a remote control, and a power inverter to run it off the van's battery. It was a snap to set up, everything went under the hood except for the button-sized lens that poked through the rubber seal on the doghouse that covered the engine, between the two front seats. In the process of installing the wiring it occurred to him that it would really be a shame if the battery went dead on him, so on his way over to Troutman Street he stopped and had it tested. He looked at the needle himself, and it stayed well up into the green zone. Feeling like a weasel, still, but a successful one, he gave the mechanic ten bucks, bought beer for the fridge, and he was ready.

11

SHE WOKE UP EARLY, EARLY FOR HER, AT LEAST, WITH AN UNFAMILIAR
feeling of excitement, and something else she could no longer
identify. This was the day, he'd told her, that strange boy from the
neighborhood. So much like a child, she'd thought him, no gang
colors, no beads or tattoos, no earrings, without, even, that self-
defensive hostility that she'd noticed in all the children of the city.
But if you looked past all of that, he bore more than a passing
resemblance to Dr. Jack. The compact build, skin color, his habitual scowl, the way his muscles bunched and pressed against his skin
from the inside. A statue, almost, she thought, maybe the statue of
an unhappy god, or of the deserted half-breed progeny of one.

He was easy for her to like, though, the way his face seemed
to soften when he looked into her eyes, or down at his shoes, the
way he'd listened to her story that was almost the truth, without
telling her what she should do. And the very idea that he could pry
her away from the clutches of Dr. Jack, of those people in that
place on St. Nick . . . She didn't think he could really do it. She

even half-hoped that he wouldn't try. How sad it would be, what they would do to him. What chance did he stand, this one boy against the likes of them?

She would tell him, she decided, when she saw him. She'd meant to do it before, Honey, I would do this for you for nothing. Just give me a hundred, anything beyond that is a waste, anyhow. A hundred bucks and I'll give him to you with a bow tied around his whoosis. She giggled at the thought of it. Such a sweet kid he was. It seemed like she hadn't really talked to anyone in such a long time, just transactional words, how much, no, I won't do that, sweetie, why is this costing me twenty a hit all of a sudden.

She took a shower, washed her hair, went through her meager possessions trying to decide what to wear. She smoked a joint while she thought of him, the other one, the one she'd be doing. She tried to remember exactly what he looked like, and a few things came back to her. His funny hair, the build of a person who eats too much and rides everywhere he goes, the way he'd stammered, licked his lips, and run away. White underwear, she thought, and a short skirt so that he'd see them when she wanted him to, and a T-shirt cut off to show her stomach. Oh, you won't get away from me this time, she thought. I own you, and you will do what I say for you to do.

She even felt a spark of desire, not for one of them or for the other, but the two, tied together in her mind somehow with the outlandish idea that she could come back to life, like Lazarus, and go back to her kitchen and her husband, wake up in the morning in that wide bed, and drink coffee. She tamped that down quickly, carefully, not killing it off altogether but keeping it very small and dim. No better way to hurt yourself, she knew, than to want something.

●   ●   ●

Tuco drove the van across Fifty-eighth Street, past the police and sanitation garages. The van needed a little TLC, the brakes tended to grab, and the steering was vague and rubbery. No big deal in either case, he and Commie Pete could deal with both of those problems in one morning. Ain't my van, he had to remind himself. I don't even want it. I don't even want to be driving it to Troutman Street, or to think about what's going to happen in it after it gets there. She'd do it anyway, he told himself, she does it all day for ten bucks per. But it's you, an inner voice said. It's you doing it.

Shut up, he thought. Leave me alone.

She was one block up from the shop, outside a deli, when he drove up. She looked the van over with a practiced eye, turned away. He rolled down the window and called to her. When she heard his voice, her whole demeanor changed, she spun back, smiling, and seeing him framed in the open window, she bounced over, Jesus, it was like being punched in the stomach, God, what a creature, and then she stuck her head in through the open window and kissed him full on the lips like no one had ever done before in his life, like he'd been sure, right up until that moment, no one ever would. She stood back, grinning, broke away; and then, laughing that musical laugh that she had, she bounced around the front of the van, got in on the passenger side, and threw her bag in the back.

He wanted to melt. He didn't, though. In fact, he was hard as a rock, and his head swam. What if we left now, he thought, just go tell the guy, Keep the money, give me the title, and drive out west to Montana or someplace, the hell with it all.

"Hey, baby," she said brightly. "This it? This where we're gonna do it?"

"Yeah," he said, his voice husky.

"Cool," she said, looking in the back. Crapped-out old truck, she thought, but it looked like nobody had ever sat in the backseat.

Probably belonged to some old fart, bought it wishing he was still seventeen, drove it all around but never got laid. "Where's the camera?"

What if we just went away?, he wanted to ask her. "You can't see it, it's right up here, looking between the seats."

She got up out of her seat and, bending over at the waist, showing her perfect legs, her perfect skin, she crawled into the back, making his heart stop once again. The backseat was already folded down, and she sat on the edge of it. "So I gotta get him right here, facing this way, so we can get his face, right?"

He inhaled, held it, stilled his shaking hands. "You sure you wanna go through with this?"

"Oh, hell," she said. "You want this guy, right?"

"Yeah."

"Well, let's go get him, then."

He threw the van into drive, pulled away from the curb. She wriggled on the edge of the seat. "Oh, baby," she said, giggling. "We are gon' burn his ass up!"

C. Maxwell Hunt stood in the middle of the floor, so angry that he quivered. His normally white face was flushed a deep red.

"What do you mean, there's no one here," he rasped through clenched teeth. There was nothing in the world that he hated more than being slighted and taken for granted. People had been doing that to him his entire life, but now, finally, he was in a position where he didn't have to put up with it anymore, and he was not going to have it, and he exploded. "Then just where the fuck are they?"

Walter stood calmly behind the counter and wondered how to handle the apoplectic white man in front of him. Stoney surely dropped the ball on this one, he thought. Probably figured he'd dodge the man for a while, but he'd read him wrong. All he really needed to have done was show up, talk to the man, let him threaten, beg for mercy. That would have bought them another week, maybe. As it was, this guy wanted someone to kill.

"Well, sir," he said, keeping the accent completely out of his voice, "I'm not sure if they told you, when you were here before, that our accountant had been murdered."

"I've spoken to the Bronx assistant DA." Maxwell was back to growling through clenched teeth.

"Well, sir, since that time one of the men you met, Thomas Rosselli, was assaulted in his home. He suffered three bullet wounds at close range. He's been in intensive care ever since." Walter tried to remember Stoney's real name but could not come up with it. "His partner, the, ah, other gentleman you met, has understandably been preoccupied since then. I have no idea where he is. Several of the other employees have either taken time off or have simply failed to show up. I'd love to cooperate in any way that I can, sir, but . . ." He spread his hands in a gesture of helplessness. "Things been quite hectic, the last few days."

C. Maxwell breathed deliberately, inhaling deeply several times. "Not as hectic," he said, once he'd calmed himself down, "as they're going to get. I don't know for sure what it is you people do here, but I intend to make it my business to find out. You tell your boss for me, if you see him still alive, that he picked the wrong person to 'dis,' as you people say." He inhaled, puffing himself up. "I can be a lot of trouble," he said, picking up his briefcase. "A lot of trouble." He pushed his way through the door, out into the bright sunshine.

Walter watched him go by the window. "Rrrahshole," he said, rolling the word off his tongue in the Bajun manner.

"This is bad," Jimmy the Hat said from behind his computer at the far edge of the counter. "He looks like the kind of guy who's gonna make life very difficult. I don't know how good Stoney is at dealing with pissed-off bureaucrats."

"Stoney?" Walter looked over at Jimmy. "From now on we ain't lettin' Stoney anywhere near that guy." He shook his head. "We gonna have to manipulate very carefully, or this whole thing could go right down the toilet."

C. Maxwell felt like a boxer who had just decked his opponent, only to hear the bell sound the end of the round. This, he told himself, is going to be enjoyable.

Oh, God, there she was! He'd almost forgotten about her. A smile spread across his face. The last time he'd seen her, she'd gotten him so worked up, he'd gone home and ambushed his wife. She hadn't gotten a thrashing like that in years! The girl was sitting right on his car, short skirt pulled up almost to her waist, her long legs crisscrossed in front of her, hanging down. She looked even better than she had when he'd first seen her. She tilted her head as she watched him coming down the sidewalk. He stopped a foot away.

"You know," he said, "you're too dangerous to be running around loose like this. Isn't there somebody supposed to be looking after you?"

"Oh, hello, again," she said. "I suppose I slipped my leash. School can be so boring. All those girls. And the nuns." She uncrossed her legs, crossed them the other way. "They don't let you have any fun at all."

"Unnnh." That flash of white was just too much to bear, and he closed the distance between the two of them, just leaned into her, really, and she wrapped those legs around his waist and held him up against the side of the car. He could feel her breasts crushed against his chest, and he reached his hand under the elastic waistband of her skirt in the back. "Unnnh."

"Easy, there, Tarzan." She pushed him away, just a bit, so that he wasn't up against her but was still stuck inside her aura. "Jane's got an idea. I borrowed my brother's van. Let's you and me go check it out."

He looked at the Ford parked behind his car. "That it?" he croaked.

"Yep." She hopped off the car, brushing up against him as she did so. She ran her hand up the inside of his pants leg. "Come on, tiger."

Tuco watched from the vestibule of the building across the street. He felt sick to his stomach, but it was too late now, too late to make another choice. The two of them made their way back to the van. Tuco thumbed the record button on the remote at the same time they opened the door, just in case the recorder made any sort of a click or a noise when it started. He didn't think that it would, but it didn't pay to take any chances. Not now, not after he'd already done it. He turned away, banged his head against the row of mail-boxes.

"Sit right here," she said, patting the spot with her hand. "Let me get you a beer." He sat, obediently, where he'd been told to sit, and she got on her knees beside him on the seat to lean into the back, where the fridge was. Her skirt rode up over her waist, and Maxwell could restrain himself no longer. She felt his nose and face pressed suddenly into her crotch from behind. Oh, Tuco, she thought, you were more right about this one than you knew. But she was confident in her intuition when it came to men. This guy was the kind of sicko that would be fun. And it was so great, even for just one day, to be part of something, to be working to some purpose, even though Tuco hadn't told her what it was, to be doing something more than just whoring and scoring.

"Owoo," she said. "Hey."

"Is that okay?" He was frightened, apologetic, ashamed.

"Oh, honey," she said, turning back around to face him. She pulled up the bottom of her abbreviated T-shirt, enough so that the bottom half of her breasts was visible, and paused. "Ain't you gonna take off that tie?"

Tuco watched, miserable. This felt like the absolute worst thing he'd ever done, or even thought about doing, and it was taking forever. Well, he thought, if there really is a hell after all, I'm sure to find it now. God, would they never finish? He started to worry that the tape would run out, that he wouldn't get anything good enough, that it would all have been for nothing.

Poor man, she thought, he just can't quite make it. No matter what she did. Not that she was doing much, he wouldn't let her. "No, leave those on," he'd said when she started to take off her underwear, so now he lay naked on top of her, sucking her breast, not quite there. He picked his head up. "I'm sorry," he said. "I just don't know . . ."

She hushed him, pushing his head back down. "Be still, now," she told him, reaching into her bag on the floor next to them. She pulled out a vibrator, clicked it on. He made no reaction to the sound, she couldn't tell if he heard it humming or not. She reached around behind him, he moved instinctively, accommodating her, and she inserted it, pushed it steadily all the way in.

•   •   •

"Aaaaaargh!" Oh, Jesus. Tuco heard the shout across the street, through the door. Oh, God. But then it came again, a long, gargling shout, but in a man's voice, not a woman's.

"Unh, unh, unh, unh, unh, oh God oh God."

She giggled, she couldn't help herself. "You see? Mama knows what you need." He lay facedown, finally, beside her. "Hold still, now," she told him, and retrieved her appliance. "Don't you feel better now?" He rolled over onto his hands and knees and faced her, looking just like a pot-bellied, red-faced, hairless basset hound.

"Uh, listen," he said, trying to catch his breath. "Please, I need for you, to do one, more thing. Please. Since we went, you know, this far."

She folded her legs underneath her, folded her hands in her lap, Buddha in white panties. "What you got in mind, sugar?"

He was already out on the stoop or he wouldn't have heard, this time, but there was no mistaking the sound of a hand striking human skin, and it was loud enough to sound serious, repetitive, smack, two seconds, smack, two more seconds, smack. Tuco grimaced, dancing out into the street, promising himself, I'll kill him if he hurts her, I'll burn the van with him inside it, I swear . . . But through the windshield he could see a hand coming back, and to his shock it was a brown one, smack, oh, God, that's gotta hurt. He went quickly back to his vestibule.

He took the beer after all, worked at it while he got dressed. She sat cross-legged, without moving, watching him. He wouldn't look at her.

"You, ah, got another one of these?"

"In the fridge, honey." She knew if there were any danger to her, it would be now. She didn't think there was, but she was not going to lean over to the fridge and find out.

"Ah, thanks." He came back around and sat down beside her. "Could I, um, see you again?"

She felt sorry for him for the first time, wondering if the camera was still rolling. "Well, that depends," she said, almost in her real voice. "You know, you really worked me over. I'm gonna need a little somethin' to calm my nerves."

"Sure I did." He could hear compassion in her voice, and he looked at the floor between his knees. He reached for his wallet, counted out five twenties. "I think I'd really love to see you again."

She reached out and took the hundred, even though she knew that it was a bad number for her. "You just look for me, sugar," she said, struggling to keep the sorrow out of her voice. "I'll be around."

Tuco didn't know how much time to give her, didn't know how he should feel. It had worked, after all, all the things that could've gone wrong hadn't, and now all that was left was the paperwork, really. Still, he leaned against the doorway, and then trudged over to the van as slowly as C. Maxwell had gone to his car.

She leaned over in her seat and ripped the sliding door open when she saw him coming. He hadn't known what to expect, but she was wearing the skirt and the T-shirt again, grinning broadly. She sat back, tipping a beer can to her lips. Tuco watched the triceps in the back of her arm flex.

"Well, baby," she said, "I hope your camera worked."

"Yeah, so do I." He got in, slid past her, wormed his way into the driver's seat. He turned around and saw her, out on the street already, tipping the can back, draining what was left in it. "Come on, get in," he said. "We gotta go."

She dropped the can on the street and kicked it under the van. "We?" she said. She reached inside for her bag. "You gonna take me home to Momma?"

Dude already paid, she started to say, thought better of it. She swung her bag out of the van and slammed the door closed. She took that one step, up next to the passenger-door window, stood looking at him. It was the first time he'd seen such a serious look on her face. He rolled the window down.

She regarded him silently, her lips pursed in disapproval. "Don't you play me," she said. "I don't need you playing me."

"Look," he said. "I live all the way the other end of Brooklyn. You can stay there, you'll be all alone, nobody will bother you. I need two or three days to handle Dr. Jack for you, and after that, you can go anywhere you want. Back out on the island, back to your parents, anything you want. I'll even drive you. Or," he said, feeling his pulse thumping in his chest, "you can stay with me. Up to you."

She almost walked away. In the end it was that tiny spark that swayed her, that idea of waking up, sitting in a kitchen with a cup of coffee. She opened the door and got in, her face clamped down hard on her fear and her sorrow. She banged the door closed. Another man, taking her off someplace.

He didn't know how to reassure her. He shrugged his shoulders. "Listen," he said. "I've gotta come back out to Queens Boulevard later, anyhow. Come with me. We'll go look. You don't like it, I'll bring you back here."

She stared straight out at the street in front of her. "Go," she said. "Go on." He started the van and drove up the block. When they got to the stop sign, she had him turn up the hill. "We gotta stop," she said. "I've gotta grab a few things."

"You sure? You think it's safe?"

She was grinning again. "He gave me twenty bucks extra for my underwear."

She could see the top of the van from her window. She stood there and smoked a joint, watching the van, and presently she began to feel better. She packed up the rest of her dope, her few stray dollar bills, and some clothes and stuffed them haphazardly into a brown paper shopping bag. She looked around the room she'd resigned herself to dying in, wondering if she'd see it again, wondering how long it would be before they started looking for her. It occurred to her for the first time that they might not even bother. Plenty more where she came from.

An hour and a half later she lay in his bed, a real one, a double, twice the size of hers, and looked out his window. The sun didn't make it all the way down to where they were, but the light hit the wall of the next building, ten feet over, way up high, and broke into a soft, misty rain of daylight that streamed through the window. There was a tree in the backyard of the next building over, she couldn't see that either, but she could hear the wind playing in the leaves. The tree was actually up higher than she was. At the end of the alley the wall went straight up about fifteen feet, and the top of it was actually ground level, and the tree was up there, in the yard.

She'd smoked another joint after he left, drank the last two beers. He'd said he was sorry he didn't have more, sorry he didn't have any food in the fridge, sorry he didn't have a TV, sorry there was no radio . . . She'd shooed him away. Didn't you say you had business, she'd said, and he'd gone off, promising to bring the world back with him when he came. She was just as happy to have it stay away while she lay in his bed, floating on a cloud, separate, apart and alone.

12

HE EXPECTED THE GUY TO HAVE AN ANSWERING MACHINE, SO WHEN a voice said, "Hello, this is Benny," he waited for it go on about the beep and a message.

"Hello?"

"Oh, hey, Benny, I was waiting for the rest of the message."

"Huh? Who is this?"

"This is Stoney. Remember me? I met you in the park the other day."

"Oh, yeah, so you did. You drink today?"

"No. You?"

"Not yet. How you doing, Stoney? You feel okay? Get over the shakes yet?"

"Not entirely. I'm getting there."

"Good, good. You eating regular?"

"Well, you know, I ain't been really—"

"Stoney. You got money for food?"

"Yeah. Yeah, I'm flush, Bennie."

"Good. Good for you. Now listen to what I tell you. It's important that you don't let yourself get hungry. Understand what I'm sayin'? Even if you don't want it, have breakfast, lunch, dinner. Carry mints in your pocket."

"Mints."

"Stoney, what do you think your body changes alcohol to, after it's done messing with your head?" He didn't wait for an answer. "Sugar. It changes to sugar. Your body is gonna crave sugar like you won't believe."

"So how come you ain't fat?"

"It don't last forever, you idiot. Besides, they don't put you in jail if you pick up a few pounds."

"Okay, Benny."

"Listen, where'd you sleep last night? You got a place to stay?"

"I don't have a problem with domicile or finance, Bennie. My problem is—"

"Your problem is you're a fucking drunk and an addict. That's what your problem is. Everything else is details, you got that?"

"Yeah. You're right, Bennie. Listen, I gotta go."

"Okay, kid, call me tomorrow."

"All right." What a crazy place Manhattan is, he thought as he hung up the phone. Fulla crazy people.

He went out to get mints. East Village, my ass, he thought. This is Alphabet City. They call it that because it is east of First Avenue, so the avenues have letters for names, A, B, C, D. It goes from Fourteenth Street down to Houston, with housing projects, a failed experiment from this century, between Avenue D and the East River, and tenements, a failed experiment from an earlier century, everywhere else. They'd been sorry when they were new, and now they were ancient, crumbling, falling down. There were even tenement buildings inside the block, surrounded on all sides by the ones that fronted on the streets, and they were more horrible yet. A few buildings, like the one Mrs. Cho's studio was in, had been restored, but most of them were in need of some natural disaster to come and knock them down. The neighborhood was a haven for refugees, always had been, from Hitler's Europe, from Bosnia, Paraguay, the sixties, reality.

East Village. Had to be a real estate salesman thought that one up.

First bodega he tried, guys were leaning on the counter drinking beer. In the second one he spent ten bucks on candy and soda. On his way back, he went over his plan again, trying to think of what it could be that was giving him that strange feeling that he'd forgotten something. Opening the door and punching in the security code, he remembered what it was. He ripped the paper off a candy bar while he dialed.

"Hello."

"Donna?"

"Hello, Stoney." It sounded like a voice that you'd use talking to your lawyer. "How's Tommy?"

"I don't know. He's still pretty heavily sedated . . ."

"Well, that's a switch."

He closed his eyes, took a deep breath. "Yeah, well. Where are the kids?"

"Outside," she said, her voice a little softer. "Dennis is teaching Marissa how to skate." She breathed into the telephone, working herself up for it. "You don't even remember, do you?"

Oh, God, he thought, oh no, please, it wasn't me . . .

"Do you?"

"No." He could tell she was crying.

"I didn't think so. I thought you were all right, the other night. I thought you only had a few beers." She covered the mouthpiece while she blew her nose. "I asked you if you thought you had a problem, if you thought you were addicted. You told me that I was an addict too. That you could make me understand. You told me to sit at the kitchen counter, and then you went around behind me. You put your hands around my neck and you said I was addicted to breathing. You can stop, if you want, you said, but not for long, and it's all you'll think about, and you'll know that you need to do it, you need it to live. Oh, yeah, I'll go back to it, I'll fucking fight for it, that's what you said . . ."

He had no memory of it at all. He'd often thought of the metaphor, but he would never hurt her, he couldn't. Could he?

"You choked me, you fucking bastard." He could hear the hurt and outrage rising in her voice. "You made me fight you . . ."

"Aah . . ."

"You made me punch you. I had to scratch you before you'd let me go. I had marks on my neck."

It was coming back to him. The first thing he remembered was the deep, raw sucking breaths, her throat making a noise he'd never heard before. She tried to scream at him but did not have the voice, and she stumbled into the far corner of the kitchen to get away. She threw the coffeemaker at him, because it was the first thing that came to hand, all ready with the water and the coffee in it for the next morning. He stood motionless, expressionless, as the coffeemaker bounced off, the glass pot breaking in a thousand pieces as it hit the floor, coffee and water flying everywhere. She was still suffering from it, that panicked, desperate, full-body, clawing thirst for air. How quickly it pushes every other thought from your mind when you need something that desperately.

"Is that true?" She had gotten some of her voice back. He had stood stock-still, watching her, his face unreadable. A sudden horrible realization had dawned on her face: If it really was like that, if he really felt that way, then there was no way to win. They were done, the two of them. She could leave or she could stay to watch him die. "Is that true?" Her voice had shaken with fear, and something like despair. He had just turned in drunken slow-motion and gone off to bed, leaving her behind in the kitchen to clean up the mess, crying desperately, on her hands and knees, looking for pieces of glass.

Stoney had never felt shame and remorse like this before. He didn't know what to say. "Donna, I—"

She wasn't listening. "Being up here for a few days is giving me a chance to think. And you know what I think, Stoney? I think it's really unfair to Dennis and Marissa. We may all be going through hell, but I really think it's hurting them the most. We can't go on like this, Stoney. After you straighten out this mess the two of you are in, you and I are going to have to make some decisions."

"Don't do anything hasty, Donna."

"Hasty? This has gone on for years, Stoney."

"I know."

"Look, be careful, okay?"

"Okay."

They used to call it the LL, now it's just the L train. It goes straight across Manhattan beneath Fourteenth Street, under the East River, and straight out into Queens. Tuco thought it had to be the original subway, the first one ever invented. Probably still running the original cars. No local and express, either, no waiting for the next train, there was no next train, just that one, you miss it, you wait until it gets all the way to the end, comes back the other way to the other end, and finally comes back for you. There was no one in the station, that time of night, just Tuco, waiting for that hot ozone breath to come huffing a century of bad breath out of the black tunnel to let him know the train was finally on its way back.

He'd considered taking a cab, but you don't see a lot of empty cabs in that part of Queens, the ones that you do see don't generally stop for a kid like Tuco, and if by some chance one does stop, he wants to go to Manhattan, where the money is, he don't wanna go down the BQE to some part of Brooklyn. So there he sat, cursing his timing; he'd dropped his token in the slot and run down the stairs to the sound of the train cranking up and clanking off down the tunnel. When he was younger he'd have hopped down on the tracks and crossed over, catch the train coming back, ride it the wrong way to the end and back. That way, at least he'd be in motion. Going nowhere, true enough, but fooling some part of himself into thinking that he was making progress. And when finally it did come, he would get on and ride it into Manhattan, in the wrong direction, away from where he was headed, so that he could change at Union Square for the A train downtown, back under the river, back into Brooklyn to the Cadman Plaza station in the Heights.

And all of this with the keys to Stoney's Lexus in one pocket and the keys to the van in the other. Didn't figure that one out, did you, you dumb bastard? The committee in his head had started right up after he'd stashed the van down by the shop and suddenly realized he didn't have a ride back. You moron, you stupid retard.

So what, he told them silently. I got him, I got the guy in living color, here's his face, here's his other end, here she is doing him with that plastic thing, good grief. Tuco hadn't believed it when he'd watched the tape, and the technician doing the stills for him hadn't believed it either, even though he'd done his best to appear jaded and bored by it all. Why would he want that, he kept asking Tuco, who had no information on the subject. Why would he pay her to do that? Why not just, you know, put it to her regular? I don't know, man, I don't know, Tuco had told him, strangely relieved.

When he'd paid the girl at the register, she'd been nice enough to address the envelope for him without asking any embarrassing questions. He'd had his lie ready, something about them recognizing his handwriting, but he hadn't needed it. Personal and confidential, he'd told her, put that on the bottom. He has to open this by himself. And just Troutman Street, Brooklyn, for the return address. It was addressed to the man's office. When will he get it, he asked them at the post office. Day after tomorrow, the lady told him, tossing the envelope into a bin. It felt odd, turning and walking away, leaving a ticking time bomb behind him. There was no note inside. He figured the stills were enough. There was always the tape, if he needed more.

By the time he got to the Cadman Plaza station, the adrenaline he'd been running on all day had ebbed away, and he trudged up the steps to the street wearily. He crossed over to Henry Street, caught the smells coming out of the pizzeria. He was too tired, he told himself, his body ached to go lie down, but there was no food in the house, nothing at all. You gotta think about these things now, he told himself. No one's going to do it for you.

He waited, collapsed in a plastic chair while they made his pizza, thinking about the girl who worked in the coffee shop down the block. Am I supposed to feel disloyal, he wondered, because I keep seeing her face? He didn't know, and he was too tired to think about it, and besides, when he got home, she was there, and she ran all those other thoughts from his mind.

She received him in silence, her gentle hands caressing him, maintaining contact as they walked down the hall together, into the kitchen, where they sat side by side at the counter and ate. He discovered that he was starving, after all. She ate a single slice, and then watched him. I'm really beat, he told her, I have to lay down, and he went into the bedroom and grabbed a pillow and some blankets, meaning to go sleep on the floor. No, she told him, her fingers soft on his arm, no, and he was startled to hear real need in her voice. She pulled him back into the bedroom, undoing the buttons on his shirt. Seeing her on the tape was nothing, nothing at all compared to this full-scale assault on his senses. The sound of her voice in the back of her throat, echoing in the still room, the feel of her hands on his chest, the taste of her lips on his, her warm breath on his neck. She yanked at his clothes with sudden intensity, and then rapidly shed the little that she was wearing. He knew that he wasn't thinking straight, realized, even, that he would reconsider later, but right there and then he wanted her, anything and everything that she was or had, her vitality, her strength, her diseases, her life and her death, her child, if they could make one.

"No, baby, no," she said, holding him back. "No, wait, baby, just one minute." She rolled him over onto his back, went off to rustle around in her bag, returned quickly. "You gotta put this on, okay? Here, hold still, I'll do it for you," she said, tearing the little package open with her teeth. This is it, Tuco thought, this is how it is to lose your head, but there was no getting it back, the water was too deep and the current too strong. He was lost.

In the morning he woke at his usual time but lay motionless, listening to the sound of her breathing. He thought of the night before with conflicting emotions. On the one hand, the physical experience of sex had been somewhat less than the years of dire warnings in church had led him to believe. On the other hand, he felt an aching desire to reach over and hold her, feel her arms around him again, pour himself into her and feel her making him whole the way she had done the night before. It can't be sex, he told himself, it had to have been something more that had made him suddenly delirious and carefree for the first time in his life, full of sunny optimism. This is it, he'd thought, this is faith, this is

believing. He had never before even conceived that such a sensation could be possible, certainly not for him. The mere memory of
it was enough to bring tears to his eyes. The idea that he could
actually connect with someone so totally and so completely had to
be something extraordinary, out of the realm of normal human
experience, miraculous. It must have been what Jesus felt, he
thought, when he walked underwater.

His cell phone started ringing, and he eased out of bed and
went to the kitchen to get it. She was awake when he came back,
half sitting up in the bed. The sight of her made him wish for
another day off. "I gotta go to work," he told her. "I'll leave you
some money, you'll have to order out."

"Are you sure you gotta go?" she said, looking down.

He wanted to melt. "Yeah," he said. "I might not be back
tonight, either. I'm gonna go see Dr. Jack, work things out."

"Oh, God," she said. "Oh, God, why don't you just forget that,
baby? They'll hurt you. They'll—"

He wasn't listening. "Nah, don't worry. I know them better
than you think. Don't answer the phone, okay?"

"No frontal assault, then?" Walter poured the El Presidente down
the center of the glass and watched it foam. "No artillery? No claymores?"

"You sound disappointed." Stoney watched him handle the
beer with hawk's eyes.

"Well, ya know." Walter drained half the glass, sighed appre-
ciatively. "T'ing been very tiresome around here, man." He emp-
tied the rest of the glass, refilled it from the bottle. "You know they
used to have a beer in Panama, Bolivar was the name. Very nice
beer for getting drunk. I never seen it in the USA."

"I figured you for a Red Stripe man."

"Well, I do indulge, from time to time, but you know, sittin' in Brooklyn, New York, drinkin' Red Stripe and eatin' flyin' fish, it ain't no way to live. Once in a while, okay, but alla time, man, seem sort of pitiful, ya know?"

"My problem is, I think I lost the handle." It just came out before he could think about it.

"Yah, we kinda noticed, man. Ya shouldn't be in a hurry, hell be hot enough when we get there. I seen it before, two a my uncles went that way, and it's a hard way to go, Stoney. It's a damn hard way to go. Just like when ya catch a fire, ya got ta burn, man, ya got ta fuckin' burn, before ya die."

Stoney tore his attention away from the beer on the table. Outside, on Troutman Street, another morning was in full swing. A crew of Ecuadorian welders from the ironworks yard came through the door, yelling their breakfast orders in Spanish at the Dominicano cooks behind the counter. Walter and Stoney were the only two speaking English in the place, but it was not the sort of thing that either of them noticed.

"Maybe I'll get lucky, get hit with a truck."

"Don't laugh, man, I knew a guy, fell asleep in an alley, back by a loadin' dock, truck backin' in run over 'is legs. Dey had to cut 'em both off, poor bastard had to roll 'imself aroun' on a skateboard. Get drunk, kept fallin' off the t'ing, twas a very sorry sight. Five, maybe six years, 'e went on that way. Finally 'is liver gave out."

"How did we get off on this topic?"

"You was preparin' to tell me what Tommy would do, 'e was us."

"So I was." Stoney lowered his voice and told Walter his plan, as far as he had it figured out, including the preparations he'd made the previous day.

"I really don't know that neighborhood at all," Walter said, dropping the accent.

"It should be perfect. If we do this right, the cops should show up just like the cavalry, we can watch it all from behind the bushes. We get the cops nervous enough, they just might shoot 'em all, we won't have to do a thing."

"I tell you what Tommy would do, he'd string it out another few days, give 'em a chance to get good and worked up. T'ing is, Tommy don't think he's so smart, not really. He just caters to the other guy's appetite."

"Not today, then?"

"Hell, no. Patience, Stoney. Make 'em go out there a few times. Let 'em smell it, you know, 'Oooh, there it is, but we can't get at it.' Know what I mean? Give yourself a little more time, let them get impatient."

"Nobody's more impatient than me. This thing has gone on long enough. I wanna wrap it up."

"Naturally, but you don't wanna mess it up. Listen, here's what Tommy would do. Let 'em follow you on up there, let 'em go smellin' around the place, see nothing bad happens. Then tomorrow they'll be ripe."

Stoney sucked in a big breath of air, blew it out. Waiting went against his nature, but he knew that Walter was right. "Okay," he said. "Today's just a dry run, then, and tomorrow we pull the string." He mulled it over, got a little more used to the idea. "You know, you're right. Today would've been too sudden. We woulda needed claymores."

"All right, man, dere you go. Listen, I almost forgot, that guy from the EPA was here yesterday, and I was not the person he wanted to talk to. He pitched a real fit, Stoney. You should have showed up, jerked him off a little. Now you really got him steaming."

"I forgot he was coming." Stoney really didn't want to think about the EPA. "Walter, I can only handle one fiasco at a time. Besides, we're gonna do what we should have done in the beginning, we're gonna hire a lawyer and let him handle it."

"All right, I tell you what, from now on, he's mine. Far as he's concerned, you retired, you ain't there. I'll find a lawyer, and all that. He hate you so bad, we got to keep 'im away from you. Tommy was around, he wouldn't let either one of us near him, he would be romancin' this guy, make the guy sorry he had to do such a t'ing to his old friend Fat Tommy. You know what I mean?"

Stoney was laughing, shaking his head. "Yeah."

"Ooh, ooh, I just got it. Here's Tommy's move. This EPA guy, you remember the way he dressed? Got the trench coat, got the unmarked police car, probably got plastic handcuffs and a pretend badge in his pocket. Bet your house, what he really wants is to be a real cop. Tommy would take him around, you know, introduce him to some of the cops that he knows. Make him feel like a tough guy, a tough guy can afford to be generous, shake 'is finger at you, tell you, 'Slow down, dammit,' and let you off with a warning."

"Yeah, well, he ain't here, and you and I ain't friendly with enough cops."

"Ain't that the truth. I'll tell ya, Tommy used to make me nervous, ya know, he knows so damn many policemen. But that's just his way, I come to see that it's just the way he is. He talks to everyone, he remembers everything. You can't bullshit him, he remembers what you told him ten years back. He don't call you on it, but ya know he remembers."

"Yeah. Tuco told me Tommy's got a pornographic memory. You know, in a way he reminds me of your cat."

"Getthefuckoutahere?"

"Yeah. The cat watches everything, don't miss a trick, just like Tommy. They both think that their survival depends on it."

"They might both be right, Stoney. You sure you got the cover on this thing nailed down nice and tight?"

Stoney shrugged. "We'll find out soon enough. You could leave your cops here with Jimmy to hold down the fort, come along, see what you think."

"Jimmy? I got a feelin' he gonna go, man. He been ready to pop, all week long. The phone ring, he jump two feet in the air, every time. Yesterday he don't come in till maybe two o'clock. Walks through the door, very agitated, says he don't feel so good, he just wants to pick up a few things, go home. He rummage around in the desk a little bit, take 'is phone book and some papers and whatnot, walks out. I ask 'im, 'You want the officer to see you home?' 'No,' he says, 'the hell with it.' I think pretty soon he gonna go find a less stimulatin' place to work."

"You think I should go have a talk with him?"

"Ya, right." It slipped out. "Leave 'im alone, Stoney. 'E got to decide what 'e want, on his own. I tell you what, though. Since you mention it, I'll get there ahead of you and settle in, watch the whole show."

"Good idea. Leave your phone on."

Tuco drove Stoney's Lexus up the BQE and over the Triborough Bridge, out of Queens. Once on the bridge, you have your choice, the Bronx or Manhattan, hence the name. "Stay left," Stoney told him. "We're going to the Bronx, up Bruckner Boulevard. Not the expressway, mind you, Bruckner Boulevard."

"That goes underneath, right?"

"Yeah. First exit to the right after you're over the bridge."

Bruckner Boulevard is the width of a superhighway, three or four lanes in each direction, islands down the middle, traffic lights every hundred yards or so, perpetually under construction. To the east run the railroad yards, down twenty feet below street level, and beyond that lies the industrial wasteland of Hunts Point. On the west side the boulevard is hemmed in by factories, some still occupied, many vacant and in various states of disrepair. Perched high over the boulevard on steel legs is the Bruckner Expressway. Stuck in traffic up there, commuters look down on the no-man's-land below. It always reminded Stoney of the tram at Busch Gardens: The people overhead labor under the misapprehension that they are safe, that the cats down below can't climb up to get at them. It seemed an obvious point to Stoney. You let them get hungry enough, they'll take the trouble to come after you, even if you are initially not to their taste or are a bit more difficult to stalk than their normal prey. It is not that far, after all, from the South Bronx to Greenwich or Rye or Scarsdale, and if you are noticeably slower or weaker than your fellows, you would be wise to bear in mind that the law of natural selection may have selected you to be deleted. That is what predators are for. Do not cluck your tongue or shake your head, all living things feed themselves on other things that are or were, themselves, alive. Remember the first rule: Watch your ass.

As Tuco braked for a red light, he and Stoney watched an old lady, four foot tall, sparse white hair, long white sweater and pink flip-flops, running across the road. "Damn, she's gotta be eighty," Tuco said as the woman continued at her improbable pace, elbows out wide, knees kicking high in the front.

"That's what chickens look like, when they run," Stoney said.

"Yeah, well, she don't wanna get squashed." The light turned green before she made it all the way across, and a cab in the right lane honked at her. She made the sidewalk, giving the cab a one-finger salute without looking back. "See?" Tuco said. "It's the traffic she's afraid of, not the street."

"Maybe she's carrying," Stoney said. "Little twenty-five automatic in your pocket do wonders for your confidence. Next light, grab the left onto Southern Boulevard."

"Damn," Tuco said. "Where we going?"

"To the bottom, my friend. We're going where evil deeds attract no attention." It was true, the neighborhood only got worse as they went along. "Pull over here," Stoney said, and Tuco stopped in front of a five-story concrete skeleton that had once been a factory. Now there was nothing left but the bones, no windows, no doors, no roof. "Not here," Stoney said. "Next one up." Tuco pulled ahead, past a street-level human-size hole in the concrete wall. As they crept past, a fortyish white guy with close-cropped yellow hair and pasty-white skin regarded them briefly before stepping through the hole into the darkness.

"Going in to cop," Tuco said. "Taking his life in his hands."

"His life is of secondary importance to him right now," Stoney said. "He's doing what he has to do."

Tuco stopped in front of the next structure, a concrete vault-like truck garage appended to the side of the ruined factory. It had a large roll-up steel door on one side, a steel personnel door in the center, and a graffiti-smeared concrete wall on the other side with grimy windows up high, behind iron bars.

Tuco got out and looked up and down the block, and across the wide boulevard. On the far side was an auto-parts store with a small parking lot to one side. A black man in a stocking hat sat on top of the wall at the back of the parking lot, drinking something out of a brown paper bag. A black Lincoln gypsy cab cruised by and continued up the boulevard. Tuco watched it pull over in the middle of the next block. He couldn't see if there were passengers inside the car. The car didn't move, and no one got out.

Stoney was banging on the steel roll-up door with an open hand. "Hey," he bellowed. "Hey, open up!"

"Go avay!" From behind the door came a high, thin voice speaking in the accent of someone who had learned English in a British school somewhere on the Indian subcontinent. "Go avay, I'm calling the police!"

"Come on, Doo-Doo, it's me. Open up."

Tuco turned to look at Stoney. "Doo-Doo?"

Stoney grinned, amusement brightening his face. Tuco heard a contactor snap closed, and the steel door began to grind up, shrieking as it went. When it got about six feet from the ground, it stopped, and a fat, dark-skinned man with great circles under his eyes stepped out.

"Hey, Doo, this's Tuco."

"Hello, Mr. Tuco."

"Doo-Doo? Is that your name?"

The Indian man rolled his eyes heavenward. "Go ahead, Doo," Stoney said. "Tell him your phone number. Go ahead, don't be afraid."

He sighed patiently. "Doo vun doo, doo doo six—"

"Okay, that's enough," Stoney said, cutting him off. "Tuco, pull that car inside. We don't want any goddamn visitors. The party's not until later."

The door squealed down behind the car, and when it was shut the three of them were enshrouded in gloom.

"Jesus, Doo, turn on some lights, willya? Tuco, climb up on top of those boxes, see if you can see out those windows." Tuco did as he was instructed.

"Yeah," he said, "it's not too bad. Can't see much beyond the end of the block, though, the angle's wrong. There was a Town Car passed us up, pulled over, next block up, and I can't see that far."

Stoney nodded in silent appreciation. "Okay, stay there, see what you see." He flipped open his phone, dialed a number, put the phone up to his ear. "Yo, Walter," he said. "Car service up one block, black Town Car. You see it?"

"Ya, man. Two stooges gettin' out, another one, plus the driver, still inside. Hang on, man. They splittin up," Walter said. "One going around the back, watch your behind."

"No back door," Stoney said. "This place is like a bunker. They got no choice but to come through the front."

Tuco stood back from the window to keep himself from being visible from the street. "One guy," he said, keeping his voice low, "coming this way. He's alone. Got a hand under his jacket. Looking us over, now he's bending down, looking at the lock, heads up. No, never mind, now he's going by, can't see him anymore."

"Another one floating around out there," Stoney told him. "Keep your eyes open." His phone crackled again.

"One come by," Walter said. "Sniff around, go on past. Went in that place next door. He better be polite in there."

"I'm sure he'll be circumspect," Stoney said dryly.

"Come back out already, going down to the corner. Here come the other one from 'round the block. They gonna cross over, comin' my way. I could take them both out right now, right from here."

"Don't do it, there's plenty more where these two came from. Our boy in the car will just call in reinforcements."

"You right, Stoney. Maybe got another team watchin' this one anyway. They're across, I'm hanging up."

"Two of them now," Tuco said, "across the street. Going into that parts store."

Stoney said a silent prayer for Walter, wondering if it was overconfidence to think those two could never get him. "You see Walter over there somewhere, hanging out?"

"Was that Walter? Was a guy in the parking lot across the street, I thought he looked familiar, but I couldn't tell, that far away. He's gone now."

Stoney laughed at himself, relieved. Don't worry about Walter, he thought. Worry about yourself.

"Still in the store," Tuco said. "One in the window, looking out." He fell silent, waiting.

"Coming out now," he said finally. "Both of them. Got a bag, must have bought something."

"Had to have an excuse to go in," Stoney said. "Wanna be just two more paying customers."

"Talking to each other," Tuco said. "Looking over here quick, not too obvious. Going on up the street. Okay, they're coming back across, still going away, though. That's it, I can't see them anymore."

"All right."

From behind the wall at the back of the parking lot, Walter watched the rear door to the store. He could also see the front door to the place through the big window on the side. He took a swig out of the quart bottle of Miller he had in a brown paper bag. Quarts weren't that easy to find anymore, but he much preferred them to the new forty-ounce cans. He liked to stay with what he was used to. No need to jump onto something new just because it claimed to be better.

Two shooters, one thinker, one driver. Easy enough to take them all, right now. That's why you should never drink beer on the job, he thought. Beer in the morning makes you reckless. Stoney was being cool, though, much more like the Stoney of a dozen years ago, a spider, motionless, calm in the center of its web, waiting patiently for its target to do something rash, carefully choosing the correct time to nip over and sink the fangs in, deliver the neurotoxin. No emotion, other than the small joy of doing something right. God, it felt good to be back at work.

He watched the two of them go out through the front door. He was surprised that they never even checked out the back, didn't even crack the door to look out. Deer hunters, he thought. Not used to stalking something that shoots back.

He screwed the cover back on the mostly full quart and left it on the ground next to an amazingly filthy white-haired man sleeping in the lee of the wall. Big heavy overcoat, no shoes. What a world, Walter thought. What a fucking world. But maybe he'd wake up and think the beer was his, finish it up. No need letting it go to waste.

He vaulted over the wall smoothly, a black shadow in a stocking hat, and slipped over to peer through the side window. From there he could see through the big windows in the front to where the two shooters were, already up to the next corner, heading back to the car. He turned his phone back on, hit the redial button.

"Back in the car," he said when Stoney answered. "Front wheels, turning, pointing out. They gonna make a U-turn, head on back this way."

"You back outta sight?"

"No need. These guys think they're shooting ducks at the carnival."

"Be careful."

"Ya, man." He flattened himself out next to the wall as the car came back down the block. The three heads in the backseat were turned away from him, looking over at the garage, but the driver was looking around, scanning the street as he drove. Walter hadn't seen his eyes, though, and he figured he had not been spotted. But it told him that they were not all morons.

"Yo, Walter."

"Ya, man."

"Why don't you stay with them, if you can. See if they head back to Troutman Street."

Walter was already running for his car, parked on the side street. "If I can? You forget who you're dealing with, whitey."

"Pardon me."

•   •   •

Tuco ducked down out of sight as they drove past. "That was them," he said. "Black gypsy cab, three guys in the backseat."

"All right," Stoney said, "that's probably it, but why don't you stay up there a little longer, just in case."

"Heading for the Triborough," Walter's voice said, "going for the BQE, I think."

"Good work, Walter, stay with them. Call me if they make any stops, otherwise I'll call you later." He snapped the phone shut. "Come on down, Tuco. That's it for today. Why don't you give Doo-Doo a ride back home. Where you live, Doo?"

"Corona," Doo said happily, relieved that he didn't have to run the gauntlet back to his home in Queens. "Thank you, sar."

Tuco jumped down from his perch, looked over at Stoney. "You gonna be all right?" He felt stupid as soon as the words had left his mouth. Stoney was the sort of guy who gave bad neighborhoods their unique flavor.

Stoney chuckled. "I am a professional," he said. "Don't try this at home. Drop Doo off in Queens, I'll call you in the morning. Tomorrow's the big day, I think."

13

SHE'LL TALK ME OUT OF IT, TUCO THOUGHT, IF I GO BACK TO DROP
the car off I'll have to stop in and see her, I won't have any choice,
and she'll talk me out of it, she won't even have to open her
mouth. I'd do anything for her, anything at all, set myself on fire
if she wanted me to. She'll want me to stay, if I go back, and I'll
have to do it. And who knows if I'd get back to this.

He'd already said he'd do it. It had started out as a bit of brava-
do, Yeah, I'll take care of you, and it had gone from that to something he needed to do for her, and now he was finding out that he
wanted to do it for himself, to see Miguel one more time, especially
after what had happened the last time. He had the premonition
that he was moving out, that more and more of his life was taking
place away from Troutman Street, for better or for worse, but this
thing with Miguel was tying him to this spot. I need to do this, he
told himself, and I need to get it over with. He decided to drop the
Lexus somewhere in the neighborhood.

He pulled the Lexus in behind the van, relieved to see it still there. All I need, he thought, is for someone to steal one of these. He began to feel butterflies, thinking of all the things that could still go wrong. He got out of the car, clicked the alarm button, and walked up to the van. Walter was sitting in the front passenger seat. Tuco sighed, shrugged, opened the door, and got in.

"Hey, ugly."

"Damn," Tuco said. "You just can't leave anything out on the street in this neighborhood."

"Any neighborhood," Walter said. "People just don't respect property anymore, although I don't think you need to worry about anyone stealin' this old shitbox." He looked around at the van's interior. "I can see you not wantin' to ride the train," he said, "but what you need with an old tank like this?"

It was not an idle question, and Tuco knew it. "I rented it," he said. "I needed it for this week."

"Yeah?" Walter was a lump of granite, sitting in the passenger seat. Tuco couldn't think of a way around him.

"First time that EPA dude was here," he said, "I was out with Commie Pete."

"I remember."

"We just pulled up in the truck when he came out. That girl was on the sidewalk, you know, that new one that's been hanging around."

"Okay."

"He almost came apart, right there. He had something for her. Big time."

"Yeah?"

"Walter, man, I'm telling you, you could feel it."

"So you decided you could scam a agent of the federal government."

"The camera lens is right by your knee."

Walter never looked at it. "Do you understand the word

'extortion'? Do you really know what blackmail is? If you make one little mistake in this game you're playing, all of us could be in deep shit. Do you understand that?"

Tuco didn't answer. He reached into the bin underneath the driver's seat and pulled out a large manila envelope. He riffled through the contents, found the shot he was looking for, pulled it out and handed it to Walter. "I don't think," he said slowly, "this man is going to the police."

"Oh my." Walter shook his head. "My, oh my. You got a few that show more of his face and less of this end?"

"Oh, yeah." Tuco started digging through the envelope. "I got—"

"No, no," Walter interrupted him hastily. "Me no wanna see 'em. I wanna be able to enjoy the company of a young lady without seein' this man's face, or he ass, either. God." He handed the print back to Tuco, who stowed it away. "Why?" he said. "Why this way, by yourself?"

"Fat Tommy used to say it all the time. It's a team sport. You guys are never gonna let me on the team because you think I'm a good guy. I had to prove I could play the game."

"It don't work exactly that way, but I see what you mean. What now?"

Tuco stared out the window. "All done with this part," he said. "I sent some prints to him at his office. No note, and just Troutman Street for a return address. Just wait for him to come back, I guess, see what he says." He looked over at Walter. "You gonna tell Stoney?"

"I ain't no rat. That's for you to do. But there's still more to this. Am I right?"

"I told the girl I'd get her out. I told her I'd get Dr. Jack to let her go."

"Man, you are nuts. Those kids shoot you for lookin' at 'em the wrong way. How you plan to go about this one?"

Tuco looked out the window again. "Dr. Jack's real name is Miguel. Miguel is my cousin. All I need to do is get in to see him. He'll let her go for me." He almost believed it himself.

"You pulled the first part off," Walter said. "You got lucky. You're gonna need help with this next part."

Tuco didn't like it, but it was Walter's idea, and once he got started there was no holding him back.

"Jesus," Tuco said. "I was just gonna go talk to the guy, I didn't want to start a war."

Walter couldn't stop laughing. "What, you just gonna march in there, ask to speak to the head asshole? They kill you for sure, man, put you down in the bottom of Newton Creek. No, I don't think so. Besides, this is gonna be fun. Oh, God, this gonna be the funniest t'ing happen 'round here for years. Come on, baby, fire this pig up and let's get back to the shop and get this mother set up."

The three of them in one room, Walter and the two ex-cops, were an imposing sight. Three big, mean, hard bastards, looking at each other, grinning broadly. "Hell, yes, we'll do it," the white one said.

"Do it for nothing," the black one said. "Shoulda done it long ago, you ask me."

"Just make sure," Walter said, "after tonight, avoid this neighborhood for a while. We gonna get the hornets all stirred up for sure. And I don't have to tell you, this is the end of this little security detail you been running for us. Ain't gonna be much left to watch over, after this, I don't think."

"That'll be the day," the black one growled at him, "I let these little shitbirds dictate where I can go."

"Yah, man, come on. No matter what happen today, they still gonna be here tomorrow. No point in bein' stupid about this. Just do like we said, go 'round and disrupt business, put a few of the little bastards in the hospital. From the time you hit their first sales team, you maybe got a half hour before they come lookin' for you, and you better be headed for home before that. And don't get caught with the dope and the guns in your car, either. Make sure ya dump alla that shit someplace where it ain't gonna do no more damage."

Tuco began to feel like a passenger on an overloaded truck with no brakes, headed down a big hill.

Two thirteen-year-old boys were hanging out on the corner of Troutman and Knickerbocker, watching the cars go by. A car pulled over to the curb, and one of them sauntered over, but when the driver's side window rolled down, he stopped in his tracks. This guy was no crack smoker.

The driver glowered at him. "You fucks," he snarled, "sold this shit to my granddaughter." He swung the car door open and got out. "I've come to give it back." Without a word, the boy backed away. From a doorway behind him, his enforcer stepped out onto the sidewalk. He was older, larger, and he was pulling a nine-millimeter pistol out of his jacket pocket.

"Get your ass back in the car," he snarled. "Back in—"

He didn't get to finish his sentence, because a large black man walking down Knickerbocker turned up Troutman behind him and hit him in the back of the head with a leather-covered sap. The kid crumpled to the sidewalk, his pistol slipping from his hand. The two thirteen-year-olds fled. The fourth kid, across the street, the one actually holding the crack, was slower to react, and the driver caught him before he'd reached the end of the block. In the next few seconds, he lost the crack he had been carrying and received several cracked ribs. The enforcer, still unconscious, got the same. The two ex-cops got into the car.

"Got the dope?"

"Yep. Got the gun?"

"Right here. Next." The scene was repeated several times in the next hour.

Tuco and Walter sat inside the Ford van. It was parked on St. Nicholas, and they watched the activity across the street, down the block. It had started with the arrival of two kids. They'd come running up the block from Troutman, gone charging into the brick building. Ten minutes later, another one showed up, coming from the other direction. A few minutes later, sirens started up.

"Ambulances," Walter said. "Cops'll be next, tryin' to stop a drug war." He chuckled.

"This is getting ugly," Tuco said.

"Told you before," Walter said, "they in a high-risk occupation." In the gathering dark they watched a steady stream of gang members leave the building. Walter waited until they were all gone.

"You ready?"

"Walter," Tuco said, "this is my problem. I don't know if I should've been smarter about this or what, but it's still my problem, and I don't want to make it yours. Most of those guys in there know me, and I know them. The worst thing that could happen is that I could take a beating, that's all. I don't want it to be worse than it has to be."

"Too late for that now," Walter said, his voice low and quiet. "It's already worse. We got something runnin' tomorrow, in case you forgot. You a part of it. What are we supposed to do if you're in the hospital with a broken head? There ain't nobody on the bench can get up and play for you. Matter-of-fact, Stoney knew we were doing this, he'd have both of our asses, and he'd be right." All this comes from drinking beer in the morning, Walter thought. It addles your thinking, and no good ever came of it. "You said you wanted to be on the team. That means you and me go in there, deliver our message, come back out in one piece. The decision you gotta make right now is, if you're on the team, you gotta start actin' like it. No more of this chargin' around on your own. Now, what's it gonna be?"

It amazed Tuco that a man as big and heavy as Walter could be so light on his feet. He'd expected him to go clomping up the steps, but Walter seemed to flow along beside him, noiseless as a house cat sneaking out the back door. Once inside, they took a quick look around. Not much to see, all of the doors and most of the interior walls on the first floor were missing, as well as the stairs to the second floor.

"It's an old trick," Walter whispered, looking around for something to stand on to reach the floor above, but there was nothing. He considered the fire escape, but something that obvious had to be booby-trapped.

"Hoist me up," Tuco whispered in his ear.

"No," Walter whispered back. "We stay together."

"There's gotta be a ladder up there, and I can't hoist you, you's obeast."

Not only fat, Walter thought, but ugly too. Have to remember to use that one on somebody. "All right," he said. "You be goddamn careful. You don't find a ladder, you come right back down."

"Yassuh."

Walter got down on one knee and motioned Tuco down next to him. "All right," he whispered in Tuco's ear. "I pick you up, just high enough to stick your head through. Bound to be someone up there. You see 'im, wave your hand, so, and I let you back down. 'Im see you, just jump down. Otherwise, I lift you the rest of the way up. Got it?"

"Yeah."

Tuco stood up and Walter grabbed him by the ankles and lifted slowly until Tuco's head cleared the opening. He was right, there was a stepladder, folded up and leaning against the hallway. There wasn't much else to see, the interior walls on the second floor were still in place. There was no lookout, not that he could see, but he could hear scratching noises coming from the back of the building. Could be anything, Tuco thought, could be a rat. He motioned Walter to lift him higher, and seconds later, his heart beating wildly, he was on the second floor.

As quietly as he could, he stepped over to the ladder, still looking around for a sentry. He started to pick up the ladder, and then cursed, but silently. The stepladder was so old and rickety that you couldn't even pick it up without it making a noise, no matter how careful you were. He heard the sharp intake of breath from somewhere in the dark. He cursed inwardly again, torn between the urge to jump back down or to try to get the ladder down to Walter, noises or not, but he did not have time to do either. He heard clomping noises now, running footsteps coming in his direction. He turned the ladder up on its side and backed away silently, reaching for the .32 in his pocket, the one he'd taken away from the street kids. His hands were shaking as he tucked himself into a dark corner. There wasn't even time to blink before the watchman came rushing down the hallway and tripped over the ladder upturned in his path. His forward momentum carried him through the empty hole, and he screamed his way down to the floor below. The scream ended abruptly, with a sickening impact noise.

Tuco rushed over to the edge of the hole, fearing that Walter had been struck down by the hurtling body of the watchman, but he hadn't. He was standing there, looking up, and the watchman lay crumpled on the floor. What had he been doing in the back, Tuco wondered, if he was the watchman, why hadn't he been up front? But then he noticed that chemistry-set reek. In the old days, Dr. Jack would ruin anyone caught smoking the product. He looked down at Walter.

"Throw the ladder down," Walter whispered. "Throw down the ladder!" But even as Tuco headed for the ladder, he heard clomping footsteps again, louder this time, coming from the floor above.

"Tuco, throw down the goddam ladder!"

It was no whisper this time, and Tuco kicked the ladder down through the opening in the floor. "Watch out!" He could hear feet rushing down the stairs from the next floor up, and he tucked himself back into a dark corner, hoping he hadn't dropped the ladder on Walter's head. As the feet got to the bottom of the stairs, he heard a frightful creaking from below as Walter yanked the stepladder open and set it up. In a flash it became horribly clear to Tuco that whoever was coming would hear it, too, that they were coming hard, and that they were going to kill Walter as he climbed up the ladder. In the darkness, he could make out the figure, black on black, skidding to a stop, hands holding a gun straight out in front. Tuco recognized the face, Miguel's friend Manny from high school, and Manny had always been a mean bastard.

"Manny, no!" he yelled at the top of his lungs. Manny, startled, swung the pistol in Tuco's direction, firing as he went. Tuco could see him in the strobe-light muzzle flashes. In the enclosed hallway the noise was deafening, and he could hardly hear the snap that the .32 made. He shot Manny in the chest three times.

That ended it.

As the echoes died away, Tuco realized that it was all over. Manny was lying on his back, trying to draw his legs up, crying. Walter was still trying to get the ladder erect. Tuco put the gun back in his pocket and went over to where Manny lay dying. He knelt down next to him.

"I'm sorry, Manny. Manny, I'm really sorry."

"It hurts, Eddie. It hurts, God . . ." He had barely enough breath to cry, but he rolled his head back and forth, making mewling sounds.

"It won't hurt long, Manny." But Manny was lost in a universe of pain and regret, and the only sounds he could make were not word sounds, they were the racking sounds of a man in agony, his chest caught in a vise. In the time it took Manny to die, which seemed like an hour, but was really only seconds, Tuco reached out to him, holding his shoulder, talking to him, telling him it was going to be okay, that it would be all right, in the end, somehow or other, mourning his passing, whatever he'd been.

Walter finally made it up. In half a second he was on his knees next to Tuco. "You all right? You all right? You get shot?" He ran his hands over Tuco hurriedly. Finding nothing wet, he shook Tuco, none too gently. "Come on, we got to move! He can't hear you, he's gone."

We ain't done yet, Tuco realized. "Okay," he said, getting to his feet, taking one last look at Manny. Manny stopped moving, and seconds later his bowels voided.

"Jesus. All right, we gotta look around for Miguel."

"Man, we got one minute, then we gone. We don't want to be anywhere around here when the cops show up."

"No one around here calls the police."

"You wanna bet fifteen to life on it? Come on, check for Miguel, and let's go!"

They headed for the stairs to the third floor. There was an emaciated junkie lying on the floor by the foot of the stairs, so wasted that he barely had enough meat to knit his bones together, barely enough skin to hold them. Most of his hair was gone and his cheeks were sunken in to the point where the shape of the skull beneath was clearly visible. There were needle tracks and cigarette burn scars up and down his arms. Walter and Tuco took little notice of him on their way by.

"Eddie!" The voice was barely audible.

Tuco froze, then spun around. He didn't recognize whoever this might have been, and he had no time to ask. He turned away to go up the stairs.

"Eddie, it's me. Miguel."

It was hard to tell, even then.

14

TUCO CARRIED MIGUEL DOWN THE LADDER, HOLDING HIM IN HIS
arms without much effort. It seemed to him that he'd carried bags
of groceries that weighed more. They paused just inside the door.
Tuco looked at the body lying where it had fallen from the floor
above while Walter scouted the street. Sirens sounded in the near
distance, but they got fainter as the patrol car got farther away.
Walter turned back, saw Tuco looking at the dead watchman.
Walter shook his head.

"Broke his neck," Walter said. "Death by misadventure." Tuco
could feel Miguel laughing feebly.

"Proud of you, Eddie," he rasped, still trying to laugh. "Two
big, bad mafa's, and you did 'em both." He looked at the look of
misery on Tuco's face, still trying to laugh, but he had a coughing
fit instead.

"Street's clear, Tuco, let's go." Tuco shifted Miguel's weight to
one arm, fished the van keys out of his pocket and handed them
to Walter. They were in the van before they heard sirens again, but

again the sounds faded away without them seeing the patrol car. Walter started the engine while Tuco laid Miguel down in the back. Walter pulled a U-turn, headed down the hill.

"Wyckoff Hospital's the other way," Tuco said.

"No, no," Miguel rasped.

"Wake up, Tuco," Walter said harshly. "Got seven or eight former badasses in there with busted ribs. You wanna go in there with him? Besides, first stop for us is down by the Grand Avenue Bridge. We got to chuck that pistol of yours into the canal. Wipe it off nice and clean."

Tuco looked around for a rag or a paper towel, but the van was empty. He took off his shirt and began wiping his prints off the .32. "I'm sorry," he told Miguel, not looking up. "I guess we hafta take you to Woodhull."

"'S' ok," Miguel answered. "I jus' wanna die in peace, without somebody squeezin' my nuts, burnin' me and askin' a lot a questions."

Tuco didn't understand what he meant. "Miguel, what happened to you?"

Miguel shrugged weakly. "Dunno. Hepatitis, AIDS, maybe. There's a virus you get from mice, coulda been that. Lotta mice, back in the house. I'm glad you come and got me, Eddie. I'm glad you come for me. I didn't think you would, after last time."

Walter turned down Metropolitan, then turned off and cut through a trucking-company parking lot. There was a high fence at the back of the lot, and a canal on the other side of the fence. There was a junkyard on the far side of the canal, and metal scrap from the junkyard spilled over the bank and down into the greasy black water, which reflected the lights of the Grand Avenue Bridge. Walter pulled the van to a stop down behind a parked semi.

"You got that wiped down real good?"

"Yeah."

"Okay. Go on, get it right into the middle, if you can." Tuco left the door open behind him and slipped through a hole in the chain-link fence. He did as he was told, and returned.

"Find a pay phone," Miguel rasped at him. "Call in shots fired, back at the house. Let the cops burn it all down." Tuco looked inquiringly over at Walter.

"Why not," Walter said. He backed the van out, drove back onto Metropolitan. Two blocks down there was a pay phone across from a gas station. He pulled over. "I'll do it," he said. "Wait here."

Miguel waited until Walter got out and chunked his door shut. "Eddie," he said, his voice very quiet. "You trust this guy? Would he fuck you?"

"I trust him," Tuco said.

"Don't answer so quick. Think about it! You trust him?"

Tuco thought, then nodded his head. "Yeah."

"Awright. Just remember, I gave you the choice."

"What are you talking about?"

Miguel waited until Walter got back in the van. "Listen care-ful, now. I ain't got the breath to do this but once. G'wan, get us away from that phone," he said. "Then pull over some place. I gotta tell you a story."

It was the money, finally, that was the problem.

Bringing in cocaine from Colombia and Peru was not a prob-lem, bringing in smack from Turkey was not a problem, distribu-tion, wholesaling, retailing, collecting the proceeds, these had all been problems once, but they had all been solved, worked out long ago. The inevitable percentages of loss had been factored into the overall equation. A certain amount of product was intercepted by the government. Sometimes it could be repurchased, sometimes it could not. A certain number of lives were lost; the work was not without its dangers, after all. But in countries where being unemployed meant starvation, and where the annual per capita income was something less than the price of a pair of box seats at Shea, there were always new recruits ready to run the risks, and the machinery hummed along.

But how do you get the money home? It was a problem that constantly needed new solutions. Every new subterfuge, every new twist and turn, sooner or later, would be met with a new initiative from the Internal Revenue Service, a new form, a new schedule this or that, another inspector asking questions. Every cash transaction over a certain amount was scrutinized. You couldn't move cash through casinos anymore. Offshore banks were not as secure as they had once been. The stock market was already a pool of sharks, half of whom owed their souls to Internal Revenue. And no tough guy ever really wanted to own a furniture store in Hackensack or a restaurant in Carlstadt. The problems those poor bastards had to deal with were generally too much for people in the dope business to handle.

It had been Dr. Jack who had come up with the newest wrinkle, and it had been simplicity itself. I have a cousin, he told them, he works in a junkyard in Brooklyn, and they ship truck parts in containers to Colombia. Why not just smuggle the money out? Pay off someone working in the place, and it would be as easy as falling out of bed.

All the parties thought about it for a while. An approach was made to someone in the junkyard, and a trial run went off smoothly. Upon further reflection, the idea seemed to have merit. The appropriate threats were made on both sides, packages were made up and inserted into oil pans, drive shafts, fuel tanks.

In the beginning, it had worked, mostly due to Dr. Jack's fearsome reputation. Everyone at the Brooklyn end had known that

he was smarter than they were, meaner, more ruthless. Still, what
he had foreseen from the beginning had, ultimately, come to pass.

Steal a brick of cocaine and it sticks to you like flypaper. It's not
as if you can cash it in somewhere. Try to sell it wholesale and you
are likely to get shot for your trouble, or arrested when your
prospective buyer turns out to work for Uncle Sam. And if word of
the transaction ever gets back to the original owner, you are dead.
Cop a one-half-inch-thick pad of C-notes, though, and everyone is
your friend. There are no risky transactions necessary to render your
newfound wealth into spendable form. You can stick a few in your
pocket anytime without fear of getting busted for possession. Take
one out, throw it across a bar or a bodega counter, and no one will
look at you twice.

Their inside man, Jimmy the Hat, had started skimming. A little here and a little there, in the vain hope that, in the flow of so
much green paper, nobody would notice. Miguel had been waiting
for it, and it was his signal to start skimming himself, but much
more seriously. He laughed as he told the story, amused by the
stunned reactions of his audience.

"But why?" Tuco asked him. "Why bother? You already had
plenty of money."

"To beat them! To win! What else is there? And I had them,
Eddie, I beat them all. Nobody knew what to do, nobody knew
where it was going. Everybody in Cali was ready to pull his brother's toenails out to make him tell what he did with the money. It
was so funny. The goons from Cali were following Jimmy the Hat
around everywhere, but they weren't sure it was him. I was gonna
steal a whole shipment. It woulda been great, except not for
Jimmy. Then, you know, I got sick . . ."

"When my lieutenants weren't afraid anymore, they got together and boxed me up in the house. I couldn't get away, couldn't
get to the doctor, couldn't watch TV, nothing. They tried really

hard to get me to tell them where I hid it." He held out a wasted arm with a row of round, angry red scars and infected, black, needle tracks. He grinned broadly. "I told them shit." Tuco turned away from the gruesome sight.

"So that was how he knew you. Every time he saw me, he would think I was you, for just a second. He told me he met you on the bus."

"Oh, he did. When this whole thing got started, we waved a little money at him, and he came right around. But we hadda make him understand that the shit was serious, you know. I think we did too good a job, for a while I thought he would never start stealing, but the money is too strong for some people. Seeing it, there in his hands, I knew it would get to be too much for him."

"Was it worth it?" Tuco looked at the wreck his cousin had become. "Look at you, man. Was it worth it?"

Miguel tried to shrug. "What the fuck," he said. "You know, once I saw this thing on TV, this thing about lions. There's one lion, the baddest one, he's the only one that gets laid. He don't hunt, his only jobs are fighting and fucking. All of the other males are trying to beat him. He only lasts a few years, then his time is over." He laid back on the seat, exhausted. "I had my turn."

"So it was Jimmy," Walter asked, "shot Marty and Fat Tommy?"

"Yeah," Miguel said, his voice feeble. "When he heard from the Colombians that they wanted an accounting, he knew he was in the crosshairs. At first, he was gonna just put the money back, but then one of my idiot lieutenants told him that we had shorted them too. Last I heard, he had cooked up some scheme to scam the money out of you guys. I guess it didn't play the way he'd thought."

"That's why 'e set up Marty," Walter said, almost to himself. "But he couldn't get anythin' out of Marty, Marty didn't know nothing, so 'e shot 'im, to give 'imself time to go after Tommy." He shook his head.

He put the van in gear, headed for Woodhull. Miguel lay limp, his head being rolled back and forth by the motions of the moving vehicle. He showed no signs of consciousness, and Tuco began to wonder if he was dead. Walter pulled the van over to the side of the road, across the street from the rusted hulk of a hospital.

"Tuco, you need a hand?"

"No," Tuco said. "I'll carry him in." He got out, and to his surprise, Miguel struggled upright and put his arm around Tuco's shoulders. He couldn't really walk, but the two of them made their way across the street. Miguel whispered in Tuco's ear on the way.

Tuco had to strain to hear him. "It's in two cardboard boxes," he said. "They're in your mother's storage closet in the basement of her building."

"How much is there?"

Miguel's voice was almost gone. "Never counted it. Couple hundred thou, maybe."

"Well, what do you want me to do with it?"

"Yours now. I don't give a shit."

They shouldered their way through the emergency-room doors. The room behind the doors was filled with unfortunates, justifiably afraid. Tuco found two empty plastic chairs.

"Nah, fuck this," Miguel said. "Lay me down on the floor and you take off. I wanna lay down in a bed one more time. If you lay me on the floor, they gotta do something with me. Okay? Then go. Listen, Eddie, it's your game now. You wanna be a lion, you wanna be a dog, 's up to you."

Tuco did not want to run out on Miguel, but he did not want to stay and watch him die, either. He wasn't sure he had the strength for it. He helped his cousin slide out of the chair and down onto the floor.

"Eddie, why'd you come?"

"Don't know. I was thinking about shooting you."

Miguel laughed for the last time. "Too late," he rasped. "You know, I always been curious, about what comes next. Is that funny or what?" He closed his eyes, and did not notice when Tuco got up and left.

15

WALTER COULDN'T QUITE DECIDE IF HE THOUGHT TUCO WAS AN exceptionally intelligent kid with a few major blind spots, or if he just had that cockroach ability to evade the descending foot, that facility for self-preservation that was of no use to anyone else. He had known plenty of people like that, people who had the sort of luck that didn't rub off. Being in their company did you no good. The grand piano falling from an upstairs window would glance off a flagpole and hit you instead of them.

The three of them sat in a coffee shop on the corner of Fourteenth Street and Avenue B, on the slum side of the street. Across the way was Stuyvesant Town. The buildings there looked like project buildings, but they were not. The people living there were unrelentingly middle class, and mostly white. Fat Tommy would never have chosen this coffee shop, under any circumstances, not when, right on the other side of Avenue A there was an exceptionally good Greek bakery. Walter sat in a back corner booth with Tuco and Stoney. He listened to Tuco telling last night's story. He'd left out the part about the pictures, the van, and the prostitute, but Walter decided to keep his peace, all that would come out later, and it didn't apply to their present problem, anyway.

The kid had covered the rest of it pretty thoroughly, though, from the two ex-cops rampaging through the neighborhood to the incursion into the gang house, the two defenders he had killed and how he'd known them from high school, to the trip to Woodhull with Miguel, and what Miguel had told them on the way.

Stoney had listened to it all in silence, but now that Tuco was done he had a question. "What were you planning to do with Dr. Jack?"

Tuco looked miserable. "If he gave me what I wanted, I guess I woulda walked out. If he didn't, I was gonna shoot him. I had it all worked out in my head, you know, why it was okay."

"After you put eight or ten of his guys in the hospital, why would he give you anything at all?"

"He woulda thought that was funny."

"What was it you wanted from him, anyway?"

Walter watched Tuco struggle with it. Gotta be hard, he thought, after everything the kid has done to try to prove he's not a moron, and now there's no way for him to tell this without laying himself open. He did it, though, Walter watched him decide to tell the truth. Not a pro yet, Walter thought. He couldn't think of a good lie fast enough. He's got it so bad for this girl, she's all he can think about, so he told Stoney why he did it, but he still skipped right over the parts about the van and the pictures.

When he was done, Stoney spoke slowly and carefully, removing all inflection from his voice. "Let me see if I understand this correctly," he said. "You fell in love with a street prostitute. You took her to your apartment and left her there, and then you went after her pimp, who happens to be the local drug kingpin, and also your cousin."

Tuco belatedly remembered what she had done for them, and started to tell that part of it. "She—"

"Did I hear all of that right? And you think she's waiting for you right now?" He backed off. "Okay, all right," he said. "We'll come back to that later. Your cousin told you that it was Jimmy the Hat who popped Tommy and Marty?"

"Yeah."

"You believe him?"

"He was dying, boss. He had nothing left to lie for. Besides, it was Jimmy skimming that got this whole mess started, he had to know that they were watching him. Probably knows that they were watching the junkyard too. That has to make you nervous, make you a little desperate, get you to do stupid things."

Stoney looked over at Walter. "You seen Jimmy? We know where he's at?"

"Nope. Don't answer the phone, nobody at his apartment."

"You went and looked?"

"Yah," Walter said sourly. "Early this morning. 'E gone."

"At least," Stoney said, "now we know what the Colombians are looking for. They still can't be sure we're the ones that have it now."

Walter sat listening to this exchange, watching Stoney sitting, drinking lousy coffee, being rational, considering someone else's feelings, even. This new Stoney was a lot like the one he'd known years ago, but he kept wondering when the other one would reassert himself, the irrational, impatient, intolerant, red-faced, damn-the-torpedoes maniac. And which one was the real one? He cleared his throat into the developing silence, and the two white faces turned in his direction and waited.

He looked from one face to the other, from the fatherless young Nuyorican to the middle-aged Italian hard-on that the kid had attached himself to. He remembered his own grandfather, long dead now, in the cold waters somewhere off the Georges Banks. In the years before the old man had gone on that last trip, he'd done his best to impart the hard-won nuggets of wisdom he'd learned: how to take a punch, how to stand up, the trouble with being unnecessarily cruel, how to be a man. He'd done all of that when he was past the age for it, having done it once already for his own son, Walter's father, who had predeceased him. Even now, Walter talked to him from time to time. He couldn't imagine the loneliness, the lost feeling from being without the company of a man who would feel that obligation, as his grandfather had, and try in some way to fulfill it.

"Those Colombians," he said, "been here for some time, seeing what's what and who's who. They know, by now, that we are an, aah, unusual enterprise. They know their money passed through the junkyard, and not all of it got home. But they still aren't sure, was it us, or was it Jimmy? Or maybe both. What's in the boxes? You want what's behind door number one or door number two? You remember that show? Trade your new couch and bedroom set for what's behind the curtain. These guys, they want the couch and the bedroom set, and what's behind the other doors too. Don't matter what it is. And after they get it, they'll shoot the game show host, that girl that stood in front of the curtain, the announcer, half of the audience. Then they'll go home. 'At's their style. Yes?"

The newer, calmer Stoney shrugged. "More or less."

"So," Walter continued, "they don't care who it was took their money, don't care what's in the boxes. They gotta figure at least some of their money's in one or two of 'em. They don't know what else we're into, but a good guess would be, if we're movin' it, it's gotta be worth taking. Then last night, we went around, they think, kicking ass and settling old scores. Means we're moving out. They're gonna want to jump us, take us down, get their money

back, my guess is they'll do it today. You got some unpleasant sur-
prises planned for them up in the Bronx?"

"Yeah. Yeah, I do."

"You sound like you got reservations."

"Nah, I suppose not. We should still be all right. But this thing
with Jimmy makes it a little stickier, you know what I mean? Him
being the one who shot Tommy, if Tuco has it right, just makes it
harder to walk away from this."

"They're in a walk-up right on Troutman. You think we'd be
better just going after them? They'd never expect that."

"No, we can't. Think like Tommy thinks. They have to go
home with the impression that they did what they came here to
do. Wrapped up all the loose ends. It's the only way to know that
when this is all over, it's really over. No, we gotta still go with the
original plan. You're right, Walter, it'll probably play even better,
after last night."

"Then let's go do it," Walter said. "This other business, Tuco's
new girlfriend, Jimmy the Hat, and Tuco's van, that can wait." He
looked at Stoney for two counts, letting him know that he still
hadn't gotten the whole story.

"Awright."

"What about Jimmy?" Tuco asked.

Stoney looked at him. "First things first," he said. "We'll get to
him later."

Tuco pointed the Lexus uptown and headed for the Queensboro
Bridge. It was one of the few left in New York City that you could
cross without paying tribute to the MTA or the Port Authority.
Stoney sat beside him with the passenger seat tilted back, idly
looking out the window. Walter was somewhat cramped, sitting in
the backseat.

"So," Walter said. "What is in the boxes?"

"When we took 'em up that first day, they were full of rags and newspapers," Stoney said. "Now they got dope in 'em. Low-grade shit, cocaine that's mostly rat poison, some very lousy weed, stuff like that. Some pistols that nobody would want. A little cop money, a few thou to our friends in blue."

"Where'd you come up with all of that in one day?"

"Guy next door," Stoney said, "in that big, empty warehouse. I went in there to tell him we had something going. We don't want him all upset, have shit going on in his own backyard he don't know about. I figured we gotta compensate him for lost business, so I bought what's in the boxes from him. I was gonna buy some hand grenades he's got in there, but I didn't want the newspapers going nuts. Too much publicity, attract too much attention. I don't think our little subterfuge needs that much extra scrutiny."

"Yah, man," Walter said dryly, "the press always overreacts so to a little ordinance."

Tuco turned down Troutman Street. They could see the cops from three blocks away.

Stoney sat up in his seat, fully awake. "Oh, boy," he said. "Turn off, Tuco, turn right here, go on down to Flushing. You guys weren't kidding, you really did stir 'em up." There was yellow plastic crime-scene tape closing off Troutman where it crossed St. Nicholas, blocking them from their junkyard just down the street. "Go on around the block, go up Wyckoff, then just back up from the corner. Park right out in front of the office door, don't bother with the parking lot." He turned in his seat. "Walter, as soon as he's stopped, you take off. You got your phone with you?"

"Yep."

"Okay, get gone as soon as you can. Tuco, you and me, we're gonna roll up the grate on the front door, go inside, grab two boxes, one each, then we're gone. Lock the front door on the way out, and we're outta here. Got it?"

"Yassuh, boss."

"No running," Stoney said as Tuco was backing up the street. "Running always attracts predators. Just nice and smooth, no wasted motion."

It was quick and easy and over almost before it started. Tuco backed right up to the door, Walter walked away calmly, and Tuco and Stoney were in and then out, carrying their boxes. Stoney locked the center lock on the front door, leaving the gate up, while Tuco put the boxes in the trunk. A few of the cops on the corner looked idly at them, but none of them moved in their direction or even paused from what they were doing. The two of them got back in the car. "No running," Stoney said again. "Drive away nice and easy."

"Take a different route," Stoney told Tuco. "Back over the Queensboro Bridge, that was good. Go straight up First, all the way uptown, and go over the Willis Avenue Bridge." He turned on his cell phone and called Walter, told him they would take a little longer to get there.

First Avenue changes character as you make your way uptown. Tuco and Stoney picked it up in Midtown, at a corner where a muscular one-legged black guy in a wheelchair has been panhandling for a generation. Turning north from there you pass by an amazing array of places to spend your money, street vendors hawking phony Rolex watches and Cartier jewelry, stores large, small, and in between. Anything anyone makes, anywhere, you can buy in Manhattan. You just have to look.

Then, as you go farther north, you pass into residential neighborhoods occupied by rich people, and the streets go quieter, cleaner, well patrolled. Trees grow through well-tended square holes in the pavement, awnings jut out from the larger buildings, where doormen in silly uniforms stand guard behind glass doors. This is a much different New York City from the one Tuco had grown up in. Even Stoney, before he had moved to New Jersey, had lived in a harsher, louder, and more hostile city than this one.

Continue north, and in the space of a few traffic lights around 106th Street, the world turns on its head as you enter a zone of ancient tenements and midrise projects, horizontal and vertical slums, loud radios, double-parked cars, car-service garages, and the occasional restored brownstone or carriage house to make you wonder what could have been. Once over the Willis Avenue Bridge, of course, and you're in the South Bronx, which is one of those places where there's no pretending. Everyone there understands that only the strong survive.

"All right," Stoney said. They were stopped at the light where Tuco was waiting to turn left onto Southern Boulevard. "We're gonna do this a little different, this time. Doo-Doo ain't there, for one thing; I got a key. I'm gonna open that personnel door, okay, you give me the boxes out of the trunk. As soon as I'm in, you take off. Go around the block, you'll see a building that used to be a Chinese laundry, still says so, there's a painted sign up on the wall. Pull down that alley, you'll see a Mercedes ragtop in there. Park next to the Mercedes. Straight in front of you will be the back of that factory building next door, go right in there, you'll see some stairs. Take the stairs to the fourth floor, I'll meet you there, up in front. Got it?"

Why does he always wait to the last minute, Tuco wondered. "Drop you, 'round the block, down the alley by the building with the painted sign, park by the Mercedes. Go up to the fourth floor. How you gonna get there?"

"I broke a hole through Doo-Doo's back wall last night," Stoncy said.

"Mercedes belong to whoever runs the warehouse?"

"Naturally. No one will mess with this car if it's parked next to his. So he tells me." Stoney called Walter on the phone again. "You all set up?"

"I had to relocate. Our friends are sitting in that same gypsy cab they had last time, but they're across the street in that parking lot next to that parts place." Stoney could hear a note of stress in Walter's voice. "Don't like this new spot. I can see but I'm too far away to help much if things go badly."

"Aaay, Walter," Stoney said, imitating Fat Tommy. "Don'a you worry, you gonna like, you'll see."

Tuco pulled up in front of the roll-up door.

"Remember what I said," Stoney told him. "No running. Nice and smooth."

"Nice and smooth." Tuco got out on the driver's side. A quick glance across the street, he saw the same Lincoln town car, a lot of heads inside. He didn't count. He opened the trunk while Stoney was opening the door. By the time he got the boxes out, Stoney was waiting for them. Stoney leaned over to speak in his ear. "Wait till I'm in. Nice and smooth, okay?"

"Yassuh, boss."

He slammed the trunk lid down, got back in behind the wheel. I should clean all the rubbish out of this car, he thought. The metal door banged closed behind Stoney, and Tuco put the car in drive and pulled away slowly.

Tuco clicked the car alarm as he walked away, for whatever good it would do. He jumped up on what had once been a loading dock and walked into the darkness. To his right was a stairwell shrouded in inky blackness. To his left he heard voices, subdued murmuring, and he assumed that off in that direction there had to be a room of some kind where the regular business of the establishment was being conducted. None of his affair.

He made his way into the stairwell, paused until his eyes adjusted somewhat, and climbed the stairs as quietly as he could, trying to see everything he could on the way up, just in case he was in a much greater hurry on the way down. At each floor some light intruded where the stairwell door had once been. On the fourth floor he went through, listening intently. He made out the subdued sound of Stoney's voice and headed in that direction.

Stoney was behind a low wall in the front of the building, looking with binoculars out through a hole where a window had once been. Hearing Tuco's approach, he put his binoculars aside and half-turned. "Tuco," he said. "This gentleman's name is William. He's been kind enough to allow us the use of his facility."

A man who Tuco had not seen sitting in the shadows about ten yards away stuffed something back into his green army fatigue jacket. He nodded.

"Tuco." His voice told of years of cigarettes and whiskey.

"William." Very polite, Tuco thought, when everybody's armed. Everybody but me.

"Tuco, do me a favor," Stoney said, "and sit down on something. You can watch if you want, but don't stand up."

"Okay." He found a place, settled in to watch.

"Hey, Walter." Stoney's voice was quiet as he spoke into the phone.

"Yah, man."

"What are our friends doing? I can see the car from here, but I can't see inside it."

"They just sitting, man. Enjoying the afternoon, takin' in the sights. You get that kid out of sight?"

"He's right here with me."

"All right, two shooters, getting out of the car. Got raincoats on. They carrying firepower under the jackets, I think. Just the two guys, plus one in the car, and a driver, same guy as yesterday. 'At's four altogether. The two shooters are moving now, taking their time, going out in front of the store. I can't see 'em anymore."

"I see 'em. They're just going up to the corner, crossing over. Out of my line of sight now. I don't wanna hang out the window to look. Can you see which way they're turning?"

"No, man, not yet, not yet, okay, here they come, headed for the front door. Okay, the one's on his knees, working on the lock, the other one's covering him with his coat. That lock should take him five, ten minutes, no more. He's pretending to drink something out of a bag. Better make the call."

Stoney hit a button on his cell phone. "Yeah, gimme Detective Earle, please. Roger Earle. Yeah, Detective Earle? We spoke yesterday? Oh, he's doing better, they tell me. I stopped in this morning, first thing. Well, semiconscious, but out of it. Don't recognize anyone, I don't think. Anyhow, that deal I told you about? Going down right now. Yeah, Southern Boulevard. No, Jesus, no, next door to there, next door, little garage building. Yes, sir. Well, thanks, when he's talking, I will tell him you asked. Thank you, sir." Stoney ended the call, and the man in the fatigue jacket snorted in amused disgust.

Stoney shrugged. "Hey," he said. "If you got a stick, you use it. Right? Shouldn't be long now." He redialed Walter.

"What's up with our buddies? They in yet?"

"Five, ten minutes, I told ya, man."

Stoney looked at his watch, tried to relax. A few minutes passed, he looked at his watch again. "Walter, what's up?"

"Still workin' on the door. Aah, looks like they got it. Goin' in live, man." From far below they heard a popping sound, like far-away firecrackers.

"Oh, nice," William rasped. "Nice people you deal with."

"Yeah," Stoney said. "You know what they say, William. Them that lives by the sword . . ."

"Dies by the sword. Will you look at all the fucking cops. You musta got the whole precinct here."

The cops ran through the drill with practiced thoroughness. Cruisers converged on the building from both directions, the first cars forming a semicircle in front of the garage, the ones lagging behind blocking the street a block away on each side. They did it quietly, no sirens, no screeching tires, no bullhorns.

Stoney sat down, rubbing his neck. He picked up his phone again. "Walter," he said. "I can't see from here. What's happening?"

"They still inside. Cops being very cool, just waiting. Still being cool. Those two still inside. Hey, maybe they got cell phones, too, I never thought of that. Their guy across the street could warn them. No, they don't, here they come, each one got a box, don't see nothing, oh, shit . . ." The crisp sound of gunfire ripped the silence, followed by shouted instructions in English and in Spanish. "First one dropped his box, went for his gun. They musta shot him eight, ten times. Other one's been winged in the leg, he's standing there on one foot, hands in the air. Now he's on the ground. Okay, dudes in flak jackets coming up the sidewalk, throwing grenades in through the door . . ."

They could both hear and feel the stun grenades going off.

"'At's it, children, the party's over."

"Yeah? What about the two in the car?"

"Oh, yeah, I forgot about them. They went inside the parts store."

"All right. Just wait, see where they go."

They waited in silence.

After ten minutes or so, William, the man in the fatigue jacket, stood up, stretched, and excused himself. "I gotta go tend to business," he said. "All them cops down there with nothing to do make me nervous."

Walter seemed to have the same thought, because a few minutes later Stoney's phone rang. "Why don't you two get out of there," he said to Stoney. "That buildin's a bad place for you and Tuco. A few of them bluebellies get curious and go lookin', you got no excuse for bein' there. I'll stay here and watch these two, they still in the store, anyway."

"You think you can stay with them, see where they go?"

"I find your lack of confidence disturbin', whitey. Anyway, I bet you this guy figures his business here is done, he gonna go and catch a plane, I think."

"You don't think he'd stick around, see to Jimmy the Hat?"

"Nope. Look at it, Stoney. He got one shooter goin' to jail, the other one goin' to the morgue. He don't want no parts of New York City right now, he goin' home. If they didn't do Jimmy already, they'll send someone else later on."

"Okay. Once those two get rolling, call me and let me know where they go."

Back in Stoney's Lexus, Tuco and Stoney headed for the Triborough Bridge. "Where to?" Tuco said.

"Manhattan."

"Downtown again, where I got you this morning?"

"Madam Cho's, you know where she is, on Third?"

"Yah."

"Don't give me that look, I just gotta drop off a key. Besides, she's closed for renovations."

"Oh, really."

"Yeah, really. Then I want to go to Port Authority. I'm taking the bus out to Jersey, I'm gonna sleep in my own bed tonight." Or on my own couch, at least, he thought. "I'll take the bus back in tomorrow, call you when I get in, you can come pick me up, we'll go wrap things up at Troutman."

"You forgetting about Jimmy?"

Stoney shot him a look. "I ain't forgetting a thing."

"You don't figure he'll be hiding in the bushes, waiting to cap you when you come walking up your sidewalk? Be a bitch if he did, after all this."

"My guess is, Jimmy is duct-taped to a chair somewhere in Brooklyn, piece of clothesline tied real tight around his neck."

Tuco shook his head. "I got a feeling he's still out there. I bet I know where too."

"Yeah? Where is that?"

"He said he had a buddy that ran a chop shop up in Hunts Point. Said the guy cut up old buses, sent the parts to South America. He told me that was where he got the idea for truck parts."

"What makes you think he's up there?"

"I dunno, just a feeling."

"Where up in Hunts Point? Did he say?"

"No, but he said you could see the place from the Bruckner."

The muscles in Stoney's jaw clenched as he ground his teeth. "Don't sound that hard to find." He looked at his watch. "All right," he said, "tomorrow, you and me, we'll take a ride, go see if you're right. Tell you the truth, I doubt we find anything, but it don't hurt to go look. We'll go into Troutman first, take care of business there, then we'll go to Hunts Point."

"You gonna close up? Sell the junkyard?"

"Nothing to sell," Stoney said. "We were subleasing, sort of. Won't take much to wind it up and move on."

"What do I do about Miguel's money?"

"Miguel, being dead, ain't got any money."

"You know what I mean."

"Yeah. I was you, I'd grab the boxes and move 'em somewhere safe. You can't be sure what Miguel said or who he talked to. Walter and I can watch your back, if you want. Beyond that, you need to talk to Fat Tommy. Financial chicanery is his department, not mine."

The stop at Madam Cho's was just a drive-by, and from there all the way to Port Authority, Stoney tried to think of what to say about Tuco's prostitute. There's no way, he wanted to tell him, that this is gonna fly. But however that worked, hormones in the blood, falling ego boundaries, temporary insanity, whatever it was, he didn't feel like he could beat it. Tuco pulled up next to the line of yellow taxis. Stoney opened his door and stuck his foot out.

"Look, Tuco," he said. "I'll leave my phone on tonight, okay? You want to talk, just call me. Okay?"

Tuco had forgotten all about the girl. His face turned red, and he gripped the steering wheel hard. He stared straight ahead. "I'll be okay."

"I ain't saying . . . anything. But I'll leave my phone on. Okay?"

"Okay."

"Talk to you in the morning."

"Okay."

The buildings of lower Manhattan were all lit up. After a while they fused together in his mind, so that he did not see them as individual things anymore, but as one single ungodly apparition hanging low in the night air, a UFO, complete with the lights of the cars on the FDR Drive and the Brooklyn Bridge blinking around the edges.

He knew it was stupid, sitting on a park bench on the promenade in the dark. It would have been suicide in most parks in the city; in Brooklyn Heights it was merely stupid. That was okay with Tuco, though, "stupid" was his theme word of the day, the way it had been so many times before, stupid, stupid, stupid.

He had wanted to tell her that there was no Dr. Jack to be afraid of anymore, that she was free. She could have then chosen to leave for that reason, but maybe she had known it all along. Then again, maybe she was not really free at all, maybe she was driven by forces he could not comprehend. In any case, she was gone, and he did not understand. It had turned out to be a horrible thing, this delusion that he had found someone, that he had connected, finally and for real, that he had escaped his prison of isolation and loneliness. To wake up and find that the bars were still there after all was more than he could bear, so he sat on the bench in the dark and cried silently. For himself or for her? He asked himself the question inwardly, but the words and ideas fell into such a yawning pit of emptiness that they lost all meaning and relevance. So far did he feel himself from human warmth and compassion that his park bench in the dark might as well have been on the moon.

Stoney's footsteps echoed in the empty house. He'd had a tingling sensation between his shoulder blades, standing on the front steps and unlocking the front door, but there had been no Jimmy waiting to shoot him.

The house didn't feel as if it had any real connection to him. His clothes were still hanging in the closet, his car would be parked in the driveway once he got his license straightened out, his tools were in the garage, but still, it had a hotel feeling to it. I sanded these floors when we bought this place, he reminded himself, but looking down into the shiny urethane finish he didn't see anything of himself looking out. There ought to be a connection, he thought. I should feel something, I should feel like I belong here, that this is my place, that this is home.

Maybe it was that night at the Royal, he thought, or staying in Mrs Cho's studio. Maybe it was just being alone, having no one to answer to. No Donna mad at me for drinking too much or not coming home, asking did I remember doing this or that. No kids to make me feel guilty for something I forgot to do, no Tommy giving me that puss first thing in the morning.

He hadn't had a drink in, what had it been, two or three days, he didn't remember how many it was, even. Long enough, anyhow, for the shakes and sweats and night horrors to back off a little. Do I miss it? he asked himself. Damn right. But I got some distance from it now.

He picked up the phone and went into the back room with it, sat in his chair. He dialed the number from memory.

"Hi, Benny, it's me, Stoney." He listened to Benny talking in his ear, only half his mind on what Benny was saying, the rest of him wondering what it was about calling Benny that he found so reassuring, so comfortable.

"What's that? I'm sorry. No, I can't go tonight, Benny. I had to come out to Jersey. Because I live here, that's why. I ain't been in the house for a few days, and I had to come back to check on it. No, she ain't here, she's at her sister's house. Yeah, well, we had a falling out. No, she didn't throw me out, but she's probably gonna. I guess I knocked her around a little bit. Easy, Benny, I don't remember doing it. Well, yeah, I was drinking, what kind of a question is that?

"Yeah, I know I need to go to a meeting, Benny, I ain't trying to stall you, but I been dodging bullets here, last few days. No, real ones. I think it's all over now. Why?" He hadn't thought of it. "I dunno, hanging out in lousy neighborhoods. Poor company.

Listen, Benny, you and me, we'll sit down in a couple days, over a plate a linguini I'll tell you the whole story. No, tomorrow's no good, I gotta tie up a few loose ends tomorrow. No, Jesus, no, nothing like that. Day after. Yeah, I promise."

"On one condition," Benny told him.

"Yeah, what's that?"

"You gotta do something for me tonight."

"What's that?"

"You got booze in the house?"

He hadn't thought of that. "Yeah, Benny, I do."

"Well, you gotta dump it. You gotta dump it right now, or you gotta go to a motel. I am goddam serious about this. You gotta do what I tell ya, 'cause I'm not wasting my time on somebody that ain't ready. You understand me?"

"Okay, Benny. You're right. Listen, Benny?" How to say it? "Thanks, man. I'll call you tomorrow." What a strange world, he thought. Bunch of people I don't know trying to shoot my ass this morning, guy named Benny who I don't know is trying to save it tonight.

He went into the kitchen and fished the gin and vodka bottles out of the cabinet. That's not bad, he thought. Better it should go to waste. There were some wine bottles in the hutch in the dining room. Benny probably didn't mean them. Did he? Shit. He dithered for a minute, and in that minute he could hear them, knew how they'd be calling his name in the nighttime. Get off the fence, he thought, and he went for them, brought them out into the kitchen and stood them on the counter. What else? Just listen, he told himself, and you'll hear them calling . . . Damn. Fridge in the garage half full of beer, Canadian Club high on a shelf. Two bottles of cognac, somewhere in the back room. Nyquil in the hall closet upstairs. Pint of scotch, under the car seat, tell Tuco to lose it. Better tell him to check the trunk too.

Scotch . . . Isn't there a bottle of single malt in here somewhere?

It took a while to hunt it all down. He began to feel a bit queasy, looking at it all, feeling the impact in his gut, remembering that burn and then the quick release, a bird catching the wind in his wings, and then the massive, thundering headache, the gorge rising in his throat . . .

He groped for the phone again, hit the redial button, but Benny's line was busy. Some other poor bastard, Stoney thought, getting his turn. Damn. He backed out of the room, went in the garage for the recycling can. Neighbors will think I'm a drunk, he thought, laughing out loud at the thought. That is, if falling asleep naked in the front yard didn't already give me away. He dragged the can into the kitchen, tried Benny again on the phone. Still busy.

Well, he thought, I gotta call her sooner or later, anyhow. He started to dial the number, then left off and hit the disconnect button. She had more power to hurt him than anyone he'd ever known. I almost wish I'd been shot, he thought, at least then she'd have to feel sorry for me. He looked at the telephone handset sorrowfully, thinking of the trouble it was going to bring him. Come on, he told himself. Don't sit here with this hanging over your head.

Her sister answered the phone. "Wait one minute," she said. "I'll get Donna." Well, he thought, you can't read anything into that, she never did like me.

He tucked the phone between his ear and his shoulder and uncorked a gin bottle. Start with something you don't like, he told himself, and upended the bottle, watching Boodle's finest gurgle down the drain.

"Hello." She sounded tired.

"Hey, kid, it's all over. You can come back, if you like."

"Did you find out who shot Tommy?"

"Yeah. It was one of our guys."

"Was it that boy you hired out of high school?"

"No. I don't know why you don't like him, he's a good kid. No, it was another guy, someone you never met. He was involved with some bad people, and he owed them money, and I guess that's why he did it."

"Is he in jail now?"

"No. No, he's not." Stoney opened another bottle. "I don't know for sure, but either the people he was doing business with got him, or he's in hiding."

"My God, Stoney." He upended the bottle, watched it go. "What are you doing?"

"You know, you got ears like a freakin' bat. You wouldn't believe me if I told you."

"Try me." Her tone was harsher than it had been.

"Following the instructions of Dr. Benjamin," he said sarcastically, "I am pouring a bottle of vodka down the kitchen sink. He says if I wanna stay here tonight, I gotta get rid of all the booze, so that's what I'm doing."

"Who's Dr. Benjamin?" She was half suspicious, half in shock.

He had just been smart-assing, saying Dr. Benjamin instead of Benny. He'd said it without even thinking. "He's just this guy, he's kind of helping me out. I talk to him, you know, now and then. I'm not drinking, for what it's worth, not since you left."

"Maybe I should stay away, if it's working this well." His heart sank, but he said nothing and continued to pour. "How did you find this guy?" she said.

Well, I was sitting on this park bench, sweating and shaking and seeing things that weren't there, and then this street dude came up to me and . . . sure. "Friend of mine, Arthur," he said, "put me in touch with him."

"Do I know Arthur?"

"You met Arthur, you'd remember him."

"Oh." She changed tacks. "How's Tommy doing?"

"They tell me he's coming around. Now that we don't have to worry about somebody shooting him —"

"What are we gonna do, Stoney? You really scared me, this time."

"Yeah, well. I'm sorry for that." She didn't answer, so he continued, uncomfortable with the silence. "I'm closing down the junkyard, and Tommy's gonna be sidelined for a while. Maybe we could take some time off, just me and you, go away somewhere, talk it over."

"Maybe we could," she said. "I'm gonna stay up here over the weekend, and come back Monday."

"All right," he said. "I'll see you then."

She sighed. "Okay."

When the bottles were all empty, he dragged the recycling can back out into the garage, trying not to inhale the vapors rising from it. God, he thought, but he couldn't finish the thought because he heard the warbling noise his cell phone made when it rang. It was Tuco.

"You were right," Tuco said, his voice low and flat. "You were right about her."

"Aw, Tuco, man . . . I'm sorry. It'll be all right, you'll be all right. Don't lose heart. The right girl is out there somewhere."

"It's okay, I guess I'm over it now. I shoulda seen it, you know, but she was such a nice person. She was so easy to talk to . . ."

"I'm sure she was. Thing is, if a person is an addict, the addict always wins out. Maybe she even felt for you what you feel for her, but there ain't shit you can do for her, not until she kicks it. She clean you out?"

"I don't know, I didn't check." There was no life in his voice.

"No," he said, when he came back. "She only took a hundred bucks."

Tuco got into bed thinking that it was over, that he'd cried himself out of it, but the bedclothes were infused with the smell of her, and it filled his head, and he started up again, alone in the dark.

16

STONEY WAS UP EARLY THE NEXT MORNING, SHOWERED AND DRESSED and out the door by six-thirty. It was clear and cool, with a stiff wind blowing, the beginning of one of those late summer days that whisper of winter coming, of ice and snow, gloves, and cold feet. It had rained the night before, and he had laid on his bed, sleepless, listening to the torrents of water beating on the roof and wondering if Donna was sleeping or if she was awake, like him, watching the rain come down in visible waves.

As he walked down his street he saw some robins eating worms that had been stranded on the blacktop. There seemed to be hundreds of worms but only a few birds, and it seemed impossible that they would be able to eat more than a tiny fraction of the worms that lay stiff and drying on the street or drowned here and there in puddles of rainwater. Two of the neighborhood kids rode their bikes up the street heedless of the lives that ended beneath their tires. Why is it, he wondered, making his way down the sidewalk, that nature is so prodigious in her use of what is so precious to each of us individually, so painfully short and irreplaceable. So many die, whether worms or birds, sperm, acorns, or humans, so many die for each one that lives up to its potential. What are your choices, anyway, if you're a worm? To be eaten by a bird, to be left to dry in the sun, or perhaps, supremely successful, to leave your dead body in the ground to nourish some other hungry, reaching thing. He turned the corner at the end of his street and headed for the bus stop, wondering if the worms got some high, some ecstasy in the rain puddles, some trip worth throwing their lives after. Then again, how much of a high could a worm get.

Fat Tommy Rosselli was lying back on a pile of pillows, looking pale and thinner than he had in years. He was in a bed in a private room. Also in the room were two nurses, three cops in uniform, and one doctor. Stoney stood outside the door, watching. Tommy was the first of the group to notice him.

"Aay, Stonada!"

It was the nickname his father had hung on him, which he had always hated. Instantly he was fourteen again, mocked, insulted, being called stupid.

"Yeah, your mother's dick." It came out before he could help it, and he was immediately sorry he'd said it, but Tommy and the cops laughed uproariously, and the doctor and the nurses smirked.

"All right," the doctor said, "this is altogether too much fun for a man in Mr. Rosselli's condition. We have to break this up."

"We gotta go, Tommy," one of the cops said. "We'll see you soon." They all filed out of the room, smiling and saying their good-byes, the doctor last. He laid a hand on Stoney's arm.

"He really does need to rest. Don't be too long, and no stress, okay?"

"Okay, Doc."

Stoney went and sat in a chair on the far side of the bed. Tommy lay back, looking at the doorway his visitors had just gone through. "Wasa my fault," he said, trying to keep his voice quiet. "He wasa too hungry, but I hire him anyway. Sometime you want something to work out, even when you know it'sa no good."

"I dunno, Tommy. I don't think there's any way you could have known."

"I feel bad. I feel very bad. I hadda make a statement, tell the cops who wasa shoot me. Now they looka for Jimmy. They gonna get him for Marty too. If he only woulda listen to me, we maybe coulda help him pulla the fat outta the fire."

"I don't think so, Tommy. Too much money missing."

"Wasa no too much," Tommy said. "Forty, fifty grand, he told me, just before I wasa get shot. He wanted me to give him fifty, pay back, maybe, maybe run away."

"Nah, it was worse than that." Stoney told him about Miguel and what he'd done, and how Tuco had flushed him out.

"Crazy inna head," Tommy said, "but nice boy, Tuco. Maybe I was right about him, anyway. Get one out of two." He shook his head sadly. "Whata you think happen to Jimmy now?"

A nurse paused in the open doorway, caught Stoney's eye, and tapped on her watch. He nodded to her, and she moved on.

"Who knows. I figure the Colombians got him, but we don't know for sure. Me and Tuco, we're gonna go sniff around a little, see if we can turn him up. I better go, Tommy, I wanna go close down the junkyard. It's gonna be a long day."

"Too bad, wasa nice, to be regular business for a while. Didn't you like?"

"It was fun for a while, but toward the end it got to be a pain in my ass, and it was a bitch of a commute." He got up to leave. "I'll come by tonight to see how you're doing."

"Aah, not tonight." Tommy's face showed a little color. "I got a nice real estate lady, she gonna bring me dinner. She told me onna phone, she know how to resuscitate me."

"I'll bet. She gives you a heart attack, at least you're in the right place."

"How's Tommy?" Tuco had the van pulled over in the no standing zone in front of Beth Israel while he waited for Stoney, and it was his first question.

"Lost a lot of weight. He seems okay, though, he's talking and whatever. He told me he wants to write a diet book, call it 'The Let Jimmy the Hat Shoot Your Ass Diet' book." He looked over at Tuco, who was showing signs of a sleepless night. "You all right?"

"I'll be okay."

Stoney waited for more, didn't get it. "This must be the van you used. Where's the camera?"

"I took it out. Stuck it in a closet. Might come in handy sometime." He glanced over at Stoney. "I'd like to stay with you guys. I think." He looked over again. "Walter tell you the rest of the story?"

"I had to drag it out of him. I appreciate what you did, but you were taking a big chance. You know that?"

"Stoney, when that guy saw the girl coming up the sidewalk, he totally wigged out. There was no way he was gonna pass her up a second time, I was sure of it." He paused. "It was ugly, though, you know what I mean? In a way I'm sorry I did it. I didn't feel too good when it was over. And then with Manny and the other guy and Angel, and Miguel, and the two kids before, and everything. Like when we went over to Vittorio's, you remember? I felt bad after that too. Is it always like that?"

"Not always. Who was Angel?"

"He died a few years ago, he was Manny's brother."

"Oh. You shoot him too?"

"No. Some Jamaicans got him. Miguel got them back."

"Oh. You know, after Tommy is up and around, he'll help you with that money from Miguel. You might be all set, know what I mean? Maybe you won't need to, ah, get involved, if you don't want to."

"I can't retire, I haven't done anything yet. Haven't done much. I'd still have to be something. I can be a guy who fixes toilets, or I can be something more. It's just that I don't want to feel terrible, every time, afterward. But you and Tommy are the only two guys who ever tried to help me."

"Yeah, well. You gonna take the bridge or the tunnel?"

"Bridge. Tunnel's backed up."

"Where'd you leave the car?"

"It's in a garage on Metropolitan."

"Oh. Well, you know, we don't steal old ladies' pension money. No pyramids, no patent medicines, nothing to do time over. We're, aah . . ."

"Adventure capitalists."

Stoney bit his lip. "Maybe that's it. We look for opportunities, and we try to get a few yucks. I tell you what. We're gonna take some time off. You do the same thing. After a few months, me or Tommy will give you a call, and we'll sit down and talk about what comes next. You want in, that's okay, you don't, no hard feelings. Fair enough?"

"Sure, okay. I rented this van, but I could buy it for a thou. Do you think I should?"

"Hell, no. You give a credit card number when you rented it?"

"I don't got a credit card, I had to pay cash."

"So you did the right thing by mistake. After you use a vehicle like you used this one, you don't want your name on it, and you don't want its smell on you. I was gonna tell you this anyway; as soon as we get to the shop, I want you to drop me off and then go get rid of this, okay?"

"All right."

"Say this guy's brother is a cop, and he sees you driving around in it. You see what I mean?"

"Yes, boss."

Tuco turned off Flushing, up St. Nicholas. When he got to the stop sign on Troutman, he could see the yellow crime-scene tape around the building up the block. A few locals stood on the sidewalk, looking in, but none of them wore Dr. Jack's colors. Memories of the night before flooded his mind but he tried to block them out as he made the turn onto Troutman.

She was up on the far end of the block, still wearing the same clothes. She was doing the junkie two-step, knees buckled, leaning impossibly far forward, bent over, head almost touching the pavement, almost losing her balance, then a shuffling half step and a slow-motion recovery, and back again, past the point of balance, back, impossibly far back, knees giving way, head rolling back . . . Stoney didn't see her, his attention was on the guy standing on the sidewalk in front of the office door. An unmarked police sedan was parked just down the block.

"This that cop that came around, the one you talked to after those two kids got it in the alley?"

"Huh?" Tuco had been lost, watching the girl.

"This guy over here. Is he—"

"A cop. He's the cop, that one from back when—"

"Okay, I get it. All right, just drop me off and go get rid of this. When you get back, we'll go up to Hunts Point."

"Yes, boss."

•   •   •

He dropped Stoney, then drove to the end of the block and pulled over. He rolled his window down and watched her, his stomach burning, and he begged silently for her to see him, Please God, let her recognize me, let her want to come back with me, let her want . . . anything. But her eyes were unfocused, even when she seemed to recover and stand somewhat upright she never focused on him or on the van. He waited a few minutes longer, wondering what to do, but then a black Mercedes pulled over in front of her and she made her way over to the driver's window and leaned down. A moment later she tottered around the front of the car and got in, and the car pulled away. I would have done it, he thought, I'd have done whatever it took to help her . . . He sat back in the driver's seat and watched the black car go straight down Troutman until it was out of sight. A kind of damp, cold fatigue settled down over him, and presently he didn't feel anything at all, just a dull and sullen anger. He dropped the shift lever into gear and drove off.

"That your guy Eddie?" The cop stood at Stoney's shoulder and watched him unlock the door.

"That's my guy Eddie."

"He doesn't have a thing for prostitutes, does he?"

Stoney turned away from the front door to peer down the block. He didn't want to watch. "Nah, just that one. She was nice to him, and he's got a soft heart."

"He's wasting his time. I know the guy used to be married to her. She's a stone junkie."

"Kid's eighteen. What're you gonna do?"

"Where did you find him, anyhow?"

"He found us. Walked right through this door, back when we

first opened. Had his hair all short, shorter than now, even, he's got on a suit, for chrissake, white shirt and a tie, shoes all shiny . . . I'm thinking, You poor fuck, you don't stand a chance. I'm in the middle of telling him we don't have anything for him, my partner, Tommy, comes in, Tommy wants to feed every lost dog he sees. Right away he thinks he's saving the kid, 'Oh,' he says, 'we need someone to do this and that, you know, how about a few days a week,' and all that. And he's still here." Stoney got the door open, looked down the block just in time to see the Mercedes drive off, with Tuco still in the van. "You coming in?"

"Thank you. So what are you guys teaching Eddie? Wasn't he better off unemployed?"

What is this guy fishing for, Stoney wondered. Don't get mad, he told himself. Be smart. "He's gaining valuable experience," he said. "He's got something to put on his resume now, and he knows a few things he didn't know before. Besides, why you worried about him? Ain't you supposed to be finding out who killed those two kids in the alley?"

"As of this morning, it ain't my case anymore."

"What's that mean?"

The cop grimaced. "It means there's a task force working the gangs in Bushwick, and it's their case now. According to them, the shootings don't have anything to do with you guys."

"So you should be happy, right?"

"Gimme a break. This don't pass the smell test. I found out this morning that the Bronx DA was doing a big investigation on you guys, because your accountant turned up with lead poisoning in a Bronx hotel room. Room was full of papers that had your name on 'em. Then your partner gets whacked, but he's in the hospital, not quite dead, and you drop out of sight. And the funny thing is, nobody on the Job wants to talk to you, instead they all go trooping over to Beth Israel. Why is that?"

"Tommy likes everybody. Even you guys."

"Oh, nice. So if I understand correctly, a guy used to work for you was trying to con some bad guys, and then he tries to put the arm on you two, now nobody knows where he is. Just between you and me, I figure he's inside an oil drum somewhere. Am I right? Am I close?"

"I object to your characterizations, Councilor. What we had here was two innocent businessmen who were unwittingly exploited by a criminal element." Stoney turned his back on the cop and unlocked Tommy's office door and shoved it open, waking the cat, who'd been sleeping on the doormat inside. The cat arched its back and spat, and Stoney stood back out of its way. The cat took its cue and departed. Stoney walked into the darkened room and sat behind the desk. "The only crime Tommy and I were guilty of was stupidity."

"You're telling me you had nothing to do with this guy going missing."

"Why don't you go talk to those guys he was running with? Wasn't it their money he was after?"

"Doesn't it bother you, some guy used to work for you, sat right here in this office, is probably at the bottom of the East River?"

No, Stoney thought. "First of all, he shot two good friends of mine. Killed one, almost killed the other. Second, I ain't his mother. And third, he was the guy that got this shit all stirred up to begin with, not me. He got taken down by his own appetites. He put his own dick in the pencil sharpener, all by himself."

"He was just trying to do what you guys do, only he just wasn't as good at it."

"Oh, that isn't true at all. I don't ever put my hand in someone else's pocket, you never know what you're gonna come up with when you do that. The objective of every business is to induce the other guy to do that of his own accord, and to shake your hand afterward."

"I guess I was misinformed about you guys. It's nice to hear what a couple of Boy Scouts you are."

"Just like you." Stoney flipped the switch by his knee, and the shoulder and back of the cop's jacket lit up a fluorescent green. "You find what you were looking for?"

"Damn." His voice was subdued. "What is this shit?"

"You'll probably have to chuck the jacket," Stoney told him. "Your car seat vinyl or cloth?"

"I got a cloth seat cover on it."

"Lucky. Chuck that too. So what did you find?"

"Nothing. And I tossed this place good too."

"You were wasting your time. We do what every other business tries to do. We look for opportunities. We find a market for something, we try to exploit it. We find someone sitting on something, they don't know what they have, we try to buy it. And since we're not General Motors, we have to be creative."

The cop shrugged off his jacket and folded it in on itself so that the infrared dye was on the inside where it wouldn't get on anything else. "So," he said, "if I wanted to buy the Brooklyn Bridge, you wouldn't sell it to me."

"Nope. But if you're looking for the da Vinci sketchbook that the Nazis stole from the Louvre back in forty-two, I know an ex-priest, used to work in the Vatican, has one that might be real."

"And you'll sell me that."

"No, but I'll put you in touch with him, for a fee."

The cop shook his head. "You know, sometimes this job sucks. This is supposed to be my day off. I'm going home."

"Don't forget to take the seat cover off, before you sit down."

He pulled the wire for the phone on Tommy's desk out of the socket, but the phones still rang out front, so he got up out of the chair and went around disconnecting them. The cat had been on the counter, asleep. It woke up when he came into the room, and it watched him as he made his way around to the phones. Although it never moved from the counter, it watched him with perfect concentration. Stoney was conscious of the unblinking focus.

"What?" he said. "You miss Walter?" He had the impression that the cat knew he was talking to it. "You don't give a shit about Walter. If he was laying here dead on the floor, you'd eat his eyeballs out. You just want to get fed, is all. That's all you care about. Why don't you go catch a rat or something?" The cat had done that on occasion, and a few times it had returned to the office with its prey still alive and squeaking to toy with it for a while before killing and eating it. Tommy had seen it twice, and both times it had put him in a funk and he had gone home early, depressed.

"You know," Stoney said to the cat, "as one mean bastard to another, I ain't such a bad guy. Watch, I'll prove it to you, if I can find where Walter keeps that swill he feeds you." He went looking, and the cat's concentration on him was total. When Stoney got to the right cupboard, the cat got up and stretched, first front, then back, but its eyes never left Stoney.

"How about that," Stoney said. "You don't even need a can opener for this crap. Oh, damn," he said, watching cat-food juice drool down over his fingers. He left the can on the floor by the cupboard and went to rinse off his hands. The cat watched, drawn to the food but still wary. "All right," Stoney said, returning, and he dumped the can unceremoniously into the cat's bowl and put the bowl on the counter. The cat growled and retreated to the far end of the counter, looking for its escape route, eyeing Stoney suspiciously.

"Relax, I ain't gonna hurt you." He backed off, sat on the window ledge. The cat sat on the far end of the counter, waiting.

"I called my old lady last night," he told the cat. "I still think I got a shot with her. You don't have that kind of trouble, do you? You just walk off to the next one. See, I could never do that. Assuming you're male, right? Go ahead, eat your breakfast. I'll stay here.

"I don't know what I'd do if she left, you know what I mean? Sometimes when I see her I feel like I can't breathe right, like I got broken ribs and I can't inhale, or something. She really got to me." He quieted, watched the cat make its slow approach.

"I mean, I wouldn't blame her if she left. All I've done lately is hurt her. I used to be able to make her laugh . . ." Stupid, he thought, talking to a cat. But who else was there?

"You know, I was never one of those guys to go chasing around. I just never had the itch, you know what I mean? She's the only woman I ever felt anything with." He shifted in his perch on the ledge and the cat left off eating to watch him. "I'll tell you something, I don't even know which way I want it to go. If she'd really be better off, I wouldn't want to hold her. I just don't know how I would make it . . .

"You figure Walter's coming back for you? You think he's gonna take you home with him? I bet you couldn't care less." The cat, he thought, lives fully present in the moment, and it don't worry about a thing. What must that be like? He turned on his cell phone and dialed.

"Hey, Walter."

"Mistah Stoney."

"You doing anything today?"

"Sitting here, waiting for the word."

"How about you go up and see Marty Cohen's partners, wrap this thing up? And don't take no for an answer, either."

"You be around if they got questions?"

"Yeah, but I don't want to hear any questions. I'm leaving this up to you, you know what to do. Listen, what about the cat?"

"Stoney, you feelin' all right? I figured you'd be drownin' him in the sink right about now."

"I would, but I can't find Commie Pete's welding gloves. I try to do it barehanded, he'd claw the shit outta me."

"Ya goin soft, Stoney. Sure, I take care a the cat, and I take care a the accountants too. After that, maybe I go away for a while. Go visit my sister in London."

"Good idea. Stop and see Fat Tommy before you go. He's sitting up, now, talking."

"Okay, man. Talk to you in about two weeks."

C. Maxwell Hunt came through the front door. The cat heard him coming first, jumped down from the counter and sought refuge. Amazing, Stoney thought. Complete focus, complete presence, and meanwhile I'm distracted and I'm missing what this pain in my ass is saying.

"Mr. Hunt," he said, interrupting him so he'd have to start over. "From the EPA."

"Yeah." C. Maxwell looked bedraggled, beaten. His coat hung listlessly from his shoulders and his hair drooped in odd lengths where he had neglected his combover, like a plant with long, dead leaves. "Mr. . . ."

"Call me Stoney."

"Whatever." He was holding a large manila envelope in one hand, and he dropped it on the counter. "What if my wife had seen these? Or my daughters?" His voice had no energy or life in it. "Did you ever think of that?"

Stoney looked up at him and was surprised to see tears. The man is crying, he thought. He was gonna hang me out to dry, and here I am feeling sorry for him. I should be laughing in his face. This is Tuco's fault, with all his talk about feeling bad afterward. He opened the envelope and took out the pictures. My God, he thought, looking at the first one, my God, will you look at the muscle tone on this girl. He leafed through the first four or five prints.

"Good grief," he said.

"You would have ruined my life," Hunt said, in a tone of quiet bewilderment. "All anyone had to do was open this envelope, and I would have been finished—at work, at home, everywhere. Didn't you think of that? Didn't you even consider it?"

"When you're running for your life, Mr. Hunt, you don't often take much notice of how the runners behind you are faring. Besides, everybody takes risks. What's the point, otherwise? But this risk is your responsibility, not mine." He went back to the first shot. A shame, he thought, what Troutman Street was going to do to one of God's masterpieces. This girl could be anywhere, she could go on television and just stand there. Instead, she would die by degrees, literally withering away, her body shriveling up, hanging on long after her spirit was dead, until, finally, it, too, would pass away. He slid the pictures back into the envelope and held it out to Hunt.

Hunt wouldn't touch it. "I can't drop the case," he said. "If I do, they'll just have someone else review it, and you'll be back to square one. But we can plead it down, you'll wind up with a fine, five thousand, probably. It's the best I can do. If I do that, do I get the negatives?"

"Negatives? I'm afraid technology has left you behind, my friend. These aren't prints, they're from a color printer. Look, you do what you said, get us out of this for five large, and I promise you that none of this stuff will ever see the light of day. Good enough?"

"You'll destroy it."

"Yeah."

Hunt sighed. "All right," he said. "I suppose I should feel happy to get this over with." He looked at the envelope in Stoney's hand, a wistful expression on his face.

"You want this?" Stoney asked him.

"Jesus." It was the loudest thing he'd said, the first sign of life. He turned away and went to look out the window. "I can't get her out of my mind," he said. "I want to go back to how I was before, but I keep seeing her. I'm afraid, if she were here, that maybe I'd do it all over again, even after all this."

"Yeah, well. Look, man, it ain't none of my business . . ."

Hunt turned back to him slowly, his face flushed a deep red and twisted into an unreadable and ugly mask. He started to say something, changed his mind.

"Easy, Max, easy. I'm trying to do the right thing, here, and I'm no good at it." Hunt's face began to return to its normal pallor. "I don't know if I'm doing you any favors or not, okay, but there's this place, okay, I want you to write it down. It's on Third Avenue in Manhattan, just north of Fourteenth. Madam Cho's Tai Chi Academy. Go in there, ask for Mrs. Cho. Tell her what happened to you, okay? You can tell her anything at all. She'll help you. Hell, you tell her you work for Uncle Sam, she might paddle you herself." Hunt took a business card off the counter and wrote on the back of it.

After he'd gone through the door, Stoney thought better of it and followed him out.

"Max, yo, Max!"

Hunt turned around, eyeing Stoney suspiciously. The hot summer breeze stirred the fronds of hair hanging down the side of his head. "What?"

"Don't tell her, Max. Don't tell her you're with the government, tell her you're an accountant or something, okay?"

Hunt turned away. "I am an accountant."

Stoney shrugged. "There you go."

• • •

Tuco parked Stoney's Lexus right out in front and walked through the door.

"You all right? Took you long enough."

"The guy didn't want to give me my deposit back. Gave me shit about keeping it too long."

"You have to reason with him?"

"I couldn't hang him out his office window, he's on the ground floor. We did have to have an ugly conversation, though." Tuco was eyeing the manila envelope that C. Maxwell Hunt had left lying behind.

"You feel bad about it afterward?"

"Give me a break, okay? But you know, I didn't. I felt good about it. The guy's a dirtbag."

Stoney was laughing. "That makes it easier." He went over and picked up the envelope. "You wanna see 'em?"

"No. I seen 'em already."

"Worked like a charm, you know. The guy was really broken."

"I didn't really mean to break him. I just thought, you know . . ."

"Hey, the guy could've walked on by. He could've thought what he wanted, when he saw her, and still passed her up and gone home to Momma, but he didn't."

"No," Tuco said, "he didn't."

"He was ready to hang us out to dry. You saved us some serious money. We owe you something, but I don't know what."

"You don't owe me anything. That ain't why I did it." He was strangely subdued. "I wanna be, you know, with you guys, you and Tommy. I wanted to show you that I wasn't, like, a moron or something, so I took a shot."

"Tuco, you and I both know that you're smart enough to do

about whatever you want." Kid thinks I'm hollering at him, Stoney thought. And I'm just trying to make him say uncle, so I'll feel better about it afterward.

"We still gonna go up to Hunts Point?"

"Let's do it."

Hunts Point is an old witch's nose sticking out into the East River. It is cut off even from what passes for normal in the South Bronx, isolated by water on three sides, and by the Bruckner Expressway and the freight yards that run in a trench parallel to it on the fourth. You have to cross a bridge over the railroad tracks to reach Hunts Point. Hunts Point Avenue runs over a bridge at the north end of the Point, and there is a narrow slice of residential neighborhood there, old tenement buildings and stores, but the rest of the Point is a place of industrial concrete buildings with bricked-up windows, chain-link fences topped with razor wire, empty streets and sidewalks, a few trucks and an occasional car, almost no pedestrians. The few people out are hurrying, trying to get where they're going, trying to get off the street.

They crossed the Leggett Avenue Bridge into the southern end of Hunts Point. "Pull over here," Stoney said. He looked at Tuco. "Safe bet you never been deer hunting, right?"

"Never."

"Okay, what you do, you put one guy up in a tree where he's got a good view, okay? The other guy, he's the walker, he goes out in a big circle. Deer are afraid, especially during hunting season. They see hunters coming, they run. A lot of times, the guy walking doesn't see a thing, doesn't know what happened until he gets to the tree his buddy is in, sees the deer dead on the ground. You with me so far?"

"Yes, boss."

"Good. I'm the walker, you're in the tree. The tree is the Hunts Point Avenue Bridge. I'm gonna get out here, and you're gonna drive up and park the car somewhere up on Hunts Point Avenue, and then you're gonna walk over to the Bruckner side of the bridge and wait there. I'm gonna walk up this first cross street right here, and if you're right, I should run into the junkyard Jimmy told you about. If Jimmy sees me coming, and you can bet, if he's there, he'll be watching, the logical thing for him to do is to try to get a cab, but he ain't gonna get one in Hunts Point. He has to cross back over to Bruckner Boulevard, and to do that he'll head north, right up to Hunts Point Avenue, over the bridge. You get it?"

"Yeah."

"You just wait for him, I should be right behind him. All you gotta do is hold him up a few minutes until I get there. If he has a gun, just let him go, call the cops on your cell phone and tell them you saw him. Got it?"

"Yeah. What are we gonna do if we catch him?"

Stoney shook his head. "Not what you think. Best thing to do is to give him to the cops. Once they put him away, the Colombians will get him."

"Right there in jail?"

"Easiest thing in the world. You ready?"

"Yes, boss."

Old busses should be easy to spot, Stoney told himself, that is, if the guy is still doing that. He passed Tiffany Street. What a name for a place like this, he thought, at this end of Tiffany, you've got Spofford juvie hall, and at the other end you can see out to where the New York State Penal Colony of Riker's Island sits in the middle of the East River. Closer to Spofford, farther from Riker's, a gray stone monastery takes up an entire city block. Stoney passed by, wondering what they were thinking in there, what they made of all this. He passed a smallish junkyard on the next block, looked inside the gate. There were brown chickens pecking at the oily dirt, and a three-legged dog came out to bark at him. Place is probably too small, he thought, and no busses. He continued on.

Tuco leaned against a column on the far end of the Hunts Point Avenue Bridge. Under the bridge a freight train moved lazily, making the rhythmic clanking noises trains always seem to make. An old Chinese man carrying a red lunch box with the cartoon image of the Tasmanian devil on it walked in Tuco's direction. A tiny girl skipped along beside him, singing to herself. Running up the sidewalk behind him, gaining fast, was Jimmy the Hat. Tuco waited. The old Chinese man caught his eye, and Tuco pointed to the other side of the street with his chin. At once the old man put a hand on the little girl's shoulder and shepherded her across to the other side of the street. Jimmy was halfway across the bridge when he saw Tuco waiting, and his eyes went wide as he skidded to a stop. More afraid of Dr. Jack than the Colombians or the cops, Tuco thought. On the far side of the bridge, Stoney turned the corner.

Probably the guy's granddaughter, Tuco thought. Probably taking her to school, carrying her lunch box. How cool must that be? Probably meets her coming out too.

"Now what," he called out.

Jimmy turned and looked at Stoney, who was waiting on the other side, then back at Tuco, who was getting closer. He went over to the green metal railing and put a foot over, looking down at the freight cars passing below.

Tuco stopped ten feet away.

"You won't make it," he said. "The drop is bigger than it looks, and besides, it's too late. Tommy came out of it, and he already talked to the cops. There's no way out. Come with me, I'll keep

Stoney away from you. I'll make sure you get to the cops, maybe they'll cut a deal, let you testify against the Colombians."

"No way," Jimmy said, still looking down. "I come with you, Stoney gets me for sure. I go to prison, the Colombians get me. I gotta run, if I run at least I have a shot."

"Was it you, did the two kids in the alley?"

"What was I supposed to do? They saw me coming over the fence."

"Does it bother you at all? Those two, plus Cohen and Bagadonuts. Would you do me now, if it would let you get away?"

Jimmy was still looking down at the freight cars, and he swung his other leg over the railing and balanced himself on the ledge outside. He looked back at Tuco, and his face looked old and tired. "I gotta go," he said, and he leaned out, hanging on to the railing, timing his leap, but pigeons had been using the ledge as a toilet for a century or so, and his foot slipped when he pushed off, and he only got about half of the distance he needed. He fell with a look of surprise on his face, and his upper body hit the outer corner of the freight car he'd been trying for. For several seconds he clung to the metal, but there was nothing for him to hold, and almost in slow motion he slid off and tumbled between the cars. There was an ungodly sound as the wheels of the car cut him in half, and then just the rhythmic clanking noise.

Stoney was waving insistently at Tuco, as if to say, Don't look, just come this way. He's right, Tuco thought, no need to look. He jogged the rest of the way across the bridge and the two of them headed for the car.

It was a quiet trip back to Troutman Street.

Tuco pulled the car over in front of the office door. Stoney looked at him.

"You gonna be all right?"

Tuco didn't look at him. "You know what I need to do? I need to go sit on a park bench on the promenade. Watch moms with their kids, people walking their dogs. Know what I mean?"

"Yeah, I do. This will all look much different after a day or two. Listen," Stoney said. "Here's what I want you to do. Take my car and park it somewhere for a few days. I have to get my license straightened out. Take tomorrow off, stay home and rest. Day after tomorrow, go in and see Tommy. Tell him about your cardboard boxes, see what he says you should do. Okay?"

"All right."

"I have to go inside and look around one more time, I need to make sure we got nothing embarrassing left behind, and then I'm gonna go home myself. Stay home and rest tomorrow, okay? You look like shit."

"Okay, boss."

17

STONEY USUALLY HAD A HARD TIME UNDERSTANDING COMMIE PETE, particularly when Pete got excited, and the telephone made it worse.

"Huh?"

"I saw them, up to the corner, I saw them taking those boys out, putting them in bags. I remember what I seen back in the fifties, Stoney, back with Stalin, I could tell you, people frozen in the snow, starved to death, piled up waiting for the spring. I'm an old man now, Stoney, I'm in the United States of America, I never expected . . ." His voice was getting higher and higher, and he was going faster and faster.

"Pete, slow down, take it easy. Those two were in the drug business, and those guys die early. Don't matter if it's Brooklyn or what. This might not be Lithuania, but it ain't paradise, either." Poor old bastard, Stoney thought. What he needs is a family, grandson to take to the ballpark. "Listen, Pete," he said. "Why don't you go see Tommy. He's much better now, they'll let you in to talk to him. Just tell them you're his uncle."

"Oh, thank God he's okay," Pete said. "What about Tuco? Is he okay too?"

"What do you mean, what about Tuco? Why shouldn't he be okay?"

"You and me, we've known each other for a long time."

"Yeah."

"Whattaya gonna teach him, Stoney? What's gonna happen to him?"

Stoney sighed. "Look, Pete, I didn't ask for this, okay? None of this was my idea. What am I supposed to do, throw him out? He doesn't have anywhere else to go. You want I should send him to college? He might have a few problems with that. You're a religious guy, ain't you? Ain't you the one believes in God? Why'nt you blame Him for this? Why is it my fault?"

"Aw, Stoney, I—"

"Listen, Pete, Tuco didn't get good cards when they dealt this hand. Maybe you didn't, either. It doesn't matter, you still have to get by the best way you can."

"Maybe so. But he looks up to you, Stoney. I'm just asking you to do right by him."

"Yeah. Look, Pete, we're gonna close up. I want you to come and get the truck, it's insured for another five or six months. Take the tools and whatnot, anything you think you could use. Otherwise someone will just break in and take 'em, okay?"

"All right. You have the title to the truck?"

"I don't know anything about a title. You gotta see Fat Tommy for that. You oughta go see him anyway."

"I was praying for him."

"Well, thank you for that, Pete. I figured you were. Say one for me, too. I could use all the help I could get."

"Stoney, I—"

"No, serious, Pete. And don't forget, come and get the truck and the tools out back. And don't forget, go on in and see Tommy. He ain't got anybody over here, Pete, you and me and Walter and Tuco are all the family he's got left. He's at Beth Israel. Drive the truck in, you could even park it at his garage."

"All right. I gonna go."

I should call Benny, Stoney thought, but he didn't want to do it. He went over and stood by the window and looked out, wondering why he was hanging around, why he didn't just go home.

There was a new girl working the street. She looked to be about fourteen but was probably much older. Thin and short, with small breasts and very short hair, at first glance he couldn't tell if she was a boy trying to pass or just a girl trying to make the best of what she had. Either way, she was driving the switch-hitters crazy, whatever she was, they wanted her. She was fussy, though, and she kept returning to the sidewalk after short conversations with the drivers who pulled over. Stoney watched one guy in a bread delivery truck try for her three times. On his third trip around the block, she wouldn't even look over at him, and he drove off angrily. Like a reluctant bass she kept circling, looking at the lure, shying away, but finally she bit. Stoney could not see the driver of the car she got into, could not even guess what made her say yes after so many nos. Some things never change, he thought. The old ones fall apart, and eventually they die, and new ones move in to take their places. No matter what bad things had happened to their predecessors, the johns still look to get off regardless of the risk, and the whores still take their money.

Addiction never sleeps.

Is it just the street, he wondered, or is it us? Is it just part of this dance we do, each one of us chasing what we have decided we need, licking our sharp teeth? Everyone's looking for a mark while simultaneously trying to watch out for whatever might be circling up behind. If you get tired and you slow down or get careless, you get taken out, the way a zebra, old or wounded or sick, gets killed and eaten by the lions.

Stoney was tired.

Maybe I just need a vacation, he thought. Maybe I ought to go down to Mexico, lay on the beach, put my feet in the water. Yeah, sure, he thought. Go broke calling Benny every five minutes. Only rest I'd get would be when I got locked up for something.

And then it was time to go, finally, for the last time. Someone might need to return to clean out the office, to take care of loose ends, but that someone would not be him. Tommy would never trust him to do it right, it wasn't his kind of job. Fob it off on Walter, he had to come back for the cat, anyhow. He walked through the place one last time, turning lights off, opening a drawer here and there to see if there was anything he wanted. He had never been one to keep souvenirs or mementos, but he had spent a chunk of his life here, and he felt as though he needed to take something of the place with him, some tangible reminder. There was nothing that spoke to him, though. Quit wasting time, he told himself. Get out, go home. He stopped in the middle of the floor, looking around, and then he went out. He locked the door behind him and rolled the grates down over the door and windows and locked them as well. Out of force of habit he headed for the parking lot, preparing to be annoyed, as he always was, if he found the gate unlocked.

The old truck was there, parked back in the corner of the lot. Something made him bend down and look underneath, and he spied a pair of blue-jean-clad legs on the far side. Penny loafers. He walked to the end of the truck as quietly as he could, stuck his head around to see.

The old man was there, sitting on the low cinder-block footing for the fence. He was tearing open a small plastic bag, shaking a needle out.

"New works?"

He looked up calmly. "Ah," he said. "Good afternoon. Yes, to your question, yes. The old one was getting dull, dull and tiresome. As luck would have it, I ran into an old student of mine. Ironic that I was finding her dull and tiresome as well, until she told me she was working at Deathhull."

Stoney walked over and sat down next to him. "I still can't believe you're doing this shit."

"Yeah, yeah," the old man said distractedly. He began the ritual of preparing his hit with a practiced hand. "Don't think of it as a drug," he said. "Think of it as a vacation, of sorts."

"I could use one," Stoney said, "but I was thinking maybe the Caribbean." He remembered how that molasses-rum smell hits you as soon as they open the door to the plane. "Or Europe, maybe."

"You still don't get it, do you? Go ahead, go to Jamaica or the Bahamas. You still have to take your wife and kids along, don't you? See what I mean? It will all still be up there in your head. Your job, your house, your relationships, career, parents, kids, cars, neighbors." He was nearly ready, intent on his preparations, but talking anyway, one part of his brain focused on what he was doing, while another part rattled away at Stoney. "How would you like to lose them all, just for an afternoon? How about that? Have all of it wiped so totally clean that it's not even part of your consciousness. All those noises in your head, all those voices, gone, even your own name, even the idea that you could have one, as if it had never been there. Just silence. How about that? You think Jamaica could compare with that? And you could be home in time for dinner."

Like a snake's tooth the needle bit into his forearm, and a tiny drop of blood stood out dark and vivid red against the white skin of his arm. The old man pulled the plunger back, the inside of the syringe turned milky white and red, and he pushed it back again, and the swirl of color was the last thing he saw before it hit him, and then he was gone.

Stoney watched, envious. But it's a fool's paradise, he told himself, because it's never like the first one, never again. He had come to know it. You'll chase that high for as long as you live, and never catch it.

He stepped back out onto the sidewalk, turned and locked the gate behind him. He headed up the sidewalk, but after a dozen steps something made him turn and look back. He saw the kid crossing the street out of the corner of his eye, but he didn't recognize him until it was too late. He was too far from the parking lot, now, too far from the office door, and both were locked and inaccessible, anyhow. The kid had his hands shoved down into his jacket pockets, and he was scowling as he looked up Troutman, checking for traffic. Or cops. If he's got a gun, Stoney thought, I'm a dead man. There was nowhere to run, so he stopped and waited.

He looked around for something, any kind of weapon, but it was like he was naked. His heart beat wildly in his chest, it felt like it was right underneath his chin, and he could hear it in his breath as he inhaled. Up the block a car pulled over to the curb, and the whore who looked fourteen got out. Right away she saw the two of them and she backed away slowly as the car drove off. She's gonna watch me die, Stoney thought, she's gonna watch me die on fucking Troutman Street, and I was almost out of here, if I'd have had Tuco drive me, I'd have made it. He was sweating now, and he thought of all the things he needed to do before he could die, insurance he'd neglected to buy, papers he needed to sign, deposit boxes he needed to tell Donna about. Yeah, and tell your son and daughter that you love them, how about that? Make up with Donna, how could you go with things the way they are now? Make up, let her forgive you, take you back. Then die, when you're ready.

Stand up, he told himself, stand up, goddam it, he hasn't shot you yet. The kid reached the sidewalk and stopped too close, and the reptile at the core of Stoney's being took note of that, adrenaline pumped into his bloodstream, and in an instant he was changed, no longer passive but tingling on the knife edge of living and dying. If you pull that hand out of your pocket, he said to himself, I'll kill you before you can clear your piece, but if you're smart enough to shoot through the jacket, you might make it, or maybe I'll get you anyway . . . He felt like a cobra, coiled, poised and tense, waiting for the rat to get within striking distance.

"Damn, what is she, fourteen, fifteen?"

Stoney had to swallow before answering. "Just don't look too close."

He still hadn't looked in Stoney's direction. "That is a girl, right? Or is it?"

"Depends on what you want."

"Damn." The kid shook his head. "What a neighborhood. You remember me, right?"

"Yeah," Stoney said. "You're Vittorio's kid, the one helped me pull him back in."

"Yeah." The kid laughed ruefully. "You know something funny? That's the last time we touched each other. It's like he hates me, now."

Stoney's adrenaline rush peaked and began to ebb as he realized the kid had come for conversation and not for revenge. "He's ashamed. You gonna quit or wait till he fires you?"

"Oh, I quit already. I couldn't take it. But a friend of mine from college got me a job where he works, down on Wall Street. I'm making twice the money, and I don't ever want to see an ice cream again. Anyway, I was just passing by on my way out to the Island, and I wanted to stop and say, you know, no hard feelings or anything. I guess it was you that got me out of there, and I was way overdue."

"Well, thanks. What's out on the Island?"

"There's a big bakery chain we heard might be going public. I gotta go sniff around, see what I can find out."

"That what you do, on Wall Street?"

"Part of it." The kid grinned. "Amazing what you can find out, buying a few drinks in a neighborhood bar."

"So I hear." He stuck out his hand, and he felt that kick back in his bloodstream, just a little this time, just in case, but the kid's hand came out of his pocket empty, and they shook.

"Good luck, kid."

"Thanks. And listen, you don't need to worry about my old man. He really won't do anything stupid."

"I know." Wasn't sure about you, though.

The kid went back across the street, eyeing the whore up the block, but she turned her back on him and walked casually in the other direction as he headed for his car.